Sue Grafton has become ~~~~~~~~~~~~~~~~ female crime writers, both here a~~~~ ~~~ US. Born in Kentucky in 1940, the daughter of the mystery writer C. W. Grafton, she began her career as a TV scriptwriter before Kinsey Millhone and the "alphabet" series took off. Her first novel, *A is for Alibi*, was inspired by Sue's own divorce: *"For months I lay in bed and plotted to kill my ex-husband, but I knew I'd bungle it and get caught so I wrote it in a book instead."*

Sue freely confesses that Kinsey is her alter ego: "I think of her as the person I might have been had I not married young and had kids; she is that stripped down piece of my personality." She writes one book a year and plans to take Kinsey all the way through the alphabet to Z when Kinsey will be forty years old.

Sue Grafton lives in Santa Barbara with her husband Steven Humphrey.

Sue Grafton

'B' IS FOR BURGLAR

PAN BOOKS

The author wishes to acknowledge the invaluable assistance of the
following people: Steven Humphrey; John Carroll; Brenda Harman,
D.D.S.; Billie Moore Squires; De De La-Fond; William Fezler, Ph.D;
Sydney Baumgartner; Frank E. Sincavage; Milton Weintraub; Jay
Schmidt; Judy Cooley; Bill Pronzini and Marcia Muller; and Joe
Driscoll of Driscoll and Associates Investigations, Columbus, Ohio.

First published in Great Britain 1986 by Macmillan

This edition published 1990 by Pan Books
an imprint of Pan Macmillan Ltd
Pan Macmillan, 20 New Wharf Road, London N1 9RR
Basingstoke and Oxford
Associated companies throughout the world
www.panmacmillan.com

ISBN 0 330 31583 8

Copyright © Sue Grafton 1986

24 26 28 27 25

A CIP catalogue record for this book is available from
the British Library.

Printed and bound in Great Britain by
Mackays of Chatham PLC, Chatham, Kent

For Steven, who sees me through

Prologue

After it's over, of course, you want to kick yourself for all the things you didn't see at the time. The Had-I-But-Known school of private investigation perhaps. My name is Kinsey Millhone and most of my reports begin the same way. I start by asserting who I am and what I do, as though by stating the same few basic facts I can make sense out of everything that comes afterward.

This is what's true of me in brief. I'm female, age thirty-two, single, self-employed. I went through the police academy when I was twenty, joining Santa Teresa Police Department on graduation. I don't even remember now how I pictured the job before I took it on. I must have had vague, idealistic notions of law and order, the good guys versus the bad, with occasional court appearances in which I'd be asked to testify as to which was which. In my view, the bad guys would all go to jail, thus making it safe for the rest of us to carry on. After a while, I realized how naïve I was. I was frustrated at the restrictions and frustrated because back then, policewomen were viewed with a mixture of curiosity and scorn. I didn't want to spend my days defending myself against "good-natured" insults, or having to prove how tough I was again and again. I wasn't getting paid enough to deal with all that grief, so I got out.

For two years, I tried an assortment of occupations, but none had the same pull. Whatever else is true of police work, it does entail the intermittent sick thrill of life on the edge. I was hooked on the adrenal rush, and I couldn't go back to the commonplace.

Eventually, I joined a small firm of private investigators and spent another two years learning the business, after which

I opened an office of my own, duly licensed and bonded. I've been at it for five years, supporting myself in a modest way. I'm wiser now than I used to be and I'm more experienced, but the fact remains that when a client sits down in the chair across the desk from me, I never know what's going to happen next.

1

I'd been in the office no more than twenty minutes that morning. I'd opened the French doors out onto the second-floor balcony to let in some fresh air and I'd put on the coffee pot. It was June in Santa Teresa, which means chill morning fog and hazy afternoons. It wasn't nine o'clock yet. I was just sorting through the mail from the day before when I heard a tap at the door and a woman breezed in.

"Oh good. You're here," she said. "You must be Kinsey Millhone. I'm Beverly Danziger."

We shook hands and she promptly sat down and started rooting through her bag. She found a pack of filter-tipped cigarettes and shook one out.

"I hope you don't mind if I smoke," she said, lighting up without waiting for a response. She inhaled and then extinguished the match with a mouthful of smoke, idly searching about for an ashtray. I took one from the top of my file cabinet, dusted it off, and passed it over to her, offering her coffee at the same time.

"Oh sure, why not?" she said with a laugh, "I'm already hyper this morning so I might as well. I just drove up from Los Angeles, right through the rush-hour traffic. Gawd!"

I poured her a mug of coffee, doing a quick visual survey. She was in her late thirties by my guess; petite, energetic, well groomed. Her hair was a glossy black and quite straight. The cut was angular and perfectly layered so that it framed her small face like a bathing cap. She had bright blue eyes, black lashes, a clear complexion with just a hint of blusher high on each cheekbone. She wore a boat-necked sweater in a pale blue cotton knit, and a pale blue poplin skirt. The bag she carried was quality leather, soft and supple, with a number of zippered compartments containing God knows what. Her nails were long and tapered, painted a rosy pink and she wore a wedding ring studded with rubies. She projected self-confidence and a certain careless attention to style, conservatively packaged like the complimentary gift wrap in a classy department store.

She shook her head to the offer of cream and sugar so I added half-and-half to my own mug and got down to business.

"What can I help you with?"

"I'm hoping you can locate my sister for me," she said.

She was searching through her handbag again. She took out her address book, a rosewood pen-and-pencil set, and a long white envelope, which she placed on the edge of my desk. I'd never seen anyone so self-absorbed, but it wasn't unattractive stuff. She gave me a quick smile then, as though she knew that. She opened the address book and turned it so that it faced me, pointing to one of the entries with a rosy fingertip.

"You'll want to make a note of the address and telephone number," she said. "Her name is Elaine Boldt. She has a condo on Via Madrina and that second one is her address in Florida. She spends several months a year down in Boca."

I was feeling somewhat puzzled, but I noted the addresses while she took a legal-looking document out of the long white envelope. She studied it briefly, as though the contents might have changed since she'd last seen it.

"How long has she been missing?" I asked.

Beverly Danziger gave me an uncomfortable look. "Well, I don't know if she's 'missing' exactly. I just don't know where she is and I've got to get these papers signed. I know it sounds dumb. She's only entitled to a ninth interest and it probably won't come to more than two or three thousand dollars, but the money can't be distributed until we have her notarized signature. Here, you can see for yourself."

I took the document and read through the contents. It had been drawn up by a firm of attorneys in Columbus, Ohio, and it was full of whereases, adjudgeds, ordereds, and whatnots, which added up to the fact that a man named Sidney Rowan had died and the various people listed were entitled to por-

4

tions of his estate. Beverly Danziger was the third party listed, with a Los Angeles address, and Elaine Boldt was fourth, with an address here in Santa Teresa.

"Sidney Rowan was some kind of cousin," she went on garrulously. "I don't believe I ever met the man, but I got this notice and I assume Elaine got one too. I signed the form and got it notarized and sent off and then didn't think any more about it. You can see from the cover letter that this all took place six months ago. Then, lo and behold I got a call last week from the attorney . . . what's his name again?"

I glanced at the document. "Wender," I said.

"Oh, that's right. I don't know why I keep blocking that. Anyway, Mr. Wender's office called to say they'd never heard from Elaine. Naturally, I assumed she'd gone off to Florida as usual and just hadn't bothered to have her mail sent, so I got in touch with the manager of her condominium here. She hasn't heard from Elaine in months. Well, she did at first, but not recently."

"Have you tried calling the Florida number?"

"From what I understand, the attorney tried several times. Apparently, she had a friend staying with her and Mr. Wender left his name and number, but Elaine never called back. Tillie had about the same luck."

"Tillie?"

"The woman who manages the building here where Elaine has her permanent residence. Tillie's been forwarding the mail and she says Elaine usually drops her a little note every other week or so, but she hasn't heard anything since March. Frankly, it's a nuisance more than anything else, but I don't have time to track her down myself." Beverly took a final drag of the cigarette and stubbed it out with a series of pecking motions.

I was still taking notes, but I suppose the skepticism was showing in my face.

"What's the matter? Isn't this the sort of work you do?"

"Sure, but I charge thirty dollars an hour, plus expenses. If there's only two or three thousand dollars involved, I wonder if it's going to be worth it to you."

"Oh, I fully intend to have the estate reimburse me out of Elaine's share since she caused all this trouble to begin with. I mean, everything's come to a screeching halt until her signature can be obtained. I must say it's typical of the way she's behaved all her life."

"Suppose I end up flying down to Florida to look for her? Even if I only charge you half my usual hourly rate for travel time, it'll cost a fortune. Look, Mrs. Danziger—"

"Beverly, please."

"All right, Beverly. I don't want to discourage your business, but in all honesty it sounds like something you could handle yourself. I'd even be happy to suggest some ways to go about it."

Beverly gave me a smile then, but it had a hard edge to it and I realized, at long last, that she was used to getting her way. Her eyes had widened to a china glaze, as blue and unyielding as glass. The black lashes blinked mechanically.

"Elaine and I are not on the best of terms," she said smoothly. "I feel I've already devoted quite enough time to this, but I promised Mr. Wender I'd find her so the estate can be settled. He's under pressure from the other heirs and he's putting pressure on me. I can give you an advance if you like."

She was back in her bag again, coming up with a checkbook this time. She uncapped the rosewood pen and stared at me.

"Will seven hundred and fifty dollars suffice?"

I reached into my bottom drawer. "I'll draw up a contract."

I walked the check over to the bank and then I retrieved my car from the lot behind the office and drove over to Elaine Boldt's address on Via Madrina. It wasn't far from the downtown area.

I figured this was a routine matter I could settle in a day or two and I was thinking with regret that I'd probably end up refunding half the money I'd just deposited. Not that I was doing much else anyway—things were slow.

The neighborhood Elaine Boldt lived in was composed of modest 1930s bungalows mixed with occasional apartment complexes. So far, the little frame and stucco cottages were predominant but the properties were being converted to commercial use one by one. Chiropractors were moving in, and cut-rate dentists who were willing to give you twilight sleep so you could have your teeth cleaned without cringing. ONE-DAY DENTURES—CREDIT. It was worrisome. What did they do to you if you missed a payment on your upper plate? The area was still largely intact—old-age pensioners stubbornly propping up their hydrangea bushes—but real-estate syndicates would eventually mow them all down. There's a lot of money in Santa Teresa and much of it is devoted to maintaining a certain "look" to the town. There are no flashing neon signs, no slums, no fume-spewing manufacturing complexes to blight the landscape. Everything is stucco, red tile roofs, bougainvillea, distressed beams, adobe brick walls, arched windows, palm trees, balconies, ferns, fountains, paseos, and flowers in bloom. Historical restorations abound. It's all oddly unsettling—so lush and refined that it ruins you for anyplace else.

When I reached Mrs. Boldt's address, I parked my car out front and locked it, taking a few minutes then to survey the premises. The condominium was a curiosity. The building itself was shaped like a horseshoe with broad arms opening onto the street; three stories high, parking level underneath, a strange combination of modern and mock-Spanish. There were arches and balconies along the front, with tall wrought-iron gates sweeping inward to a palm-planted courtyard, but the sides and back of the building were flat and unadorned, as though the architect had applied a Mediterranean veneer to a plain plywood box, adding a lip of red tile at the top to suggest an entire roof when there was none. Even the palms looked like cardboard cutouts, propped up with sticks.

I passed through the courtyard and found myself in a glass-enclosed lobby with a row of mailboxes and door buzzers on the right. On my left, through another set of glass doors, apparently kept locked, I could see a set of elevator doors and an exit leading to a set of fire stairs. Huge potted plants had been artfully arranged throughout the entranceway. Straight ahead; a door led out into a patio where I caught sight of a pool surrounded by bright yellow canvas deck chairs. I checked the tenants' names, which were punched out on strips of plastic tape and pasted alongside each apartment buzzer. There were twenty-four units. The manager, Tillie Ahlberg, occupied apartment 1. An "E. Boldt" was listed at apartment 9, which I guessed was on the second floor.

I gave "E. Boldt" a buzz first. For all I knew, she'd answer on the intercom and then my job would be done. Stranger things had happened and I didn't want to make a fool of myself looking high and low for a lady who might well by now be at home. There was no response so I tried Tillie Ahlberg.

After ten seconds, her voice crackled into the intercom as though the sound were being transmitted from outer space.

"Yes?"

I placed my mouth near the box, raising my voice slightly.

"Mrs. Ahlberg, my name is Kinsey Millhone. I'm a private detective here in town. Elaine Boldt's sister asked me to see if I could locate her and I wondered if I might talk to you."

There was a moment of white noise and then a reluctant reply.

"Well. I suppose. I was on my way out, but I guess ten minutes won't hurt. I'm on the ground floor. Come through the door to the right of the elevator and it's down at the end of the hall to the left." The buzzer sounded and I pushed through the glass doors.

Tillie Ahlberg had left her front door ajar while she collected a lightweight jacket, her purse, and a collapsible shopping cart that rested against the hall table. I tapped on the doorframe and she appeared from my left. I caught a glimpse of a refrigerator and a portion of kitchen counter.

Tillie Ahlberg was probably in her sixties, with apricot-tinted hair in a permanent wave that looked as if it had just been done. The curl must have been a little frizzier than she liked because she was pulling on a crocheted cotton cap. An unruly fringe of apricot hair was still peeking out, like Ronald McDonald's, and she was in the process of tucking it away. Her eyes were hazel and there was a powdery patina of pale

8

ginger freckles on her face. She wore a shapeless skirt, hose, and running shoes, and she looked like she was capable of covering ground when she wanted to.

"I hope I didn't seem unsociable," she said comfortably. "But if I don't get to the market first thing in the morning, I lose heart."

"It shouldn't take long anyway," I said. "Can you tell me when you last heard from Mrs. Boldt? Is she Miss or Mrs.?"

"Mrs. She's a widow, though she's only forty-three years old. She was married to a man who had a string of manufacturing plants down south. As I understand it, he dropped dead of a heart attack three years ago and left her a bundle. That's when she bought this place. Here, have a seat if you like."

Tillie moved off to the right, leading the way into a living room furnished with antique reproductions. A gauzy golden light came through the pale yellow sheers and I could still smell the remnants of breakfast: bacon and coffee and something laced with cinnamon.

Having established that she was in a hurry, she seemed ready to give me as much time as I wanted. She sat down on an ottoman and I took a wooden rocking chair.

"I understand she's usually in Florida this time of year," I said.

"Well, yes. She's got another condominium down there. In Boca Raton, wherever that is. Near Fort Lauderdale, I guess. I've never been to Florida myself, so these towns are all just names to me. Anyhow, she usually goes down around the first of February and comes back to California late July or early August. She likes the heat, she says."

"And you forward mail to her while she's gone?"

Tillie nodded. "I do that about once a wee.. in batches, depending on how much has accumulated. Then she sends me back a note every couple of weeks. A postcard, you know, just to say hi and how the weather is and if she needs someone let in to clean the drapes or something of that nature. This year she wrote me through the first of March and since then I haven't heard a word. Now, that's not like her a bit."

"Do you still have the postcards by any chance?"

"No, I just threw 'em out like I always do. I'm not much for collecting things like that. There's too much paper piling up in the world if you ask me. I read 'em and tossed 'em and never thought a thing of it."

"She didn't mention taking a side trip or anything like that?"

"Not a word. Of course, it's none of my business in the first place."

"Did she seem distressed?"

Tillie smiled ruefully. "Well, it's hard to seem upset on the message side of a postcard, you know. There isn't but that much room. She sounded fine to me."

"Do you have any guesses about where she might be?"

"Not a one. All I know is it's not like her not to write. I tried calling four or five times. Once some woman friend of hers answered but she was real abrupt and after that, there wasn't anything at all."

"Who was the friend? Anyone you knew?"

"No, but now I don't know who she knows in Boca. It could have been anyone. I didn't make a note of the name and wouldn't know it if you said it to me right this minute."

"What about the mail she's been getting? Are her bills still coming in?"

She shrugged at that. "It looks that way to me. I haven't paid much attention. I just shipped on whatever came in. I do have a few I was about to forward if you'd like to see them." She got up and crossed to an oak secretary, opening one of the glass doors by turning the key in the lock. She took out a short stack of envelopes and sorted through them, then handed them to me. "This is the kind of thing she usually gets."

I did the same quick sorting job. Visa, MasterCard, Saks Fifth Avenue. A furrier named Jacques with an address in Boca Raton. A bill from a John Pickett, D.D.S., Inc., right around the corner on Arbol. No personal letters at all.

"Does she pay utility bills from here too?" I asked.

"I already sent those this month."

"Could she have been arrested?"

That sparked a laugh. "Oh no. Not her. She wasn't anything like that. She didn't drive a car, you know, but she wasn't the type to get so much as a jaywalking ticket."

"Accident? Illness? Drink? Drugs?" I felt like a doctor interviewing a patient for an annual physical.

Tillie's expression was skeptical. "She could be in the hospital I suppose, but surely she would have let us know. I find it very peculiar to tell you the truth. If that sister of hers hadn't come along, I might have gotten in touch with the police myself. There's just something not right."

"But there are lots of explanations for where she might be," I said. "She's an adult. Apparently she's got money and no pressing business. She really doesn't have to notify anybody of her whereabouts if she doesn't want to. She might be on a cruise. Or maybe she's taken a lover and absconded with him. Maybe she and this girl friend of hers took off on a toot. It might never occur to her that anyone was trying to get in touch."

"That's why I haven't really done anything so far, but it doesn't sit well with me. I don't think she'd leave without a word to anyone."

"Well, let me look into it. I don't want to hold you up right now, but I'll want to see her apartment at some point," I said. I got up and Tillie rose automatically. I shook her hand and thanked her for her help.

"Hang on to the mail for the time being, if you would," I said. "I'm going to chase down some other possibilities, but I'll get back to you in a day or two and let you know what I've come up with. I don't think there's any reason to worry."

"I hope not," Tillie said. "She's a wonderful person."

I gave Tillie my card before we parted company. I wasn't worried yet myself, but my curiosity had been aroused and I was eager to get on with it.

2

On the way back to the office, I stopped off at the public library. I went to the reference department and pulled the city directory for Boca Raton, checking the address I had for Elaine Boldt against the addresses listed. Sure enough, she was there with a telephone number that matched the one I'd been given. I noted the names of several other owners of adjacent condominiums, jotting down telephone numbers. There seemed to be a number of buildings in the same complex and I guessed that it was an entire "planned community." There was a general sales office, a telephone number for tennis courts, a health spa, and a recreational facility. I made notes of everything just to save myself a possible trip back.

When I reached the office, I opened a file on Elaine Boldt, logging the time I'd put in so far and the information I had. I tried the Florida number, letting it ring maybe thirty times without luck, and then I put in a call to the sales office of the Boca Raton condominium. They gave me the name of the resident manager in Elaine Boldt's building, a Roland Makowski, apartment 101, who picked up on the first ring.

"Makowski here."

I told him as briefly as possible who I was and why I was trying to get in touch with Elaine Boldt.

"She didn't come down this year," he said. "She's usually here about this time, but I guess she had a change of plans."

"Are you sure?"

"Well, I haven't seen her. I've been up and down and around this building day in and day out and I never laid eyes on her. That's all I know. I guess she could be here if she's always someplace where I'm not," he said. "That friend of hers, Pat, is here, but Mrs. Boldt went off someplace else is what I was told. Maybe she could tell you where. I just bumped into her

anging towels out on the rail which we don't allow. The
alcony's not a drying rack and I told her as much. She kinda
vent off in a huff."

"Can you tell me her last name?"

"What?"

"Can you tell me Pat's last name? Mrs. Boldt's friend."

"Oh. Yes."

I waited a moment. "I've got a pencil and paper," I said.

"Oh. It's Usher. Like in a movie theater. She's sublet, she
aid. What's your name again?"

I gave him my name again and my office number in case
e wanted to get in touch. It was not a satisfactory conver-
ation. Pat Usher seemed to be the only link to Elaine Boldt's
whereabouts and I thought it essential to talk to her as soon
s possible.

I put in another call to Elaine's Florida number, letting it
ing until *I* got annoyed with the sound. Nothing. If Pat Usher
vas still in the apartment, she was resolutely refusing to an-
wer the phone.

I checked the list I'd made of neighboring apartments and
ried the telephone number of a Robert Perreti, who appar-
ntly lived right next door. No answer. I tried the number
or the neighbor on the other side, dutifully letting the phone
ng ten times as the telephone company advises us. At long
ast, someone answered—a very old someone by the sound
f her.

"Yes?" She sounded as if she were feeble and might want
weep. I found myself speaking loudly and carefully as though
the hearing-impaired.

"Mrs. Ochsner?"

"Yes."

"My name is Kinsey Millhone. I'm calling from California
nd I'm trying to reach the woman who's staying next door
you in apartment 315. Do you happen to know if she's in?
ve just called and I let the phone ring about thirty times with
o luck."

"Do you have a hearing problem?" she asked me. "You're
eaking very loudly, you know."

I laughed, bringing my tone down into a normal range "I'm sorry," I said. "I wasn't sure how well you could hear me."

"Oh, I can hear perfectly. I'm eighty-eight years old and I can't walk a step without help, but there's nothing wrong with my ears. I counted every one of those thirty rings through the wall and I thought I'd go crazy if it went on much longer."

"Has Pat Usher stepped out? I was just on the line to the building manager and he said she was there."

"Oh, she's there all right. I know she is because she slammed the door not moments ago. What was it you wanted, if it's not too impertinent of me to ask?"

"Well, actually I'm trying to locate Elaine Boldt, but I understand she didn't make it down this year."

"That's true and I was awfully disappointed. She's part of a bridge foursome when Mrs. Wink and Ida Rittenhouse are here and we count on her. We haven't been able to play hand since last Christmas and it's made Ida very cranky if you want to know the truth."

"Do you have any idea where Mrs. Boldt might be?"

"No, I don't and I suspect the woman in there is on her way out. The condominium bylaws don't permit sublets and I was surprised that Elaine agreed to it. We've complained aplenty to the association and I believe Mr. Makowski has asked her to vacate. The woman has her back up, of course claiming her agreement with Elaine covers through the end of June. If you want to have a conversation with her yourself you'd do well to get down here soon. I saw her bringing up some cartons from the liquor store and I believe . . . well, should say I *hope* she's packing up even as we speak."

"Thanks. I may do that. You've been a big help. If I get down there, I'll stop by."

"I don't suppose you play bridge, do you, dear? We've been reduced to playing hearts now for the last six months and Ida's developing quite a mean mouth. Mrs. Wink and I can take too much more of this."

"Well, I've never played but maybe I could give it a try," said.

14

"A penny a point," she said brusquely, and I laughed.

I put in a call to Tillie. She sounded out of breath, as though he'd had to run for the phone.

"Hi, Tillie," I said. "It's me again. Kinsey."

"I just got back from the market," she panted. "Hang on until I catch my breath. Whew! What can I do for you?"

"I think I better go ahead and take a look at Elaine's apartment."

"Why? What's going on?"

"Well, the people in Florida say she's not there, so I'm hoping we can figure out where else she might have gone. If I come back over there, could you let me in?"

"I guess so. I'm not doing anything except unloading groceries and that won't take but two shakes."

When I reached the condominium again, I called her on the intercom and she buzzed me through and then met me at the elevator door with a key to Elaine's apartment. I told her the details of my conversation with Elaine's building manager down in Florida, filling her in as we rode up to the second floor.

"You mean nobody down there has seen her at all? Well, something's wrong then," she said. "Definitely. I know she left and I know she fully intended to go down to Florida. I was looking out the window when the cab pulled up out front and gave a toot and she got in. She had on her good fur coat and that fur turban that matched. She was traveling at night, which she didn't like to do, but then she wasn't feeling good and she thought the change in climate might help."

"She was sick?"

"Oh, you know. Her sinuses were acting up and she'd had that awful head cold or allergy or whatever it was. I don't mean to criticize, but she was a bit of a hypochondriac. She called me and said she'd decided to go ahead and fly on down, almost on the spur of the moment. She wasn't really scheduled to go for nearly two weeks, but then the doctor said it might do her good and I guess she booked the first flight she could get."

"Do you know if she used a travel agent?"

"I'm almost sure she did. Probably one close by. Since she didn't drive, she liked to deal with businesses within walking distance where she could. Here it is."

Tillie had paused outside of apartment 9, which was on the second floor, directly above hers. She unlocked the door and then followed me in.

The apartment was dim, drapes drawn, the air dry and still. Tillie crossed the living room and opened the drapes.

"Nobody's been in since she left?" I asked. "Cleaning lady? Tradesmen?"

"Not as far as I know."

Both of us seemed to be using our public-library tones, but there's something unsettling about being in someone else's place when you're not supposed to be. I could feel a low-level electrical current surging through my gut.

We did a quick tour together and Tillie said it looked all right to her. Nothing unusual. Nothing out of place. She left then and I went through on my own, taking my time so I could do it right.

This was a corner apartment, second-floor front, with windows running along two sides. I took a minute to stare down at the street. There were no cars passing. A boy with a Mohawk haircut was leaning up against a parked car directly below. The sides of his head were shaved to a preexecution gray and the strip of hair that remained stood up like dry brush in the center divider of a highway. It was dyed a shade of pink that I hadn't seen since hot pants went out of style. He looked to be sixteen or seventeen, wearing a pair of bright red parachute pants tucked down into combat boots, and an orange tank top with a slogan on the front that I couldn't read from where I stood. I watched him roll and light a joint.

I moved to the side windows which looked down at an angle through the ground-floor windows of the small frame house next door. The roof had been gnawed by fire, the eaves of the house showing through like the frail bones of an overcooked fish. The door was boarded up, the glass broken out.

f the windows, apparently by the heat. A FOR SALE sign was ammed into the dead grass like a flimsy headstone. Not much f a view for a condominium that I estimated must have cost Elaine more than a hundred thousand dollars. I shrugged to myself and went into the kitchen.

The counters and appliances gleamed. The floor had apparently been washed and waxed. The cupboards were neatly stacked with canned goods, including some 9-Lives Beef and Liver Platter. The refrigerator was empty, except for the usual door full of olives and pickles and mustards and jams. The electric stove had been unplugged, the cord dangling across the clockface, which read 8:20. An empty brown paper sack had been inserted in the plastic wastebasket under the sink, a cuff neatly turned down at the top. It looked as if Elaine Boldt had systematically prepared the apartment for a long absence.

I left the kitchen and wandered out into the entrance hall. The layout seemed to be a duplicate of Tillie's apartment downstairs. I moved down a short corridor, glancing to my right into a small bathroom with a sink shaped like a sunken marble shell, gold-plated fixtures, gold-flecked mirrored tiles on one wall. The small wicker wastebasket under the sink was empty except for a delicate gray-brown clump of hair clinging to the side like the light matting when a hairbrush has been cleaned.

Across from the bathroom was a small den, with a desk, a television set, an easy chair, and a sofa bed. The desk drawers contained the usual assortment of pens, paper clips, note cards, and files, which for the moment I saw no reason to examine more closely. I did come across her social-security card and made a note of the number. I left the den and moved into a master suite with an adjoining bathroom.

The bedroom was gloomy with the drapes pulled, but again everything seemed in order. To the right, there was a walk-in closet large enough to rent out. Some of the hangers were empty and I could see gaps in the articles lined up on the shelves where she'd probably packed an item. A small suitcase was still tucked down in one corner, one of the expensive designer types covered with somebody else's name all done in curlicues.

I checked dresser drawers randomly. Some still contained wool sweaters in plastic cleaner's bags. A few were empty except for a sachet or two left behind like tiny scented pillows. Lingerie. A few pieces of costume jewelry.

The master bath was spacious and orderly, the medicine cabinet stripped of all but a few over-the-counter remedies. I moved back to the door and stood there for a moment, surveying the bedroom. There was nothing to suggest foul play or haste, burglary, vandalism, illness, suicide, drunkenness, drug abuse, confusion, or recent occupancy. Even the faint powdering of household dust on the glossy surfaces seemed undisturbed.

I left, locking the door behind me. I took the elevator down to Tillie's and asked her if she had any photographs of Elaine.

"Not that I know," she said, "but I can describe her if you like. She's just about my size, which would make her five foot five, a hundred and thirty pounds. She has streaked blond hair which she wears pulled back. Blue eyes." Tillie stopped. "Oh wait, maybe I do have a picture. I just remembered one. Hold on."

She disappeared in the direction of the den and after a few moments returned with a Polaroid snapshot that she handed to me. The picture had an orange cast to it and seemed sticky to the touch. Two women stood in the courtyard, a full-length shot, taken from perhaps twenty feet back. One I guessed immediately was Elaine, smiling happily, trim and elegant in a pair of well-cut slacks. The other woman was thick through the middle, with blue plastic eyeglass frames and a hairdo that looked as if it could be removed intact. She appeared to be in her forties, squinting into the sun self-consciously.

"This was taken last fall," Tillie said. "That's Elaine on the left."

"Who's the other woman?"

"Marty Grice, a neighbor of ours. Now that was an awful

18

thing. She was killed . . . oh gosh, I guess six months back. It doesn't seem that long ago."

"What happened to her?"

"Well, they think she interrupted a burglar breaking into the house. I guess he killed her on the spot and then tried to burn the place down to cover it up. It was horrible. You might have read about it in the paper."

I shook my head. There are long periods when I don't read the paper at all, but I remembered the house next door with its charred roof and windows broken out. "That's too bad," I said. "Do you mind if I keep this?"

"Go right ahead."

I glanced at it again. The image was faintly disturbing, capturing a moment not that long ago when both women grinned with such ease, unaware that anything unpleasant lay ahead. Now, one was dead and the other missing. I didn't like that combination at all.

"Were Elaine and this woman good friends?" I asked.

"Not really. They played bridge together now and then, but they didn't socialize aside from that. Elaine is a bit stand-offish where most people are concerned. Actually, Marty used to get a little snippy about Elaine's attitude. Not that she ever said anything much about it to me, but I can remember her being a bit snide once in a while. Elaine does treat herself well—there's no doubt about *that*—and she tends to be insensitive to the idea that people really can't afford to live as well as she does. That fur coat of hers is a case in point. She knew Leonard and Marty were in financial straits, but she'd wear the coat over there to play bridge. To Marty, that was just like waving a red flag in front of a bull."

"That's the same coat she was wearing when you saw her last?"

"Yes, indeed. A twelve-thousand-dollar lynx fur coat with a matching hat."

"Wow," I said.

"Oh, it's beautiful. I'd give my eyeteeth to have a coat like that."

"Can you remember anything else about her departure that night?"

"I can't say that I do. She was carrying some sort of luggage—I guess a carry-on—and the cab driver brought down the rest."

"Do you remember what cab company?"

"I really didn't pay much attention at the time, but she usually called City Cab or Green Stripe, sometimes Tip Top, though she didn't like them much. I wish I could be more help. I mean, if she left here on her way to Florida and never got there, where did she end up?"

"That's what I want to know," I said.

I gave Tillie what I hoped was a reassuring smile, but I was feeling uneasy.

I went back to the office and did a quick calculation of the expenses I'd run up so far; maybe seventy-five bucks for the time spent with Tillie and the time going through Elaine's apartment, plus the time in the library and on the telephone and the long-distance charges. I've known P.I.s who conduct entire investigations on the phone, but I don't think it's smart. Unless you're dealing with people face-to-face, there are too many ways to be deceived and too many things to miss.

I called a travel agent and got myself booked round-trip to Miami. The fare was ninety-nine bucks each way if I flew in the dead of night and didn't eat, drink, or go to the john. I also reserved a cheap rental car on the far end.

My plane didn't leave for hours yet, so I went home and got in a three-mile jog, then stuck a toothbrush and toothpaste in my purse and called it packing. At some point, I was going to have to track down Elaine's travel agent and find out what airline she had taken and whether perhaps she'd booked herself through to Mexico or the Caribbean. In the meantime, I hoped I could catch Elaine's friend in Florida before she flew the coop, taking with her my only link to Elaine's whereabouts.

3

It was still dark when the plane touched down in Miami at
4:45 A.M. The airport was sparsely populated at that hour,
the lighting as subdued as a funeral home's. In the baggage
claim area, stacks of abandoned suitcases were piled together
in shadowy glass-fronted cabinets. All the airport shops were
closed. Travelers slept here and there on the unyielding plastic seats, resting their heads on bulging canvas totes, their
jackets hunched up over their shoulders. The intercom paged
a passenger to the white courtesy telephone, but the name
was garbled and I didn't think anyone would respond. I had
only managed to sleep for about an hour on the plane and I
felt rumpled and out of sorts.

I picked up my rental car and a sheet map and by 5:15 was
headed north on U.S. 1. Twenty miles to Fort Lauderdale,
another fifteen to Boca Raton. Dawn was turning the sky a
pearly translucent gray and clouds were piled up like heads
of cauliflower in a roadside stand. The land on either side of
the highway was flat, with white sand creeping up to the edges
of the road. Patches of saw grass and stunted cypress cut into
the horizon and Spanish moss hung from the trees like tattered rags. The air was already moist and balmy and the
streaks of orange from the rising sun hinted at a hot day to
come. To kill some time, I stopped at a fast-food place and
ate some brown and yellow things that I washed down with
a carton of orange juice. All of it tasted like something the
astronauts would have to reconstitute.

By the time I reached the community where Elaine Boldt
had her Florida condominium, it was nearly seven o'clock and
the sprinkler system was sending out jets of water across the
closely clipped grass. There were six or seven buildings of
poured concrete, each three stories high, with screened-in

porches punctuating the low clean lines. Hibiscus bushes added touches of bright red and pink. I circled through the area, driving slowly along the wide avenues that curved back as far as the tennis courts. Each building seemed to have its own swimming pool cradled close and there were already people stretched out on plastic chaise longues sunning themselves. I spotted the street number I was looking for and pulled into a small parking lot out in front. The manager's apartment was on the ground floor, the front door standing open, the screen door secured against the onslaught of big Florida bugs that were already making warning sounds in the grass.

I knocked against the aluminum frame.

"I'm right here." It was a woman's voice, disconcertingly close.

I cupped one hand, shading my eyes so that I could see who I was talking to through the screen door.

"Is Mr. Makowski here?"

The woman seemed to materialize on the other side, her face level with my knees.

"Hold on. I've been doing my sit-ups and I can't get to my feet yet. Lord, that hurts." She hauled herself into a kneeling position, clinging to the arm of a chair. "Makowski's off fixing the toilet in 208. What can I do you for?"

"I'm trying to get in touch with Elaine Boldt. Do you have any idea where she might be?"

"You that investigator who called from California?"

"Yes, that's me. I thought I should talk to someone down here and see if I could get a lead on her. Did she leave a forwarding address?"

"Nope. I wish I could help you out, but I don't know much more than you do. Here, come on in." She lurched to her feet and held the screen door open. "I'm Charmaine Makowski, or what's left of her. Do you exercise?"

"Well, I jog, but that's about it," I said.

"Good for you. Don't ever do sit-ups. That's my advice. I do a hundred a day and it always hurts." She was still winded, her cheeks tinted pink from the effort. She was in her late forties, wearing a bright yellow sweat suit, her belly protruding in pregnancy. She looked like a ripe Florida grapefruit.

"You got it," she said. "Another one of life's little jokes. I thought it was a tumor 'til it started to kick. Know what that is?"

She was pointing to a bump just below her waist. "That's what a belly button looks like turned inside out. It's embarrassing. Makowski and I didn't think we could have any kids. I'm almost fifty and he's sixty-five. Oh hell, what difference does it make? It's more fun than menopause, I guess. Have you talked to that woman up in 315? Her name is Pat Usher, but you probably know that. She claims Elaine let her sublet, but I doubt that."

"What's the story on that? Mrs. Boldt never talked to you about the arrangement?"

"Nope. Not a word. All I know is this Usher woman showed up a few months ago and moved in. At first nobody objected because we all just figured it was a two-week visit or something like that. People in the building can have any kind of company they want for short periods of time, but the rules say you can't sublet. Prospective buyers are screened real carefully and if we allowed sublets it would just be an invitation for any Tom, Dick, or Harry to move in here. The whole community would start to deteriorate. Anyway, after a month, Makowski went up to have a little chat with her and she claims she paid Elaine for six months and doesn't intend to move. It's driving Makowski around the bend."

"Does she have a signed lease?"

"She has a receipt showing she's paid Elaine some money, but it doesn't say for what. Makowski's had her served with an eviction notice, but she's taking her sweet time getting out. You haven't met her yet, I take it."

"I'm just on my way up. Do you know if she's in?"

"Probably. She doesn't go out much except to the pool to work on her tan. Tell her 'drop dead' from the management."

Three-fifteen was located on the third floor in the crook of the L-shaped building. Even before I rang the bell, I had the feeling that I was being inspected through the fisheye spy hole in the middle of the door. After a moment, the door opened to the width of the burglar chain, but no face appeared.

"Pat Usher?"

"Yes."

"My name is Kinsey Millhone. I'm an investigator from California. I'm trying to locate Elaine Boldt."

"What for?" Her tone was flat, guarded, no lilt at all and no graciousness.

"Her sister's been trying to get in touch with her to sign a legal document. Can you tell me where she is?"

There was a cautious silence. "Are you here to serve me papers?"

"No." I took out the photostatic copy of my license and passed it through the crack. The license disappeared smoothly, like a bank card being sucked into an instant-cash machine. After an interval, it came back.

"Just a minute. I'll see if I can find her address."

She left the door ajar, still secured by the chain. I felt a little flash of hope. Maybe I was making progress. If I could track Elaine down in another day or two, I'd feel pretty smug, which sometimes counts as much as money whatever business you're in. I waited, staring down at the welcome mat. The letter *B* was defined in dark bristles, surrounded by bristles in a lighter shade. Did they have enough mud in Florida to justify a mat like that? It was coarse enough to rip the bottom of your shoe off. I glanced to my left. Just off the balcony, I could see palm trees with little beaded skirts near the top. Pat Usher was back, still talking through the crack.

"I must have thrown it out. She was in Sarasota last I heard."

Already, I was tired of talking to the door and I felt a surge of irritation. "Do you mind if I come in? It's about the settlement on somebody's estate. She could pick up two or three thousand dollars if I can just get her signature." Appeal to greed, I thought. Appeal to the secret yearning for a windfall. Sometimes I use it as a ploy when I am tracking down a deadbeat who's run out on a bill. This time it was even true, so my voice had this wonderful sincere ring to it.

"Did the manager send you up here?"

"Come on, would you quit being paranoid? I'm looking for Elaine and I want to talk to you. You're the only person so far who seems to have any idea where she is."

Silence. She was pondering this as though it were an I.Q. test and she could pad the results. I had to struggle with the urge to bite. This was the only lead I had and I didn't want to blow it.

"All right," she said reluctantly, "let me get some clothes on first."

When she finally opened the door, she was wearing a float, one of those gauzy print caftans you slip over your head when you're too lazy to put on your underpants. She had adhesive tape across her nose. Her eyes were puffy and circled with bruises that were fading from blue to green. She had a strip of clear tape under each eye and her tan had dimmed to a sallow hue that made her look like she had a mild case of hepatitis.

"I was in a car accident and broke my nose," she said. "I don't like for people to see me like this."

She moved away from the door, the caftan sailing out behind her as though there were a breeze. I followed her in, closing the door behind me. The place was done in rattan and pastels and smelled faintly of mildew. Sliding glass doors on one side of the living room opened out onto the screened-in porch, beyond which there were only lush green treetops visible and clouds piling up like a bubble bath.

She took a cigarette out of a lead crystal box on the coffee table and lit it with a matching table lighter that actually worked. She sat down on the couch, propping her bare feet up on the edge of the table. Her soles were gray.

"Sit down if you want."

Her eyes were an eerie, electric green, tinted by contact lenses I had to guess. Her hair was a tawny shade, with a luster I've never been able to coax out of mine. She stared at me with interest now, her manner faintly amused. "Whose estate is it?"

She had this way of asking certain questions with no tilt at the end, soliciting information by making flat statements that

I was supposed to respond to. Odd. It made me wary somehow and I found myself taking care with what I said.

"A cousin, apparently. Someone in Ohio."

"Isn't it a bit radical to hire a private detective so you can hand out three thousand bucks?"

"There are other inheritors involved," I said.

"You have some kind of form you want her to sign."

"I want to talk to her first. People are worried because they haven't heard from her. I'd like to include something in my report about where she's been."

"Oh my God, now we got a report. She was restless. She's been traveling. What's the big deal."

"Do you mind if I ask you about your relationship with her?"

"No, I don't mind. We're friends. I've known her for years. She came down to Florida this time and she wanted some company."

"When was this?"

"Middle of January. Something like that." She paused, watching the ash on her cigarette. Her eyes came up to mine again, her expression remote.

"And you've been staying here ever since?"

"Sure, why not? I'd just lost the lease on my place and she said I could move in."

"Why'd she take off?"

"You'd have to ask her that."

"When did you last hear from her?"

"Two weeks ago, something like that."

"And she was in Sarasota then?"

"That's right. Staying with some people she met."

"Can you tell me who?"

"Look, she wanted me to keep her company, not baby-sit. It's none of my business who she hangs out with, so I don't ask."

I felt as if we were playing a parlor game that I couldn't possibly win. Pat Usher was having a better time than I was too, and I resented that. I went at it again. Was it Mrs. Peacock in the library with the rope?

"Can you tell me anything else you think might help?"

"I wasn't aware I'd helped so far," she said with a smirk.

"I was trying an optimistic approach," I snapped.

She shrugged. "Sorry to dim your little ray of hope. I've told you everything I know."

"I guess we'll have to let it go at that. I'll leave you my card. If she calls again, would you have her contact me?"

"Hey, sure. No sweat."

I took a card out of my wallet and put it on the table as I got up. "I understand you're getting some hassles from people here."

"Can you believe that? I mean, what's it to them? I've paid my rent. No parties, no loud music. I hang my laundry out and the manager comes unglued. Threw a fit. I don't get it." She got to her feet and led me to the door. The caftan billowing out behind her made her seem like a larger woman than she was. As I went past the kitchen, I caught sight of some cardboard boxes stacked up near the sink. She turned and followed my gaze.

"I'll probably find a motel close by if it comes to that. The last thing in the world I need is the sheriff on my case. That's who I thought you were, as a matter of fact. They got women sheriffs these days, did you know that? Sheriffettes."

"So I've heard."

"What about you?" she asked. "How'd you become a detective. That's a weird way to make a living, isn't it?"

She was becoming real chatty now that I was on my way out and I wondered if I might pump her for more information. She seemed eager to prolong the contact, like someone who's been cooped up too long with a pack of preschool kids.

"I sort of backed into detective work," I said, "but it beats selling shoes. You don't work yourself?"

"Not me. I'm retired. I don't ever want to work again."

"You're lucky. I don't have much choice. If I don't work, don't eat."

She smiled for the first time. "I used to spend my life waiting for a break. Then I figured out I better make my own luck,

27

you know what I mean? Nobody gives you nothing in this world, that's for sure."

I feigned agreement, glancing down toward the parking lot.

"I better be on my way," I said. "But could I ask you one more thing?"

"Like what."

"Do you know Elaine's other friends? There must be someone who knows how to get in touch with her, don't you think?"

"I'm the wrong one to ask," she said. "She used to visit me down in Lauderdale, so I don't know friends of hers up here."

"How'd you connect up this time? I understand she flew down almost on impulse."

She seemed momentarily perplexed at that, but regained her composure. "Yeah, that's right, she did. She called me from the airport in Miami and then picked me up on her way through."

"In a rented car?"

"Yeah. An Oldsmobile Cutlass. White."

"How long was she here then before she took off?"

Pat shrugged again. "I don't know. Not long. A couple of days, I guess."

"Did she seem at all nervous or upset?"

She became faintly irritated at that. "Wait a minute. What are you getting at? Maybe I could come up with something if I knew what was on your mind."

"I'm not sure," I said mildly. "I'm just fishing around, trying to figure out what's going on. The people who know her in Santa Teresa think it's unusual that she'd disappear without a word."

"But she told *me*. I've been telling you that. What is she some kind of kid that she has to call home all the time and tell someone where she is and what time she's getting in? What's the problem?"

"There isn't one. Her sister wants her to get in touch. That's all it amounts to."

"Yeah, all right. I get touchy now and then. I've been under a lot of pressure and I don't mean to take it out on you. She's probably call at some point and I'll give her your name and number, okay?"

"Great. I'd appreciate that."

I held out my hand and she shook it briefly. Her fingers were dry and cold.

"It's been nice talking to you," I said.

"You too," she replied.

I hesitated, glancing back at her. "If you do move into a motel, how will Elaine know where to reach you?"

The smirk was back, but there was something else in her eyes. "How about I'll leave a forwarding address with Makowski, my friendly building manager downstairs. That way you'll know how to reach me too. Will that do the trick?"

"Probably so. Thanks much."

4

I moved off toward the stairs. I could feel her eyes on my back and then I heard the door close. I continued on down to the parking lot and got in my car and drove off. I wanted to talk to Mrs. Ochsner in the next apartment, but I thought it was better to wait. Something about Pat Usher bothered me. It was not just the fact that some of what she'd told me was untrue. I'm a born liar myself and I know how it's done. You stick as close to the truth as you can. You pretend to volunteer a few bits of information, but the facts are all carefully selected for effect. Pat's problem was that she was having to wing far too much and she'd started to embroider where she should have kept her mouth shut. That business about Elaine Boldt picking her up in Fort Lauderdale in a rented white Cutlass was crap. Elaine didn't drive. Tillie had told me that. At the moment, I couldn't figure out why Pat had lied about it, but it must have been significant. What really bothered me about her was that she had no class and it struck me as odd that Elaine Boldt had chosen her for a friend. From what Tillie and Beverly told me, I had the feeling Elaine was a bit of a snob and Pat Usher didn't seem quite glossy enough to satisfy.

I found a drugstore half a block away and bought two packs of index cards so I could make some notes and then I put in a call to Mrs. Ochsner in 317. Finally, she picked up.

"Hello?"

I identified myself and told her where I was. "I've just been up there talking to Pat Usher and I don't want her to know that I'm talking to you. Is there some way we can get together?"

"Well, what fun," Mrs. Ochsner said. "What shall we do? I could take the elevator down to the laundry room. It's right near the parking lot, you know, and you could pick me up."

"Let's do that," I said. "I'll swing by in ten minutes."

"Make it fifteen. I'm slower than you think."

The woman whom I helped into the front seat of the car had hobbled out of the laundry room with a cane. She was small, with a dowager's hump the size of a backpack and off-white hair that stood out around her head like dandelion fuzz. Her face was as soft and withered as an apple doll and arthritis had twisted her hands into grotesque shapes, as though she intended to make geese heads in shadow on the wall. She was wearing a housedress that seemed to hang on her bony frame and her ankles were wrapped in Ace bandages. She had two garments over her left arm.

"I want to drop these off at the cleaner's," she said. "You can run them in. I want to stop by the market, too. I'm out of my cereal and half-and-half." Her manner was energetic, her voice wavering but excited.

I went around to my side of the car and got in. I started the car, glancing at the third floor to make sure Pat Usher wasn't standing there watching us. I pulled out. Mrs. Ochsner peered at me avidly.

"You don't look at all like you sounded on the phone," she said. "I thought you'd be blond with blue eyes. What are they, gray?"

"Hazel," I said. I lowered my sunglasses so she could see for herself. "Where's the cleaner's from here?"

"Right next door to that drugstore you telephoned from. What do you call that haircut?"

I glanced at myself in the rearview mirror. "I guess I don't call it anything. I do that myself with nail scissors every six weeks. I keep my hair short because I don't like to fool with . Why, do you think it looks bad?"

"I don't know yet. It probably suits, but I don't know you well enough to say. What about me? Do I look like I sound?"

I glanced over at her. "You sound like a hell-raiser on the phone."

"I was when I was your age. Now, I have to be careful I'm

31

not just written off as a crank like Ida. All my dear friends died and I got stuck with the crabby ones. What kind of luck are you having with Elaine?"

"Not a lot. Pat Usher says she was actually in Boca for a couple of days and then took off again."

"No, she wasn't."

"Are you sure?"

"Of course I am. She always knocked on the wall when she got in. It was like a little code. She's been doing it for years. She'd come over within the hour and make arrangements to play bridge with us because she knew how much it meant."

I parked in front of the cleaner's and picked up the two dresses she'd placed over the seat. "I'll be right back," I said.

I took care of both errands while Mrs. Ochsner waited and then we sat in the car and talked. I filled her in on my conversation with Pat Usher.

"What do you think of her?" I asked.

"She's too aggressive," Mrs. Ochsner said. "She tried to cultivate me at first, you know. Sometimes I'd sit out on the balcony in the sun and she'd talk to me. She always had that sooty smell people get when they smoke too much."

"What'd you talk about?"

"Well, it wasn't culture, I'll tell you that. She talked about food most of the time, but I never saw her put anything in her mouth except cigarettes and Fresca. She drank pop incessantly and that mouth of hers flapped all the time. So self centered. I don't believe she ever asked me one word about myself. It simply never occurred to her. I was bored to death of course, and began to avoid her whenever I could. Now she's rude because she knows I disapprove of her. Insecure people have a special sensitivity for anything that finally confirms their own low opinion of themselves."

"Did she mention Elaine?"

"Oh yes. She said Elaine was off on a trip, which struck me as odd. I'd never known her to come down here only to go someplace else. What would be the point?"

"Can you tell me who else Elaine might have kept in touch with? Any other friends or relatives down here?"

"I'll have to think about that. I don't know of anyone offhand. I assume that most of her good friends are in California, since that's where she lives most of the time."

We talked on for a while, but mostly about other things. At 11:15, I thanked her and took her back to the parking lot, gave her my business card so she could call me if she needed to, and then watched her hobble to the elevator. Her gait was irregular, like a marionette's being worked from above by strings. She waved to me with her cane and I waved back. She hadn't told me much, but I was hoping she'd be able to report on what was happening here after I flew back.

I drove out to the beach then and sat in the parking lot with my index cards, making notes of everything I could remember about my search to this point. It took an hour and my hand was cramped, but I needed to get it down while the details were fresh. When I finished, I took my shoes off and locked the car, walking the beach. It was too hot to jog and the lack of sleep had left me torpid anyway. The breeze coming in off the ocean was dense with the smell of salt. The surf seemed to roll in at half speed and there were no whitecaps. The ocean was a luminous blue and the sand was littered with exotic shells. All I'd ever seen on the California beaches were tangles of kelp and occasional Coke-bottle bottoms worn smooth by the sea. I longed to stretch out on the beach and nap in the hot sun, but I had to be on my way.

I ate lunch at a roadside stand built of pink cinder block while a radio station blared out Spanish-language programs as foreign to me as the food. I feasted on black-bean soup and a bolsa—a sort of pouch made of pastry holding a spicy ground meat. By four o'clock that afternoon, I was on a plane, headed for California. I'd been in Florida for less than twelve hours and I wondered if I was any closer to finding Elaine Boldt. It was possible that Pat Usher was being straight with me when she claimed Elaine was in Sarasota, but I doubted it. In any event, I was anxious to get home and I slept like the dead until the plane reached LAX.

When I got to the office at nine the next morning, I filled out a routine form for the Driver's License Records at the Department of Motor Vehicles in Tallahassee, Florida, and a second form for Sacramento on the off-chance that Elaine might have been issued a driver's license in her own name sometime in the last six months. I also sent similar requests to the Vehicle Registration Records in both places, not so much with the expectation of the inquiries paying off, but just to cover my bets. I stuck all four envelopes in my out box and then I pulled out the phone book and started checking addresses for travel agents located within walking distance of Elaine's condominium. I was hoping to establish her travel arrangements and find out if a plane ticket had been used. So far, I had only Pat Usher's word that Elaine had ever arrived in Miami. Maybe she never even reached the airport in Santa Teresa, or maybe she got off the plane at some point en route. In any event, I was going to have to check it out item by item. I felt as if I were on an assembly line, inspecting reality with a jeweler's loupe. There's no place in a P.I.'s life for impatience, faintheartedness, or sloppiness. I understand the same qualifications apply for housewives.

Most of my investigations proceed just like this. Endless notes, endless sources checked and rechecked, pursuing leads that sometimes go no place. Usually, I start in the same place, plodding along methodically, never knowing at first what might be significant. It's all detail; facts accumulated painstakingly.

It's hard to remain anonymous these days. Information is available on just about anyone: credit files on microfiche, service records, lawsuits, marriages, divorces, wills, births, deaths, licenses, permits, vehicles registered. If you want to remain invisible, pay cash for everything and if you err, don't get caught. Otherwise, any good P.I. or even a curious and persistent private citizen can find you out. It amazes me that the average person isn't more paranoid. Most of our personal data is a matter of public record. All you have to know is how to look it up. What your state and city government don't have on file, your next-door neighbor will usually share without so much as a dollar changing hands. If there was no way to get

34

a line on Elaine Boldt directly, I'd try an oblique approach. She'd left for Boca two weeks early, traveling at night, which, according to Tillie, was something she didn't like to do. She'd told Tillie she was ill, leaving town on doctor's orders, but at this point, there was no verification of that claim. Elaine might have lied to Tillie. Tillie might be lying to me. For all I knew Elaine had left the country, planting Pat Usher behind her to promulgate the notion that she was in Sarasota instead. I hadn't any idea why she'd do such a thing, but then I had a lot of ground to cover yet.

Having narrowed the list of travel agencies to six possibilities, I put in a call to Beverly Danziger and filled her in on my excursion to Florida. I wanted to bring her up to date even though the trip hadn't netted me much. I also had a couple of questions for her.

"What about family?" I asked. "Are your parents alive?"

"Oh, they've both been gone for years. We were never a close-knit family in the first place. I don't even think there were uncles or cousins she'd kept in touch with."

"What about jobs? What sort of work has she done?"

Beverly laughed at that. "You must not have a clear sense of Elaine quite yet. Elaine never lifted a finger in her life."

"But she does have a social-security card," I said. "If she's worked at all, it gives me one more avenue to pursue. For all we know, she's waiting tables someplace for a lark."

"Well, I don't think she's ever had a job, and if she did, it's not something she'd ever do again," Beverly said primly. "Elaine was spoiled. She felt she should be handed everything and what she wasn't handed, she took right out from under your nose anyway."

I really wasn't much in the mood to listen to Beverly unload past grievances. "Look, let's skip to the bottom line here. I think we ought to file a missing persons report. That way we can open up the scope of this thing. It should also eliminate some possibilities and believe me, at this point, everything helps."

The silence was so complete, I thought she'd hung up on me.

"Hello?"

"No, I'm here," she said. "I just don't understand why you want to talk to the *police* of all people."

"Because it's the next logical step. She may well be somewhere in Florida, but suppose she's not. At the moment, we only have Pat Usher's word for that. Why not get some broadscale coverage? Let the cops put out an APB. Let the Boca Raton P.D. get some sort of inquiry routed through Sarasota and see what they come up with. They can circulate a description through the state and local police down there and at least determine that she's not ill or dead or under arrest."

"Dead?"

"Hey, I'm sorry. I know it sounds alarming, and it may be nothing like that, but the cops will have access to information I just can't get."

"I don't believe this. I just wanted her signature. I hired you because I thought it would be the quickest way to find her. I don't think it's really a police matter. I mean, I simply don't want you to do that."

"All right. What, then? You can't ask me to find your sister for you and then start cutting off lines of inquiry."

"I don't see why not if I don't think it's appropriate. I don't see why you can't just let it go at this."

This time I was silent, wondering at the nature of her uneasiness. "Beverly, did I miss something here? Are you telling me to drop it?"

"Well, I don't know. Let me think about it and I'll call you back. I just didn't think it would be a problem and I'm not sure I want you to go on with this. Maybe Mr. Wender can proceed without her. Maybe he can find some loophole that will let him hold out only her portion of the estate until she turns up."

"You didn't seem to feel that way two days ago," I said.

"Maybe I made a mistake," she said. "Let's just don't worry about it right now, okay? I'll be in touch if I want you to go on with it. In the meantime, why don't you send me a report and an itemized bill of some kind? I'll have to talk to my husband about what to do from here."

"All right," I said with puzzlement, "but I have to tell you, I'm worried."

"Well, don't be," she said and the phone clicked in my ear.

I stared at the receiver. Now what was all that about? Her anxiety had been unmistakable, but I couldn't ignore the message. She hadn't fired me outright, but she'd put me on hold and I wasn't technically supposed to proceed without her instructions to do so.

Reluctantly, I went back through my index cards and typed up a report. I was stalling for time and I knew it, but I wasn't ready to let go. I put a carbon in my files and slipped the original in an envelope, which I addressed to Beverly, enclosing an itemization of my expenses to that point. Beyond the seven-hundred-and-fifty-dollar retainer she'd given me, she'd authorized an additional two hundred and fifty dollars for a total "not to exceed one thousand dollars without further written notice"—which was contractual double-talk for the fact that so far, we were covered. With the plane fare, the rental car, long-distance calls, and approximately thirty hours of my time, the charges came to $996 plus change. She owed me two hundred and forty-six bucks. I suspected she'd pay me off and wash her hands of it. My guess was that she'd enjoyed hiring a detective, officiously stirring up trouble for Elaine, who'd annoyed her by not signing on the dotted line as she'd been asked. Now suddenly, she must have realized that she'd opened up a big can of worms.

I locked up the office and dropped the report in a mailbox on my way home. Elaine Boldt was still among the missing and that didn't sit well with me.

5

My phone rang at 2:08 A.M. I picked up the receiver automatically, my brain still blank with sleep.

"Kinsey Millhone." The voice was male and the tone was neutral, like someone reading at random from a telephone book. Somehow I knew it was a cop. They all sound like that.

"Yes. Who's this?"

"Miss Millhone, this is Patrolman Benedict of the Santa Teresa Police Department. We've been called on a 594 at 2097 Via Madrina, apartment 1, and a Mrs. Tillie Ahlberg is asking for you. Would it be possible for you to lend some assistance? We have a policewoman with her, but she's asked for you specifically and we'd appreciate it if you could respond."

I raised up on one elbow, a few brain cells switching to ignition. "What's a 594?" I said. "Malicious mischief?"

"Yes ma'am."

It was clear Patrolman Benedict didn't want to risk anything by rushing right in with a lot of facts.

"Is Tillie okay?" I asked.

"Yes ma'am. She's unharmed, but she's upset. We don't mean to disturb you, but the lieutenant okayed us to get in touch."

"I'll be there in five minutes," I said and hung up.

I pushed the quilt back and grabbed for my jeans and sweatshirt, pulling on boots without ever getting up off the couch. I usually sleep naked in a fold of quilt because it's so much easier than opening the sofa bed. I went into the bathroom, brushed my teeth and splashed water on my face, combing my unruly hair with my fingers as I snatched up my keys and moved to the car. I was wide awake by now, wondering what kind of 594 we were talking about. Tillie Ahlberg was clearly not the perpetrator or she'd have called an attorney instead.

The night air was cold and the fog had rolled in off the beach and halfway across town, filling the empty streets with a fine mist. Stoplights blinked dutifully from red to green to red again, but there was no traffic and I ran the lights every chance I got. There was a black-and-white parked out in front of 2097 and the lights in Tillie's ground-floor apartment were all on, but things seemed quiet; no flashing red lights, no neighbors gathered on the sidewalk. I announced myself on the intercom and somebody buzzed me in. I pushed through the door to the right of the elevator and moved quickly down the corridor to Tillie's apartment at the end. Several people in robes and pajamas stood in the hall near the door, but a patrolman in uniform was encouraging them to go on back to bed. When he spotted me, he approached, hands on his hips as though he didn't know what else to do with them. He looked like he'd probably still be asked for his I.D. when he ordered a drink, but up close I could see signs of age: fine lines near his eyes, a slight loosening of the taut skin along his jaw. His eyes were old and I knew he'd already seen more of the human condition than he could assimilate.

I held out my hand. "Are you Benedict?"

"Yes ma'am," he said, shaking hands with me. "You're Miss Millhone, I take it. Nice to meet you. We appreciate this." His grip was firm, but brief. He nodded toward the door to Tillie's apartment, which stood ajar. "You can go on in if you want. Officer Redfern is with her, taking down particulars."

I thanked him and moved into the apartment, glancing to my right. The living room looked like something left in the path of a tornado. I stopped and stared for a moment. Vandalism in a place like this? I moved into the kitchen. Tillie was sitting at the table with her hands tucked between her knees, the freckles standing out on her pale face like red pepper flakes. A uniformed policewoman, maybe forty years old, was seated at the table taking notes. She had short-cropped blond hair and a birthmark like a patch of rose petals on one cheek. Her name tag identified her as Isabelle Redfern and she talked to Tillie in low, earnest tones like someone trying to persuade a flier not to leap off a bridge.

When Tillie caught sight of me, tears spilled out of her eyes and she began to shake, as though my appearance were tacit permission to fall apart. I knelt down beside her, taking her hands. "Hey, it's okay," I said, "what's going on?"

She tried to speak, but nothing came out at first except a wheezing sound like someone stepping on a rubber duck. Finally, she managed to choke out a response. "Someone broke in. I woke up and saw this woman standing in the door to my room. My God, I thought my heart would stop. I couldn't even move I was so terrified. And then . . . and then, she started . . . it was like this hissing sound and she ran in the living room and started tearing everything up. . . ." Tillie put a handkerchief over her mouth and nose, closing her eyes. Officer Redfern and I exchanged a look. Bizarre stuff. I put my arm around Tillie's shoulders, giving her a little shake.

"Come on, Tillie," I said, "it's over now and you're safe."

"I was so scared. I was so scared. I thought she was going to kill me. She was like a maniac, like a totally crazy person, panting and hissing and crashing around. I slammed the bedroom door shut and locked it and then dialed 911. Next thing I knew it got quiet, but I didn't open up the door until the police got here."

"That's great. You did great. Look, I know you were scared, but you did it just right and now it's okay."

The policewoman leaned forward. "Did you get a good look at this woman?"

Tillie shook her head, beginning to shake again.

This time the policewoman took Tillie's hands. "Take a couple of deep breaths. Just relax. It's over now and everything's fine. Breathe deeply. Come on. Do you have any tranquilizers on hand or alcohol of some kind?"

I got up and moved over to the kitchen cabinets, opening doors at random, but there didn't seem to be any liquor at all. I found a bottle of vanilla extract and poured the contents into a jelly glass. Tillie downed it without even looking.

She began to breathe deeply, calming herself. "I never saw her before in my life," she said in somewhat more ordered tones. "She was crazy. A lunatic. I don't even know how she got in." She paused. The air smelled like cookies.

The policewoman looked up from her notes. "Mrs. Ahlberg, there was no sign of forced entry. It had to be someone who had a key. Have you given a key to anyone in the past? Maybe someone who was house-sitting? Someone who watered your plants when you were away?"

At first Tillie shook her head and then she stopped and shot a look at me, her eyes filled with sudden alarm.

"Elaine. She's the only one who ever had one." She turned to the policewoman. "My neighbor in the apartment right above me. I gave her a key last fall when I took a little trip to San Diego."

I took over then, filling in the rest; Elaine's apparent disappearance and her sister's hiring me.

Officer Redfern got up. "Hold on. I want Benedict to hear this."

It was 3:30 in the morning by the time Redfern and Benedict were finished, and Tillie was exhausted. They asked her to come down to the station later that morning to sign a statement and in the meantime, I said I'd stay with her until she had herself under control again.

When the cops finally left, Tillie and I sat and stared at each other wearily.

"Could it have been Elaine?" I asked.

"I don't know," she said. "I don't think so, but it was dark and I wasn't thinking straight."

"What about her sister? Did you ever meet Beverly Danziger? Or a woman named Pat Usher?"

Tillie shook her head mutely. Her face was still as pale as a dinner plate and there were dark circles under her eyes. She anchored her hands between her knees again, tension humming through her like a wind across guitar strings.

I moved into the living room and surveyed the damage more closely. The big glass-fronted secretary had been tipped over and lay facedown on the coffee table, which looked to have collapsed on impact. The couch had been slashed, the foam hanging out now like pale flesh. Drapes were torn down. Windows had been broken, lamps and magazines and flowerpots flung together in a heap of pottery shards and water and paper pulp. This was what insanity looked like when it was on the loose. That or unbridled rage, I thought. This had to be connected to Elaine's disappearance. There was no way I'd believe it was an independent event, coincidental to my search for her. I wondered if there was a way to find out where Beverly Danziger had been tonight. With her porcelain good looks and her blinking china blue eyes, it was hard to picture her loping around all looney-tunes, but how did I know for sure? Maybe she'd driven up to Santa Teresa the first time on an institutional pass.

I tried to imagine what it would be like to wake in the dead of night to some hissing female on the rampage. An involuntary shiver took me and I went back into the kitchen. Tillie hadn't moved, but her eyes came up to my face with a look of dependency.

"Let's get it cleaned up," I said. "We're neither of us going to sleep anyway and you shouldn't have to do this by yourself. Where do you keep your dustpan and broom?"

She pointed to the utility room and then with a sigh she got to her feet and we went to work.

When order had been restored, I told Tillie I wanted the key to Elaine's apartment. "What for?" she asked apprehensively.

"I want to check it out. Maybe she's up there."

"I'll come with you," she volunteered promptly. I wondered vaguely if she was going to follow me around for life like Yogi Bear and Boo-Boo. Still, I gave her a quick hug and told her to wait a minute while I made a quick trip to my VW. She shook her head and followed me outside.

I took my semi-automatic out of the glove compartment, hefting it in my hand. It was a nondescript .32 with a crosshatched ivory grip and a clip that would hold eight rounds. The life of a private eye is short on gun battles, long on basic research, but there are times when a ball-point pen just doesn't get it. I had visions of some deranged female flying out of the darkness at me like a bat. A .32 may not have much stopping power, but it can sure slow you down. I wedged the gun in the back of my jeans and headed back to the elevator with Tillie at my heels.

"I thought it was against the law to carry a concealed weapon like that," she said uneasily.

"That's why I have a permit," I said.

"But I always heard handguns were so dangerous."

"Of course, they're dangerous! That's the point. What do you want me to do? Go in there with a hunk of rolled-up newspaper?"

She was still giving that one some thought when we reached the second floor. I took out the automatic and eased the safety off, pulling back the slide on the barrel to cock it. I slipped the key to Elaine's lock and then I opened the door and let it swing back. Tillie was holding on to my sleeve like a little kid. I waited a moment, staring into the gloomy interior with my heart thumping. There was no sound . . . no movement inside. I felt for the light switch and flipped it on, peering around the doorframe quickly. Nothing. I indicated that Tillie was to wait where she was and I moved through the apartment quietly, turning lights as I went, using a modified version of my best junior G-man stance every time I entered a room. As far as I could tell, there was no sign that anyone had been there. I checked the closets and took a quick peek under the bed and then sighed, realizing that I'd been holding my breath. I went back to the front door and had Tillie come in, closing and locking it behind us. I moved back down the hallway to the den

I went through Elaine's desk quickly, checking her files. In the third drawer down, I found her passport and flipped through the pages. It was still valid, but it hadn't been used since a trip to Cozumel one April three years back. I tucked the passport in my back pocket. If she was still around, I didn't want her using her passport to slip out of the country. There was something else knocking around in the back of my head, but I couldn't figure out what it was. I shrugged to myself, assuming it would surface in due course.

I deposited Tillie at her door.

"Look," I said, "when you have a chance, take a careful look around and see if anything's missing. When you go down to the police station, they'll want a list of stolen property if you know of any. Do you carry any homeowner's insurance that might cover the damages?"

"I don't know," she said, "I guess I can check. Would you like some tea?" Her expression was wistful and she clung to my hand.

"Tillie, I wish I could, but I've got to go. I know you're uneasy, but you'll be okay. Is there somebody in the building who can keep you company?"

"Maybe the woman in apartment 6. I know she's up early. I'll try her. And thanks, Kinsey. I mean that."

"Don't worry about it. I was glad to help. I'll talk to you later. Get some sleep if you can."

I left her looking after me plaintively as I headed toward the lobby. I got in the car and tucked the gun in the glove compartment again, and then I headed for my place. My head was full of questions, but I was too tired to think. By the time I crept back in the folds of my quilt, the sky was a predawn gray and an enterprising rooster somewhere in my neighborhood was heralding the day.

The phone shrilled again at 8:00 A.M. I'd just reached that wonderful heavy stage of sleep where your nervous system turns to lead and you feel like some kind of magnetic force has just fused you to the bed. Consistently waking someone from a sleep like that could generate psychosis in two days.

"What," I mumbled. I could hear static in the line, but nothing else. Oh goody, maybe I'd been wakened by a long-distance obscene phone caller. "Hello?"

"Oh, that's you! I thought I'd dialed the number wrong. This is Julia Ochsner down in Florida. Did I wake you up?"

"Don't worry about it," I said. "I thought I just saw you. What's happening?"

"I've come across some information I thought you might like to have. It looks like that woman next door was telling the truth when she told you Elaine flew down here in January, at least as far as Miami."

"Really?" I said, sitting up. "What makes you say that?"

"I found the plane ticket in the garbage," she said with satisfaction. "You'll never believe what I did. She was packing up to go and she'd set several boxes full of discards and trash out. I'd been down to the manager's apartment and on my way back I spotted the ticket. It was right near the top, shoved down half out of sight, and I wanted to see whose it was. I didn't think I could come right out and ask her so I waited until she made a trip down to the parking lot with a load of clothes and I just scampered out there and stole it."

"You scampered?" I said, with disbelief.

"Well, it wasn't 'scampering' exactly. More like a fast creep. I don't think she even missed it."

"Julia, what made you do that? Suppose she'd caught you!"

"What do I care? I'm having a ball. When I got back, I had to go lie down I was laughing so hard!"

"Yeah, well you'll never guess what's happened here," I said. "I got fired."

"Fired?"

"More or less. Elaine's sister told me to lay off for the time being. She got nervous when I told her I thought we should file a missing persons report with the cops."

"I don't understand. Why would she object?"

"Beats me. When did Elaine leave Santa Teresa? Do you have the date?"

"It looks like January ninth. The return was left open."

"Well, that helps some. Why don't you drop that in the mail to me if it's not too much trouble. Beverly may back down yet."

"But that's ridiculous! What if Elaine's in trouble?"

"What can I do? I'm paid to follow instructions. I can't just bop around doing anything I please."

45

"What if I hired you myself?"

I hesitated, taken aback by the idea but not opposed to it.

"I don't know. That could get sticky. I suppose I could terminate my relationship with her, but there's no way I could release information to you that I'd uncovered for her. You and I would have to start from scratch."

"But she couldn't *prevent* me from hiring you, could she? I mean, once you've settled your account with her?"

"God, it's too early in the morning for me to worry about this stuff, but I'll mull it over and see what I can come up with. As far as I know, I could turn around and work for you as long as it doesn't represent any conflict of interest. I'd have to advise her what's going on, but I don't see how she could interfere."

"Good, then do it."

"Are you sure you want to spend your money that way?"

"Of course I am. I have lots of it and I want to know what's happened to Elaine. Besides, I'm having the time of my life! Just tell me what we do next."

"All right. Let me nose around some and I'll call you back. And Julia, in the meantime, would you watch out for yourself?" I said, but she just laughed.

6

I stayed in the shower until the hot water ran out and then got dressed, pulling on jeans and a cotton sweater, zipping boots up to my knees. I plopped on a soft leather hat with a wide brim and studied the effect in the bathroom mirror. It would do.

I headed for the office first and wrote a letter to Beverly Danziger, terminating our professional relationship. I was pretty sure she'd be thoroughly disconcerted by that and it gave me a nice feeling. I went next door to the offices of California Fidelity Insurance and made a photocopy of my itemized bill to her, marked it "final," and tucked it in with the letter and a copy of my final report. Then I headed over to the police station on Floresta and talked to a Sergeant Jonah Robb about a missing persons report on Elaine Boldt, watching his fingers fly across the keys as he typed the information I gave him on the form.

He looked like he was in his late thirties, his body compact in his uniform. He was maybe twenty pounds overweight, not an unattractive amount, but something he'd have to cope with soon. Dark hair trimmed very short, smooth rounded face, a dent in his left ring finger where he'd recently worn a wedding ring. He shot a look at me at that point. Blue eyes flecked with green.

"Anything you want to add to this?"

"Her next-door neighbor down in Florida is sending me a plane ticket she apparently used. I'll take a look at it and see if it tells us anything else. A friend of hers named Pat Usher swears up and down she spent a couple of days with Elaine Boldt before she went off to Sarasota, but I don't believe much of what she says."

"She'll probably show up. They usually do." He took a file

folder out and inserted a clamp. "You used to be a cop, didn't you?"

"Briefly," I said. "But I couldn't make it work. Too rebellious I guess. What about you? How long have you been on the force?"

"Eight years. I was a detail man before that. Sold drugs for Smith, Kline, and French. I got tired of driving around in a late-model car, hitting up on doctors. It was all hype anyway. Just like selling anything else. Sickness is big business." He looked down at his hands, then back at me. "Well. Anyway, I hope you find your lady. We'll do what we can."

"Thanks," I said, "I'll give you a call later in the week."

I picked up my bag and moved toward the door.

"Hey," he said.

I looked back.

"I like the hat."

I smiled.

As I passed the front counter on my way out, I caught sight of Lieutenant Dolan in Identification and Records, talking to a young black clerk in uniform. His glance slid past me and then came back with a look of recognition. He broke off his conversation with her and ambled over to the counter. Lieutenant Dolan is in his fifties, with a square, baggy face and a bald spot he tries to disguise with tricky arrangements of what hair remains. It's the only evidence of any vanity on his part and it cheers me up somehow. I imagine him standing in front of his bathroom mirror every morning, trying to cope with the creeping expanse of naked scalp. He was wearing rimless bifocals, apparently new, because he couldn't quite get me in range. He peered at me first from above the little half-moons and then from below. Finally, he slipped the glasses off and tucked them in the pocket of his rumpled gray suit.

"Hello, Kinsey. I haven't seen you since the shooting. How are you doing with that?"

I felt myself flush with discomfort. I'd killed someone in the course of an investigation two weeks before and I was studiously avoiding the subject. The moment he mentioned it I realized how completely I'd willed it away. It hadn't even crossed my mind and his reference to it seemed as startling as that dream where you find yourself stark-naked in a public place.

"I'm fine," I said briefly, breaking off eye contact. In a flash, I saw the beach at night, that slat of light when the big trash bin I was hiding in was opened and I looked up. My little semiautomatic had jumped in my hand like some kind of reflex test and I'd squeezed off more rounds than were really necessary for getting the job done. The blast in that confined space had been deafening and my ears had been ringing ever since, a high-pitched hiss like gas escaping from a faulty valve. In a flash, the image was gone again and Lieutenant Dolan was standing there, maybe wishing he'd kept his mouth shut judging from the look on his face.

My relationship to Con Dolan has always been adversarial, remote, based on grudging mutual respect. He doesn't like private investigators as a rule. He feels we should mind our own business, whatever *that* is, and leave law enforcement to professionals like him. My fantasy has always been that one day we'll sit down and exchange criminal gossip like little old ladies, but now that he'd introduced a personal note, I could feel myself withdraw, disconcerted by the shift. When I met his eyes again, his gaze was flat, his expression bland.

I shook my head. "Sorry," I said, "you took me by surprise. I guess I haven't quite sorted it through." Actually what took me by surprise was realizing I'd killed someone and didn't much care. No, that wasn't true. I did care, but if my life was threatened, I knew I'd do it again. I'd always believed I was a good person. Now I didn't know what "good" meant. Surely good people didn't kill other human beings, so where did that put me?

He said, "What are you doing down here?"

I shook my head again slightly and focused on the subject at hand. "I just filed a missing persons report for a client," I said. I hesitated, wondering if he'd encountered Elaine during his investigation of the incident next door. "Did you handle the Grice homicide back in January of this year?"

He stared at me, his face closing up like sea anemone. Apparently he had. "What about it?"

"I wondered if you interviewed a woman named Elaine Boldt. She lives in the condominium next door."

"I remember the name," he said carefully. "I spoke to her myself by phone. She was supposed to come down and talk to us, but I don't think she ever showed up. She your client?"

"She's the one I'm looking for."

"How long she been gone?"

I detailed the information I had and I could see him run through the possibilities in the same way I had. In Santa Teresa County, some four thousand persons, male and female, are reporting missing every year. Most are found again but a few remain somewhere out in the ether.

He shoved his hands down in his pockets, rocking on his heels. "When she does turn up, tell her I want her down here for an interview," he said.

I was startled. "That case hasn't been wrapped up yet?"

"No, and I won't discuss it with you either. Department policy," he said. His favorité phrase.

"Jesus, Lieutenant Dolan. Big deal. Who asked you?" I knew he was protecting the integrity of his case, but I get tired of his being such a tight-ass. He thinks he is entitled to any information I have, while he never gives me a thing. I was hot and he knew it.

He smiled at me. "I just thought I'd head off that tendency of yours to stick your nose where it doesn't belong."

"I'll help you out sometime too," I said. "And meanwhile if you want to talk to Elaine Boldt, you can find her yourself."

I pushed away from the counter, heading toward the exit

"Well, you don't need to take that attitude," he called. I glanced back. He was looking entirely too self-satisfied for my taste.

"Right," I said and pushed on out the double doors.

I came out of the police station into the flat overcast day and stood for a moment, collecting myself. The man gets to me. No doubt about it. I took a deep breath.

The temperature was in the mid-sixties. Pale remnants o

sunlight shone through the clouds, tinting the neighborhood with lemon-colored light. The shrubbery had taken on a chartreuse glow and the grass seemed dry and artificial from the lack of moisture. It hadn't rained for weeks and the month of June had been a monotonous succession of foggy mornings, hazy afternoons, and chilly nights. Actually, Lieutenant Dolan had opened up a possibility and I wondered if Elaine's departure was coincidental with the murder of Marty Grice or connected in some way. If the vandalism at Tillie's was related, why not this? Could she have taken off to avoid the lieutenant's questioning? I thought it might help to pin down some dates.

I headed over to the newspaper office six blocks away and asked the clerk in the newspaper morgue to track down the file clips on Marty Grice's death. There was only one clip, a small article, maybe two inches long, stuck back on page eight of local news, dated January 4.

BURGLAR KILLS HOUSEWIFE, THEN BURNS BODY, POLICE SAY

A Santa Teresa housewife was bludgeoned to death during an apparent burglary in her westside residence early last night. According to homicide detectives, Martha Renée Grice, 45, of 2095 Via Madrina, was struck repeatedly with a blunt instrument and doused with flammable liquid. The victim's body was discovered, badly burned, in the foyer of the partially destroyed single-family dwelling after Santa Teresa fire fighters battled the blaze for thirty minutes. The fire was first spotted by neighbors at 9:55 P.M. Two adjacent homes were evacuated, but no other injuries were reported. Details of the arson were withheld pending further investigation.

The crime seemed pretty spectacular to get such small play. Maybe the cops hadn't had much to go on and had tried to minimize the coverage. That might explain Dolan's attitude. Maybe he wasn't being uncooperative. Maybe he had no evidence. Nothing makes a cop any tighter than that. I took down the pertinent information in my notebook and then I walked over to the public library and checked the Santa Teresa city directory that had come out last spring. Martha Grice was listed at 2095 Via Madrina along with a Leonard Grice, bldg. contrctr. I assumed he was the husband. The newspaper account had made no mention of him and I wondered where he'd been when the whole thing went down. The directory listed the neighbors next door at 2093 as Orris and May Snyder. His occupation was "retired" but the directory didn't say from what. I jotted down the names and the telephone number. It might be interesting to see if I could find what went on and whether Elaine might have seen something she didn't want to talk about. The more I thought about it, the better I liked that idea. It gave me a whole new line to pursue.

I retrieved my car from the lot behind my office and circled back around to Via Madrina. It was now twelve o'clock straight up and high-school students were spilling out onto the streets; girls in jeans, short white socks and high heels, guys in chinos and flannel shirts. The wholesome California sorts outnumbered the punkers about three to one, but most of them looked like they'd been dressed out of ragbags. Some kids were wearing outrageous designer jumpsuits and some wore whole outfits in camouflage fabric as though prepared for an air attack. About half the girls sported three to four earrings per ear. In hairstyles, they seemed to fancy the wet look, or ponytails sticking up out of the sides of their heads like waterspouts.

As I pulled up in front of the condominium, a cluster of six girls were clumping down the sidewalk, smoking clove-scented cigarettes. Shoulder pads and green nail polish, dark red lipstick. They looked like they were on their way to a USO dance in 1943.

I caught just a fragment of their conversation.

"So I'm all 'What the fuck did you think I was talking about, dick-head?!' and he goes like 'Hey, well, I never did anything to you, bitch, so I don't know what your problem is.' "

I smiled to myself, and then looked over at the Grice house with interest. It was white frame, a story and a half, with a squat L-shaped porch across the front, resting on fat red-brick pillars topped with short pyramids of wood. It looked as if it had been jacked up somehow and might, at any moment, collapse. Most of the porch roof had burned away. The yard was scrappy and a row of pale pink-and-blue hydrangea bushes crowded the porch, still looking browned and wilted from the fire, though new growth was bravely showing through. The front window frames on the first floor were capped with lintels of black soot where the fire had licked the framing. A sign had been posted warning trespassers away. I wondered if the salvage crew had already gone in to clean up. I was hoping not, but I was probably out of luck on that. I wanted to see the house as it had been on the night of the fire. I also wanted to chat with Leonard Grice, but there was no indication whatever that the house was inhabited. Even from the street, I could still pick up the six-month-old cologne of charred wood and grinding damp where the firemen's hoses had penetrated every seam and crevice.

As I headed toward Elaine's condominium, I spotted some-one coming out of a small wooden utility shed in the Grices' backyard. I paused to watch. A kid, maybe seventeen. He had a Mohawk haircut, three inches of what looked like bright pink hay with a path mown on either side. He had his head down, his hands shoved into the pockets of his army fatigues. With a start, I realized I'd seen him before—from Elaine's front window the first time I searched her place. He'd been standing in the street below, rolling a joint at a leisurely pace. Now what was he up to? I veered, picking up my pace so my path would intersect his just about at the property line.

"Hello," I said.

He looked up at me, startled, flashing the sort of polite smile kids reserve for adults. "Hi."

His face didn't match the rest of him. His eyes were deep-set, a jade green set off by dark lashes and dark eyebrows that feathered together at the bridge of his nose. His skin was clear, his smile engaging, slightly snaggle-toothed. He had a dimple in his left cheek. He glanced to one side, moving past me. I reached out and caught him by the sleeve.

"Can I talk to you?"

He looked at me and then quickly back over his shoulder.

"You talking to me?"

"Yes. I saw you coming out of that shed back there. You live around here?"

"What? Oh. Sure, couple of blocks away. This is my Uncle Leonard's house. I'm supposed to check and make sure nobody's bothering his stuff." His voice was light, almost feminine.

"What stuff is that?"

The jade-green eyes had settled on me with curiosity. He smiled and his whole face brightened. "You a cop or something?"

"Private investigator," I said. "My name is Kinsey Millhone."

"Wow, that's great," he said. "I'm Mike. You guarding the place or something like that?"

I shook my head. "I'm looking into another matter, but I heard about the fire. Your aunt was the one who was killed?"

The smile flickered. "Yeah, right. Jesus, that was terrible. I mean, her and me were never close, but my uncle really got messed up over that. He's a fuckin' basket case. Oh. Sorry 'bout that," he said sheepishly. "He's like vegged out or something, staying with this other aunt of mine."

"Can you tell me how to get in touch with him?"

"Well, my aunt's name is Lily Howe. I don't remember the number offhand, or I'd help you out."

He was beginning to blush and the effect was odd. Pink hair, green eyes, rosy cheeks, green army fatigues. He looked like a birthday cake, innocent and festive somehow. He ran a hand across his hair, which was standing straight up on top like a whisk broom.

I wondered why he was so ill at ease. "What were you doing back there?"

He glanced back at the shed with an embarrassed shrug. "I was checking the padlock. I get like really paranoid, you know? I mean, the guy pays me ten bucks a month and I like to do right by him. Did you want something else? Because I have to go grab some lunch and get back to class, okay?"

"Sure. Maybe I'll see you later." ‾

"Right. That'd be great. Anytime." He smiled at me again and then moved away, walking backward at first, his eyes latched to mine, turning finally so that I was watching the narrow back and slim hips. There was something disturbing about him, but I couldn't think what it was. Something didn't jibe. That goody-two-shoes helpfulness and the look in his eyes. Artless and cunning . . . a kid whose conscience is clear because he doesn't have one. Maybe I'd check him out too, as long as I was at it. I went into the condominium courtyard.

7

I found Tillie spraying down the walk, a rolling tumble of leaves and debris pushed along by the force of the jet. Water dripped from the feather palms, the rubbery scent of hose mingling with the odor of wet earth. Stepping-stones were tucked in among the giant ferns, though why anyone would want to walk back in there was beyond me. It looked like a shadowy haven for daddy longlegs. Tillie smiled when she saw me and released the trigger nozzle, shutting off the spray. She was wearing jeans and a T-shirt, her spare form giving her a girlish look even in her sixties.

"Did you ever get any sleep?" I asked.

"No, and I'm not going to stay in that apartment 'til the windows are fixed. I may have an alarm system put in too. I came out here just to busy myself. Hosing the walks is restful, don't you think? It's one of the pleasures of adulthood. When I was a kid, my dad never would let me have a turn."

"Have you been down to the police station yet?"

"Oh, I'll go in a bit, but I don't look forward to it."

"I went by a little while ago and filed a missing persons report on Elaine."

"What'd they say?"

I shrugged. "Nothing much. They'll do what they can. I ran into a homicide detective who worked on Marty Grice's murder. He says Elaine was supposed to come in for an interview and never showed up. Do you remember how soon afterward she went to Florida?"

"Well, I'm not sure. It was that same week. I do know that much. She was terribly upset about the murder and that's one reason she left. I thought I mentioned that."

"You said she was sick."

"She was, but she always seemed to have something wrong

with her. She said the murder had her crazy with anxiety. She thought getting out of town would help. Hang on," Tillie said. She went into the bushes and turned off the water at the faucet, using the last of the water pressure to empty the hose before she coiled it up again. She emerged from the shrubbery, wiping her damp hands on her jeans. "Are you thinking she knew something about Marty's death?"

"I think it's worth looking into," I said. "Her side window looks right down into the Grices' entryway. Maybe she saw the burglar."

Tillie made a skeptical face. "In the dark?"

I shrugged. "It doesn't seem likely, does it, but I don't know what else to think."

"But why wouldn't she have gone to the police if she knew who it was?"

"Who knows? Maybe she wasn't thinking straight. People panic. They don't like to get involved in these things. Maybe she felt she was in jeopardy herself."

"Well, she *was* nervous," Tillie said. "But then we were all a bundle of nerves that week. You want to come in?"

"Actually I do. I think I ought to take a look at those bills of hers. At least we can see how recently she's used her charge accounts and where she was at the time. Has anything else come in?"

"Just a couple of things. I'll show you what I've got."

I followed Tillie through the lobby and into the corridor beyond.

She unlocked her front door and moved into the living room, crossing to the secretary. Since the glass had been broken out of the doors, there was no need to unlock anything, but I saw her hesitate, nonplussed, putting an index finger on the side of her cheek like someone posing for a photograph. "Now, that's odd."

"What?" I asked. I crossed to the secretary and looked in. We'd replaced the tumble of books the night before, and there was nothing else on the shelves now except a small brass elephant and a framed snapshot of a puppy with a stick in its mouth.

"I don't see Elaine's bills and they should be there," she said. "Now, isn't that strange." She glanced at the shelves again and then opened the drawers one by one, sorting through the contents.

She moved into the kitchen and dug into the big black plastic bag where we had dumped all the broken glass and debris the night before. There was no sign of them.

"Kinsey, they were in the secretary yesterday. I saw them myself. Where could they have gone?"

She looked up at me. It didn't take a massive leap of intelligence to arrive at the obvious possibility.

"Could *she* have taken them?" Tillie asked. "That woman who broke in last night? Is that what she was really up to?"

"Tillie, I don't know. Something about it bothered me at the time," I said. "It didn't make sense to think someone would break in while you were here just to tear the place apart. Are you sure you saw them yesterday?"

"Of course. I put the new batch of bills with the other ones on the shelf. They were right here. And I don't remember seeing them at all when we cleaned up. Do you?"

I thought back, chasing it around in my memory. I'd only seen the bills once, the first time I'd talked to her. But why would someone bother to steal them? It didn't make sense.

"Maybe she deliberately scared the pants off you to keep you out of the way while she searched the place," I said.

"Well, she sure had the right idea. I wouldn't have come out of my room on a dare! But why would she do that? I don't understand."

"I don't either. I can always get duplicates of the bills, but it's going to be a pain in the ass and I'd rather not do it if I don't have to."

"I want to know who has a key to my apartment. That makes my blood run cold."

"I don't blame you. Listen, Tillie. Nothing makes me crazier than sixteen unanswered questions in a row. I'm going to see what I can find out about this murder next door. It has to be connected somehow. Have you talked to Leonard Grice recently?"

"Oh, he hasn't been there since it happened," she said. "I haven't seen him at any rate."

"What about the Snyders on the other side? Do you think they could be of any help?"

"They might. Do you want me to talk to them?"

"No, don't worry about it. I'll check with them myself. Just one more thing. Leonard Grice has a nephew . . . a kid with a pink Mohawk."

"Mike."

"Yeah, him. Is there any chance he might have been the person who broke in last night? I just talked to him outside and he's not a big guy. He might well have looked like a woman in the dark."

"I don't think so," she said, skepticism plain. "I couldn't swear to it, but I don't think it was him."

"Well. Just a thought. I don't like to make assumptions about gender. It really could have been anyone. I'm going to go next door and see what the Snyders have to say. You take care of yourself."

The house at 2093 was similar in feeling to the house that burned . . . the same-size lot, same ill proportions, the same white frame and red brick. The brick itself was roughly textured, a cunning imitation of fired clay. There was a FOR SALE sign out front with a banner pasted across it boasting SOLD! as though an auction had been enacted just before I started up the walk. A large tree shaded the yard down to a chill, and dark ivy choked the trunk, spreading out in all directions in a dense mat that nearly smothered the walk. I went up the porch steps and knocked on the aluminum screen door. The front door had a big glass panel in it, blocked by a sheer white curtain stretched between two rods. After a moment, someone moved the curtain aside and peered out.

"Mr. Snyder?"

The curtain was released and the door opened a crack. The man appeared to be in his seventies, corpulent and benign. Old age had given him back his baby fat and the same look of grave curiosity.

I held out a business card. "My name is Kinsey Millhone. Could I have a few minutes of your time? I'm trying to track down Elaine Boldt, who lives in that big condominium over there, and Tillie Ahlberg suggested I talk to you. Can you help me out?"

Mr. Snyder released the catch on the screen door. "I'll do what I can. Come on in." He held the screen door open and I followed him inside. The house was as dark as the inside of a soup can and smelled of cooked celery.

From the rear of the house, a shrill voice called out.

"What's that? Who all is out there, Orris?"

"Someone Tillie sent!"

"Who?"

"Hold on a minute," he said to me, "she's deaf as a yard of grass. Take a seat."

Mr. Snyder lumbered toward the back. I perched on an upholstered chair with wooden arms. The fabric was a dark maroon plush with a high-low pattern of foliage, some nondescript sort that I'd never seen in real life. The seat was sprung; all hard edges and the smell of dust. There was a matching couch stacked with newspapers and a low mahogany coffee table with an inset of oval glass barely visible for all the paraphernalia on top: dog-eared paperbacks, plastic flowers in a ceramic vase shaped like two mice in an upright embrace, a bronze version of praying hands, six pencils with erasers chewed off, pill bottles, and a tumbler that had apparently held hot milk which had left a lacy pattern on the sides of the glass like baby's breath. There was also an inexplicable pile of pancakes wrapped in cellophane. I leaned forward, squinting. It was a candle. Mr. Snyder could have moved the entire table outside and called it a yard sale.

From the back end of the house, I could hear his exasperated explanation to his wife. "It's nobody selling anything," he snapped. "It's some woman Tillie sent, says she's looking for Mrs. Boldt. Boldt!! That widda woman lived upstairs of Tillie, the one played cards with Leonard and Martha now and again."

There was a feeble interjection and then his voice dropped

"No, you don't need to come out! Just keep set. I'll take care of it."

He reappeared, shaking his head, his jowls flushed. His chest was sunken into his swollen waistline. He'd had to belt his pants below his big belly and his cuffs drooped at the ankles. He hitched at them irritably, apparently convinced he'd lose them if he didn't hang on. He wore slippers without socks and all the hair had been worn away from his ankles, which were narrow and white, like soup bones.

"Switch on that light there," he said to me. "She likes to pinch on util'ties. Half the time, I can't see a thing."

I reached over to the floor lamp and pulled the chain. A forty-watt bulb came on, buzzing faintly, not illuminating much. I could hear a steady thump and shuffling in the hall.

Mrs. Snyder appeared, moving a walker in front of her. She was small and frail and her jaw worked incessantly. She stared intently at the hardwood floor and her feet made a sticky sound as she walked, as though the floor had been shellacked and had never dried properly. She paused, hanging on to her walker with shaking hands. I stood up, projecting my voice.

"Would you like to sit here?" I asked her.

She surveyed the wall with rheumy eyes, trying to discover the source of the sound. Her head was small, like a little pumpkin off the vine too long, looking shrunken from some interior softening. Her eyes were narrow inverted V's and one tooth protruded from her lower gum like a candle wick. She seemed confused.

"What?" she said, but the question had a hopeless ring to it. I didn't think anybody answered her these days.

Snyder waved at me impatiently. "She's fine. Just leave her be. Doctor wants her on her feet more anyway," he said.

I watched her uncomfortably. She continued to stand there, looking puzzled and dismayed, like a baby who's learned how to pull itself up on the sides of a crib, but hasn't figured out how to sit down again.

Mr. Snyder ignored her, settling on the couch with his knees spread. His belly filled the space between his legs like a duffel bag, as cumbersome on him as a clown suit with a false front. He put his hands on his knees, giving me his full attention as though I might be soliciting his entire history for inclusion on "This Is Your Life."

"We been in this house forty year," he said. "Bought it back in nineteen and forty-three for four thousand dollar. Bet you never heard of a house that cheap. Now it's worth one hunnert and fifteen thousand. Just the lot we're settin' on. That don't even count the house. They can knock this place down and build anything they want. Hell, she can't even get that walker into the commode. Now Leonard, next door, nearly sold his house for a hunnert and thirty-five, had it in escroll and everything and then the deal fell out. That about done him in. He's the one I feel sorry for. House burnt. Wife dead. You know what the kids these days would say . . . his carnal was bad."

He went right on talking while I took mental notes. This was better than I'd hoped. I had thought I'd have to tell a few fibs, leading the conversation around judiciously from Elaine's whereabouts to the subject of the murder next door, but here sat Orris Snyder giving testimony extemporaneously. I realized he'd stopped. He was looking at me.

"You've sold this house? I saw the sign out front."

"Sold," he said with satisfaction. "We can move us up to that retirement place when the kids get everything here packed up. We've got a regular reservation. We're on the list and everything. She's old. She doesn't even know where she is half the time. Fire broke out in this place, she'd lay there and cook."

I glanced at his wife, who had apparently locked her knees. I was worried she would pass out, but he didn't seem to give it much thought. She might as well have been a hall tree.

Snyder went on as though prompted by questions from an unseen audience. "Yessir, I sold it. She like to have a fit, but the house is in my name and I own it free and clear. Paid four thousand dollar. Now I call that a profit, wouldn't you?"

"That's not bad," I said. I glanced over at his wife again. Her legs had begun to tremble.

"Why don't you get on back to bed, May?" he said and then looked at me with a disapproving shake of his head. "She can't hear good. Hearing comes and goes. Got tintypes of the ear and all she can see is living shapes. She got the leg of that walker hung up on the broom-closet door last week and stood there for forty-six minutes before she got loose. Old fool."

"You want me to help you get her back to bed?" I asked.

Snyder floundered on the couch, turning himself sideways so he could get up. He pushed himself to his feet and then went over to her and shouted in her face. "Go lay down awhile, May, and then I'll get you some snackin' cake," he said.

She stared steadfastly at his neck, but I could have sworn she knew exactly what he was talking about and was just feeling stubborn and morose.

"Why did you put the light on? I thought it was day," she said.

"It only costs five cent to run that bulb," he said.

"What?"

"I said it's pitch-black night outside and you got to go to bed!" he hollered.

"Well," she said, "I think I might in that case."

Laboriously, she thumped the walker around, navigating with effort. Her eyes slid past me and she seemed suddenly to discern me in the haze.

"Who's that?"

"It's some woman," Snyder broke in. "I was telling her of Leonard's bad luck."

"Did you tell her what I heard that night? Tell about the hammering kept me awake. Hanging pictures . . . bang, bang, bang. I had to take a pill it made my head hurt so bad."

"That wasn't the same night, May. How many times I told you that? It couldn't have been because he wasn't home and he's the one did that kind of thing. Burglars don't hang pictures."

He looked over at me then, twirling his index finger beside his temple to indicate that she was rattlebrained.

"Banged and banged," she said, but she was only muttering

to herself as she thunked away, moving the walker in front of her like a clothes rack.

"She hasn't a faculty left," he said to me over his shoulder. "Pees on herself half the time. I had to move every stick of dining-room furniture out and put her bed in there right where the sideboard stood. I told her I'd outlive her the day I married her. She gets on my nerves. She did back then too. I'd just as soon live with a side of meat."

"Who's at the door?" she said insistently.

"Nobody. I'm talkin' to myself," he said.

He shuffled into the hallway behind her. His hovering had a tender quality about it in spite of what he said. In any event she didn't seem aware of his aggravation or his minor tyrannies. I wondered if he'd stood there and timed her for the forty-six minutes while she struggled with the broom-closet door. Is that what marriages finally come down to? I've seen old couples toddle down the street together holding hands and I've always looked on faintly misty-eyed, but maybe it is all the same clash of wills behind closed doors. I've been married twice myself and both ended in divorce. I berate myself for that sometimes but now I'm not sure. Maybe I haven't made such a bad tradeoff. Personally, I'd rather grow old alone than in the company of anyone I've met so far. I don't experience myself as lonely, incomplete, or unfulfilled, but I don't talk about that much. It seems to piss people off—especially men.

8

Mr. Snyder returned to the living room and sat down heavily on the couch. "Now then."

"What can you tell me about that fire next door?" I asked. "I saw the place. It looks awful."

He nodded, preparing himself as though for a television interview, staring straight ahead. "Well now, the fire engine woke me up ten o'clock at night. Two of 'em. I don't sleep good anyhow and I heard the siren come right up here close so I got up and went out. Neighbors was runnin' from ever' which way. Black smoke outen that house like you never saw. These firemen, they bashed their way in and pretty soon flames it up the front porch. Whole backside got saved. They found Marty, that was Leonard's wife, layin' on the floor. It'd be right about over there," he said, pointing toward the front door. "I never seen her myself, but Tillie said she was charred head to foot. Just a bunch of stumps, like a piece of wood."

"Oh really. Tillie didn't mention that to me."

"She seen the smoke and called right up. Nine-one-one it was. I was sound to sleep. Woke up when the fire engine come blastin' down the road. I thought they'd go right on by, but then I seen the lights and I got up and put a robe on and went out. Poor Leonard wasn't even home. He drove up about the time they got the fire out. Collapsed right on the street when he heard she was dead. I never saw a man so tore up. My wife, May, she never woke up at all. She'd tooken a pill and she's deaf as a broom anyway. You've seen that yourself. Fire broke out here, she'd been roast pork."

"What time was it when Mr. Grice got home?"

"I don't know the exact time. Fifteen, twenty minutes after the fire engines come as best I recollect. He was out to dinner with his sister as I hear tell and he comes home to find his own wife dead. His knees give out and down he went. Right on the sidewalk with me standin' not this far away. Turned white and dropped like a big hand had give him a thump and knocked him out. It was the awfullest thing you ever saw. They brought her out zipped up in a plastic sack—"

"How'd Tillie happen to see her?" I interrupted. "I mean if she was zipped up in a body bag?"

"Oh, that Tillie, she sees everything. Ask her. She prob'ly pushed though when the door got bashed in and seen the body for herself. Makes me sick to think of it."

"I understand Leonard's been staying with his sister since then."

"That's what I heard, too. Her name is Howe. Lives on Carolina. It's in the book if you want to get in touch."

"Good. I'll try to see him this afternoon. I'm hoping he can tell me something about where Mrs. Boldt might have gone."

I got up and held out my hand. "You've been a big help."

Mr. Snyder struggled to his feet and shook my hand, walking to the door with me.

I looked over at him with curiosity. "What do you think your wife was referring to when she mentioned the hammering that night? Do you have any idea what she meant?"

He waved impatiently. "She don't know what she's talkin about. She got that all confused."

I shrugged. "Well, I hope Mr. Grice is doing all right at any rate. Did he have good insurance coverage? That would be a big help, I'm sure."

He shook his head, pulling at his chin. "I don't think he come out too good on that. Him and me has the same insurance comp'ny, but his policy didn't amount to much as I understand it. Between the fire and his wife's being gone now he's about ruined. He collects disability for a bad back, you know, and she was sole support."

"God, that's terrible. I'm sorry to hear that," I said, and then took a chance. "What insurance company?"

"California Fidelity."

Ahh. I felt my little heart go pitty-pat. This was the first break I'd had. I worked for them.

California Fidelity Insurance is a small company that handles all the ordinary coverage: life and health, homeowner's, auto, and some commercial lines, with branches in San Francisco, Pasadena, and Palm Springs. Santa Teresa is the home office, occupying the second floor of a three-story building on State Street, which cuts straight through the heart of town. My corner consists of two rooms—one inner, one outer—with a separate entrance. Early in my career, I worked for CFI, doing insurance investigations on fire and wrongful-death claims. Now that I'm out on my own, we maintain a loose association. I cover certain inquiries for them every month in exchange for office space.

I let myself into the office now and checked the answering machine. The light was blinking, but the tape was blank except for some hissing and a couple of high-pitched beeps. For a while, I had a live answering service, but the messages were usually botched. I didn't think prospective clients were that keen to confide their troubles to some twenty-year-old telephone operator who could barely spell, let alone keep the numbers straight. An answering machine is irritating, but at least it tells the caller that I am female and I pick up on the second ring. The mail wasn't in yet, so I went next door to talk to Vera Lipton, one of the California Fidelity claims adjusters.

Vera's office is located in the center of a warren of cubicles separating adjusters. Each small space is equipped with a desk, a rolling file, two chairs and a telephone, rather like a little bookie joint. Vera's niche is identifiable by the pall of smoke hovering above the shoulder-high partitions. She's the only one in the company who smokes and she does so with vigor, piling up stained white filter tips like ampules of distilled nicotine. She's also addicted to Coca-Cola and she usually has a row of empty bottles marching around her desk, accumulating them at the rate of one every hour. She's thirty-six, single, and she collects men with ease, though none of them seems to suit her. I peered into her cubicle.

"What'd you do to your hair?" I asked when I caught sight of it.

"I was up all night. It's a wig," she said. She stuck a fresh cigarette between her teeth, biting gently while she lit up. I've always admired her smoking style. It's jaunty and sophisticated, dainty and tough. She pointed to the wig, which was streaked with blond, a wind-blown effect.

"I'm thinking of dyeing my hair this shade. I haven't been a blond for months."

"I like it," I said. Her usual color was auburn, a mix of several Clairol offerings that varied in hues from Sparkling Sherry to Flame. Her glasses today had tortoiseshell rims and big round lenses tinted the color of iced tea. She wore glasses so well it made other women wish their eyesight would fail.

"You must have a new man in your life," I said.

Vera shrugged dismissively, shaking her head. "I got two actually, but I wasn't up doing what you think. I read a book on how the new technology works. Lasers and analog-to-digital converters. I got curious about electricity yesterday, you know? Turns out nobody really knows what it is, which is worrisome if you ask me. Great terminology though. 'Pulse amplitude' and 'oscillation.' Maybe I'll run into a guy I can say that to. What's with you? You want a Coke?"

She had already opened her bottom file drawer where she kept a little cooler packed with ice. She pulled out a Coke in a bottle about the size of a Playtex nurser, and uncapped it by wedging it under the metal drawer handle and giving a quick downward snap. She proffered the bottle, but I shook my head and she drank it down herself. "Have a seat," she said then and set the bottle on the desk top with a thunk.

I moved aside a stack of files and sat down in the extra chair. "What do you know about a woman named Marty Grice who was murdered six months ago? I heard she was insured through CFI."

Vera touched daintily at the corners of her mouth with her thumb and index finger. "Sure, I was assigned to that one. I went out and took a look at the place two days after it happened. God, what a mess. I don't have the proof of loss yet, but Pam Sharkey said she'd get it to me in the next couple of weeks."

"She's the agent on it?"

Vera nodded, taking a drag of her cigarette. She blew the smoke straight up. "The big life-insurance policy lapsed, but there was a little twenty-five-hundred-dollar policy in effect. That's probably not enough to bury a dog these days. There's also a homeowner's for the fire loss, but the guy was desperately underinsured. Pam swears up and down she advised him to upgrade, but he didn't want to be saddled with the added expense. You know how people get. They try to save six bucks and end up blowing two-three hundred thousand when the bottom drops out." She tapped the cigarette on the lip of the empty Coke bottle, neatly knocking the ash into it.

"Why's the settlement taking so long?"

Vera's mouth turned down and she lowered one eyelid—a gesture that conveyed the message "big deal," though I don't know how. "Who knows?" she said. "The guy's got a year to file the claim. Pam says he's been a basket case since his wife died. He can hardly manage to sign his own name."

"Did she leave a will?"

"Not that I heard. The whole thing's been sitting in probate court for the last five months or so, in any event. What's your interest in it? Are you looking into her death?"

"Not really. I'm looking for a woman who lived next door when it happened. She left town a couple of days afterward and hasn't been seen since then by the people who count. I keep thinking there's a connection. I was hoping you'd tell me there was a great big policy in effect."

"The cops had the same idea. Your buddy Lieutenant Dolan was over here practically sitting in my lap for days. I kept saying, 'Forget it! The guy's broke. He's not going to net a dime.' I guess I finally convinced him because I haven't heard from him since. What are you thinking, that Grice and this doll next door were in cahoots?"

"It did cross my mind. I haven't met him yet and I have no idea whether there could have been a relationship between them, but it does look suspect. From what I'm told, she left town abruptly and she was upset. My first instinct was that

69

maybe she'd seen something and took off to avoid getting caught up in it."

"Maybe so." Vera sounded dubious.

"But you don't believe it."

"I'm just looking at his end. If the guy killed his wife for fun and profit, he sure went about it wrong. Why let a policy lapse like that? If he were smart, he'd have jacked the face value up two-three years ago, let enough time pass so it didn't look too obvious and then . . . whap, his wife is dead and he collects. If he killed her with no payoff, he's an idiot."

"Unless he just wanted her out of his way. Maybe that was all he cared about. Maybe letting the policy lapse was a ploy."

"Hey, listen, what do I know? I'm not a homicide dick."

"Me neither. I'm just trying to figure out why this woman disappeared and where she might have gone. Even if you're right and Grice had nothing to do with it, she still might have witnessed something. This burglar business sounds too tidy for words."

Vera smiled cynically. "Hell, maybe she did it herself."

"God, you're more suspicious than I am."

"Well, you want Grice's number? I got it somewhere here." Vera paused to toss the tag end of her cigarette into the Coke bottle. There was a quick spitting sound as the ember touched the thimbleful of Coke that remained. She extracted a file from the bottom of a stack and found the telephone number and the address.

"Thanks," I said.

She gave me a speculative look. "You interested in an unemployed aerospace engineer? He's got bucks. He invented some little dingus they use now in all the satellites."

"How come you don't want him?" I asked. Vera tended to offer up her rejects like hostess gifts.

She made a face. "He was fine for a while, but now he's on a health kick. Started taking algae pills. I don't want to kiss a man who eats pond scum. I thought you might not object since you live so clean. Maybe you two could jog together and nibble dried seaweed snacks. If you're interested, he's yours."

"You're too good to me," I said. "I'll keep an eye out. I might run into someone who's up for him."

"You're way too picky about men, Kinsey," she said reprovingly.

"*I'm* picky?! What about you?"

Vera stuck another cigarette between her teeth and I watched her flick a tiny gold lighter into play before she spoke.

"I figure guys are like Whitman's Samplers. I like to take a little bite out of each and then move on before the whole box gets stale."

9

It was 1:30 by now and as nearly as I could remember, I
hadn't eaten lunch. I pulled into a fast-food restaurant, parked,
and went in. I could have hollered my order into a clown's
mouth and eaten in the car as I drove, but I wanted to show
I had class. I wolfed down a cheeseburger, fries, and a Coke
for a dollar sixty-nine and was back on the streets again in
seven minutes flat.

The house where Leonard Grice was supposedly staying
was located in a dingy tract of houses just off the freeway, a
neighborhood of winding streets that had been named after
states, starting with the East Coast. I rambled down Maine,
Massachusetts, New York, and Rhode Island Drives, getting
stuck in tricky cul-de-sacs where Vermont and New Jersey
turned into dead ends. It looked like the builder had gotten
as far as Colorado Avenue before the money ran out or his
knowledge of geography failed. There was a long stretch of
vacant lots with stakes visible at intervals, each tied with a little
white rag to mark off the undeveloped parcels of land.

Most of the houses had gone up in the fifties. The trees
had flourished, overpowering the small lots. The houses were
alternately pale pink and pale green stucco, mirror images of
one another like a whole tray of loaf cakes on a bakery shelf.
All had the same rock-covered roofs, as though some volcano
nearby had erupted, raining down a thin debris. The whole
tract seemed dominated by wide-mouthed garages and I was
subjected to untidy views of lawn equipment and camper shells,
toys, tools, dusty luggage, banged-up refrigerators. There were
surprisingly few cars visible and the impression I got was of
a community abandoned in the wake of some natural disaster.
Maybe a plague had passed this way or maybe toxic waste

had risen up through the soil, killing all the dogs and cats and burning holes in children's feet. At the intersection of Maryland and Virginia, I turned right.

On Carolina, a few enterprising souls had faced their homes with fieldstone or cedar shingle, and some had opted for an Oriental effect—trellises of plywood with geometric cutouts that were meant to look Chinese, the roof corners tilted up for that gala 1950s pagoda look. Compared to more recent tracts on the outskirts of Santa Teresa, these houses were shabby and the evidence of poor construction floated on the surface like chicken fat on homemade soup. There were cracks in the stucco, window shutters askew. The veneer on the front doors was peeling off in strips. Even the drapes were hung crookedly and I could imagine bathroom plaster bulging out in places, faucet handles frozen with rust.

The Howes had traded their front lawn for a rock garden, apparently burying the scruffy grass under tons of sand, topped with gravel beds in shades of mauve and green. I could still see a strip of black plastic "mulch" peeping out around the edge where some attempt had been made to suppress the weeds. The Bermuda grass had risen to the challenge and it was snaking its way through the gravel at a leisurely pace. There was a birdbath tucked among the succulents and a poured-concrete squirrel seemed to pop up out of the cactus in an attitude of perpetual, stony optimism. I doubted there was a live squirrel within blocks.

I parked the car and walked up to the house, taking the clipboard I keep in the backseat of my car. The Howes' garage door was closed, making the place look blank and unoccupied. The long, low line of the porch was obscured with ivy, looking picturesque, but capable, I knew, of lifting the roof right off. The drapes were closed. I rang the bell, but there was no reassuring "ding-dong" within. A minute passed. I knocked.

The woman who came to the door was subdued, her faded blue eyes searching my face hesitantly.

"Mrs. Howe?"

"I'm Mrs. Howe," she said.

It felt like Lesson One on a foreign-language record. There were dark circles under her eyes and her voice was as flat and dry as a cracker.

"I understand Leonard Grice is staying here. Is that correct?"

"Yes."

I held my clipboard up. "I'm from the insurance company and I wonder if I might have a word with him." It's a marvel God doesn't reach right down and rip my tongue out by the roots for the lies I tell.

"Leonard's taking a rest. Why don't you come back another time." She was closing the door.

"I'll just take a minute," I said quickly. I stuck the clipboard into the crack. She'd never get the door shut that way.

She paused. "The doctor still has him on sedatives." A non sequitur but the point was clear.

"I see. Well, of course, I wouldn't want to disturb him, but I'd really like to see him, as long as I've driven all the way out here." I tried to sound winsome, but apparently failed.

She stared at me stubbornly and I could see the color rise in her face. She glanced sideways as though she were consulting an invisible companion. Abruptly, she moved back and let me into the house with the attitude of someone using the ʃ word under her breath. Her hair was gray, shoulder-length and thin, turned under in a tight pageboy. She had bangs along her forehead in a hairstyle I hadn't seen since those June Allyson movies where she was so loving and so long-suffering. Mrs. Howe wore a plain white blouse and a sensible charcoal-gray wool skirt. She was chunky through the waist. What is it about middle age that makes a woman's body mimic pregnancy?

"I'll see if he'll talk to you," she said and left the room.

I waited just inside the front door, taking in with a quick glance the cotton shag carpeting, brick fireplace painted white, an oil painting above it of waves crashing on rocks. She'd apparently used the painting as the focal point of her decorating scheme because the couch and wing chairs were upholstered in the same passionate shade of turquoise, in a fabric

74

that looked faintly damp. I hated this part of my job—asserting myself persistently into somebody else's pain and grief, violating privacy. I felt like a door-to-door salesman, pushing unwanted sets of nature encyclopedias complete with fake walnut case. I also hated myself vaguely for being judgmental. What did I know about hairstyles anyway? What did I know about waves crashing on rocks? Maybe the turquoise said exactly what she'd meant to say about the room.

When Leonard Grice appeared, I could feel my heart sink. He didn't look like a man who'd murdered his wife, as much as that theory appealed to me. He was probably in his early fifties, but he moved like an old man. He was not bad-looking, but his face was pallid, cheeks sunken as though he'd recently lost some weight. His manner was vacant and he held his hands in front of him when he walked as though he were blindfolded. He had all the airs of a man who has stumbled painfully over something in the dark and wants to be certain he doesn't get caught by surprise again. It was possible, of course, that he'd killed her and was consumed now by guilt and remorse, but the killers I've run into in my brief career are either cheerful or matter-of-fact, like they can't understand what all the fuss is about.

Leonard's sister walked beside him, her hand near his elbow, watching where he placed his feet. She eased him toward a chair and shot me a look, clearly hoping I was satisfied at the trouble I'd caused. I did feel crummy, I'll confess.

He sat down. He seemed to be coming to life, reaching automatically for a pack of Camels in his shirt pocket while Mrs. Howe perched on the edge of the couch.

"Sorry to have to bother you," I said, "but I've just been talking to the adjuster at California Fidelity and there were a few details we wanted to clarify. Do you mind answering some questions for me?"

"He can hardly afford not to cooperate with the insurance company," she interjected peevishly.

Leonard cleared his throat, striking a match twice without effect against a paper matchbook. His hands were trembling and I wasn't sure he'd ever manage to match the flame to the end of his cigarette even if he could conjure one up. Mrs. Howe reached over, took the packet, and struck the match for him. He inhaled deeply.

"You'll have to pardon me," he said, "the doctor has me on some medicine that does this to me. I'm on disability for my back. What is it exactly that you want?"

"I've just recently been assigned to this case and I thought it might be helpful to hear your own account of what happened that night."

"What on earth for!" Mrs. Howe said.

"That's all right, Lily," he broke in, "I don't mind. I'm sure she's got her reasons for wanting to know." His voice was stronger now, dispelling the original impression of feebleness. He took a deep drag of his cigarette, letting it rest in the fork between his index and third fingers.

"My sister's widowed," he said, as though that might explain her belligerence. "Mr. Howe died of a heart attack eighteen months ago. After that, Marty and I got in the habit of taking Lil out to dinner every week. Mostly it was a way to keep up with each other and visit back and forth. Well that night, Marty planned to go as usual, but she said she felt like she was coming down with the flu, so at the last minute she decided to stay home. It was Lil's birthday and Marty was disappointed because she knew we were going to have a little cake brought to the table and waiters singing . . . you know how they do. She wanted to see the look on Lily's face. Anyway, she felt if she wasn't well, she might spoil everybody's evening so she didn't go." He paused, taking a deep drag of his cigarette. He'd accumulated a long ash and Lily pushed an ashtray toward him just as it tumbled.

"Did you tend to go out the same night of the week each time?" I asked.

He nodded. "Tuesdays as a rule."

I made a note dutifully on the legal pad on my clipboard. I hoped I looked like I had some legitimate reason to be asking all this stuff. I pretended to consult a form or two, flipping back a page. I thought the clipboard was a nice touch. I guess

Lily did too. She peered over, wanting to see me write down something she said too.

"That's the best night for me," she ventured. "I get my hair done on Tuesdays and I like to go out when it's looking nice."

"Hair on Tues.," I wrote. "How many people knew you went out on Tuesday nights?"

Leonard's eyes slid over to mine with a curious look. The medication had opened his pupils to the full, perfect black holes that looked like they'd been made with a paper punch.

"Pardon?"

"I wondered how many people knew about your nights out. If the intruder was someone you knew, he might have thought she'd be out with you as usual."

His expression flickered with uncertainty. "I don't understand what this has to do with the insurance claim," he said.

I had to be careful how I framed my reply because he'd put his finger on the flaw in my charade. My questions had nothing to do with anything except trying to figure out if Elaine could have seen a murder. So far, I didn't even know what had actually happened that night and I was trying to weasel the information out of him. Lieutenant Dolan wasn't going to tell me, that was for sure.

I smiled briefly, keeping my tone light. "Naturally we're interested in seeing this crime solved," I said. "We may need a determination on the case before the claim is paid."

Lily glanced at Leonard and then back to me, alerted by his wariness. "What kind of 'determination'?" she asked. "I don't understand what you mean."

Leonard shifted back to his original attitude. "Now, Lil, it can only help," he said. "The insurance company wants to get to the bottom of this just like we do. The police haven't done anything on it for months." He glanced at me again. "You'll have to pardon Lil. . . ."

She flashed him a look. "Don't apologize for me when I'm sitting right here," she snapped. "You're too trusting, Leonard. That's what's wrong with you. Marty was the same way. If she'd been a little more cautious, she might be alive today!"

She faltered, clamping her mouth shut, then surprised me by filling in some details. "She was on the phone to me that night and someone came to the door. She rang off to see who it was."

He chimed in. "The police said it's possible she knew the person, or it might have been someone off the street. Police said a lot of times a burglar rings the bell if the lights are on. If someone answers the door, he can act like he's got the wrong address. Nobody answers, he might go ahead and break in."

"Were there signs of a struggle?"

"I don't think so," Leonard said. "Not that I ever heard. I went through the house myself, but I couldn't see anything missing."

I looked back at Lily. "What had she called about?" I asked. "Or did you call her?"

"I called her myself when we got in," she said. "We got back here a little later than we thought and Leonard didn't want her to worry."

"And she sounded all right when you talked to her?"

Lily nodded. "She sounded fine. She sounded just like she always did. Leonard talked to her for a bit and then I got back on with her and we were just winding down when she said there was someone at the door and she had to go see who it was. I was going to offer to stay on the line, but we were done anyway so I just said good-bye and hung up."

Leonard pulled a handkerchief out of his pants pocket and pressed it to his eyes. His hands had begun to shake badly and there was a tremor in his voice. "I don't even know what her last moments were like. Police said the guy must have hit her square in the face with a baseball bat, something that size. She must have been terrified—"

He broke off.

I could feel myself squirm, but I didn't say anything. What actually occurred to me, as tacky as it sounds, is that a baseball bat in the face doesn't leave time to feel much of anything. Crack! You're gone. No terror, no pain. Just lights out, home run.

Lily reached over and placed her hand on his. "They were married twenty-two years."

"Good years too," he said, his tone almost argumentative. "We never went to bed mad. That was a rule we made early. Anytime we had a quarrel, we got it settled. She was a fine woman. Smarter than me and I'm not ashamed to admit it."

Tears glittered in his eyes, but I felt oddly removed, like the only sober person at a party full of drunks.

"Did the police mention any possibility of witnesses? Someone who might have seen or heard something that night?"

He shook his head, mopping at his eyes. "No. I don't think so. I never heard that."

"Possibly someone in the building next door?" I suggested. "Or someone passing by? I understand you've got people across the street from you too. You'd think someone would have noticed *something*."

He blew his nose, recovering his composure. "I don't think so. Police never said anything to us."

"Well, I've taken up enough of your time and I'm sorry I've caused you so much distress. I'd like to go through the house and assess the fire damage if you don't mind. One of our adjusters has already been through, but I'll need to see for myself so I can make my report."

He nodded. "My neighbor has a key. Orris Snyder right next door. You go knock on his door and tell him I said it was all right."

I got up and held my hand out to him. "Thanks for talking to me."

Leonard got to his feet automatically and shook my hand. His grip was solid, his flesh almost feverishly hot.

"By the way," I said as if it had just occurred to me, "have you heard from Elaine Boldt lately?"

He focused on me, apparently perplexed by the reference. "Elaine? No, why?"

"I was trying to get in touch with her on another matter and I realized she lived in that condominium right next door," I replied with ease. "Someone mentioned that she was a friend of yours."

"That's right. We used to play bridge together before Marty died. I haven't talked to her for months. She's usually in Florida this time of year, I believe."

"Oh, that's right. I think somebody else mentioned that. Well, maybe she'll call when she gets back," I said. "Thanks again."

By the time I got back out to my car again, both my armpits were ringed with sweat.

10

It was now nearly three o'clock and I was feeling frazzled. I'd been up since two A.M. with just a brief time-out for sleep at dawn before the long-distance call from Mrs. Ochsner had wakened me. I couldn't face the office again, so I headed for my apartment and changed into my running clothes. I use the word *apartment* here in its loosest sense. Actually I live in a converted one-car garage, maybe fifteen feet square, tricked out as living room, bedroom, kitchen, bathroom, closet, and laundry facility. I've always liked living in small spaces. For months as a child, just after my parents were killed, I spent my spare time in a cardboard box that I filled with pillows and pretended was a sailing vessel on its way to some new land. It doesn't take an analyst to interpret this excursion on my part, but it's carried over into my adult life, manifesting itself now in all sorts of things. I drive small cars and I favor "littleness" in any form, so this place suits me exactly. For two hundred dollars a month I have everything I want, including a debonair eighty-one-year-old landlord named Henry Pitts.

I peered in his back window on my way out, and spotted him in the kitchen rolling out puff pastry dough. He's a former commercial baker who supplements his social security these days doing up breads and sweets, which he sells to or trades with local merchants. I tapped on the glass and he motioned me in. Henry is what I like to think of as an octogenarian "hunk," tall and lean with close-cropped white hair and eyes that are periwinkle blue, full of curiosity. Age has boiled him down to a concentrate, all male, compassionate and prudent and wry. I can't say that the years have invested him with spirituality, or infused him with any special wisdom, second sight, profundity, or depth. I mean, let's not overstate the case here. He was smart enough when he first started out and age hasn't diminished that a whit. Despite the fifty years' difference in our ages, there's nothing of the pundit in his attitude toward me, and nothing (I hope) of the postulant in my attitude toward him. We simply eye one another across that half a century with a lively and considerable sexual interest that neither of us would *dream* of acting out.

That afternoon, he was wearing a red rag around his head pirate-style, his tanned forearms bare and powdered with flour, his fingers as long and nimble as a monkey's as he gathered the dough and turned it halfway. He was using a length of chilled pipe as a rolling pin and he paused to flour it while he worked, coaxing the pastry into a rectangle.

I perched up on a wooden stool and retied my shoes. "You making napoleons?"

He nodded. "I'm catering a tea for someone up the street. What are you up to, besides a run?"

I filled him in briefly on my search for Elaine Boldt while he folded the dough in thirds and wrapped it, returning it to the refrigerator. When I got to the part about Marty Grice I saw his brows shoot up.

"Stay away from it. Take my advice and leave it to the homicide detectives. You're a fool if you get involved in that end of it."

"But what if she saw who killed Marty? What if that's why she took off?"

"Then let her come forward with the information. It's not up to you. If Lieutenant Dolan catches you messing around with his case, he'll have your rear end."

"Actually, that's true," I said ruefully. "But how can I back off? I'm running out of places to look."

"Who says she's lost? What makes you think she's not down in Sarasota someplace lapping up gin and tonic on the beach?"

"Because somebody would have heard from her. I mean I don't know if she's up to something or maybe in big trouble herself, but until she shows up I'm going to beat the bushes and bang on pans and see if I can run her to ground."

"Make-work," he said. "You're chasing your own tail."

"Well, that's probably true, but I gotta do something."

Henry gave me a skeptical look. He opened a bag of sugar and weighed out a mound. "You need a dog."

"No, I don't. And what's that got to do with it? I hate dogs."

"You need protection. That business at the beach would never have happened if you'd had a doberman."

That again. God, even my recent brush with death had taken place in a garbage bin . . . someplace small and cozy with me sobbing like a kid.

"I was thinking about that stuff today and you want to know the truth? All this talk about women being nurturing is crap. We're being sold a bill of goods so we can be kept in line by men. If someone came after me today, I'd do it again, only this time I don't think I'd hesitate."

Henry didn't seem impressed. "I'm sorry to hear that. I hope you haven't started a trend."

"I mean it. I'm tired of feeling helpless and afraid," I said.

Henry puffed his cheeks up and blew a raspberry, giving me a bored look. Big talk, his face said, but you don't fool me a bit. He cracked an egg on the counter and opened it up with one hand, letting the white slip through his fingers into a cup. He put the yolk in a bowl and took up another egg, repeating the process with his eyes pinned on me.

He said, "So defend yourself. Who's arguing with that? But you can drop the rhetoric. It's bullshit. Killing is killing and you better take a look at what you did."

"I know," I said, with less energy. The look in his eyes was making me squirm and I wasn't all that crazy about his tone. "Look, maybe I haven't really dealt with that. I just don't want to be a victim anymore. I'm sick of it."

Henry cradled the bowl in his arms, whisking the eggs with a practiced ease. When I do that, the eggs always slop out the side.

He said, "When were you ever a victim? You don't have to justify yourself to me. You did what you did. Just don't try to turn it into a philosophical statement, because it doesn't ring true. It's not as if you made a rational decision after months contemplating the facts. You killed somebody in the heat of the moment. It's not a platform for a political campaign and it's not a turning point in your intellectual life."

I smiled at him tentatively. "I'm still a good person, aren't I?" I didn't like the wistful tone. I meant to show him I was a grown-up, coping with the truth. Until the words came out of my mouth, I hadn't even known I felt so unsure.

He didn't smile back. His eyes rested on my face for a moment and then dropped back to the eggs. "What happened to you doesn't change that, Kinsey, but you have to keep it straight. Blow somebody's brains out and you don't brush that off. And you don't try to turn it into an intellectual stance."

"No, you don't," I said uneasily. I had a quick flash of the face that peered into the garbage bin just before I fired. By some remarkable distortion, I could have sworn I saw how the first bullet stretched the flesh like elastic before smashing through. I shook the image away and hopped down. "I have to run," I said, feeling anxious.

I left the kitchen without glancing back, but I know what the look was on Henry's face. Caution and sorrow and pain.

Once outside, I had to put it out of my mind again. Back the subject went, into its own little box. I did a quick stretch, concentrating on my hamstrings. I don't run fast enough or far enough to justify much of a warm-up. Other joggers, I know, would argue with that, citing injuries that result from insufficient stretching before a run, but I find exercise loathsome enough without adding contortions up front. For a time, I tried it, dutifully lying on my back in the grass with one leg straight out and the other cocked sideways toward my waist as though broken at the hip. I could never get up afterward unless I flopped about like a bug and I finally decided it was worth a possible groin-muscle pull to avoid the indignity. I've never been injured running anyway. I've never thrilled to it either. I'm still waiting for the rumored "euphoria" that apparently infuses everyone but me. I headed over to the boulevard at a brisk walk, keeping my mind blank.

I generally do three miles, jogging along the bicycle path that borders the beach. The walkway is stenciled with odd cartoons at intervals and I watch for those, counting off the quarter-miles. The tracks of some improbable bird, the mark of a single fat tire that crosses the concrete and disappears into the sand. There are usually tramps on the beach; some who camp there permanently, others in transit, their sleeping bags arranged under the palm trees like large green larvae or the skins shed by some night-stirring beast.

That afternoon the air seemed heavy and chill, the ocean sluggish. The cloud cover was beginning to break up, but the visible sky was a pale washed-out blue and there was no real sign of sun. Out on the water a speedboat ran a course parallel to the beach and the path of the wake was like a spinning ribbon of silver winding along behind. On the landward side, the mountains were dark green. At this distance, the low-growing vegetation looked like soft suede, with rock face showing through along the ridges as though the nap had worn away from hard use.

I did the turnaround at East Beach and ran the mile and a half back, then walked the block to my apartment as a cool-down. I'm big on cool-downs. I showered and dressed again and then hopped in my car and headed up to Pam Sharkey's office on Chapel. Pam was the insurance agent who'd written up the policies for Leonard Grice and I wanted to probe that issue before I set it aside. I trust Vera, but I don't like taking people's word for things. Maybe Grice had taken out a massive policy from some other company. How did I know?

The Valdez Building is located at the corner of Chapel and Feria, a Spanish word meaning "fair." I only know that because I looked it up. I've been thinking I should take a Spanish class one of these days, but I haven't gotten around to it yet. I can say *taco* and *gracias* but I'm real short on verbs. The Valdez is typical of the architecture in this town: two stories of white stucco with a red tile roof, big arches, windows faced with wrought-iron gratings. There are azure blue awnings and the landscaping consists of small plots of perfect grass. Palm trees grace the courtyard and there's a fountain capped by a small naked boy doing something wicked with a fish.

Pam Sharkey's office is on the first floor and sports the same network of cubicles I'd seen at California Fidelity. Nothing architecturally innovative for the insurance game these days. It must be like doing business in a series of playpens. The company she works for, Lambeth and Creek, is an independent agency that writes policies for a number of companies, CFI being one. I'd only dealt with Pam once, when I was bird-dogging an errant husband. His wife, my client, was in the process of divorcing him and was hoping for evidence of his philandering as a negotiating tool when it came down to the settlement. Pam had taken offense, not because I'd uncovered her affair with the man, but because I'd turned up two other women involved with him at the same time. None of this was ever brought up in court, of course, but her name was prominent in my report. She had never forgiven me for knowing too much. Santa Teresa is a small town and our paths cross now and then. We're polite to one another, but the civilities are undercut with spite on her part and sly amusement on mine.

Pam is petite, a bristly little chihuahua of a human being. She's the only woman I ever met who claims to be ten years older than she actually is so that everyone will tell her how young she looks. On that basis, she swears she's thirty-eight. Her face is small, her skin dusky and she applies pancake makeup in varying shades in a vain attempt to add "planes" to her cheeks. I got news for her. There's no way to disguise the bags under your eyes by the skillful use of "cover." From most angles anybody with a brain can see the bags sitting right there, only looking phantom white instead of gray. Who's fooled by this? Why not go for the dark circles and at least look exotic and worldly-wise . . . Anna Magnani, Jeanne Moreau, Simone Signoret perhaps. Pam had also taken lately to a permanent wave, so her pale brown hair looked frizzy and unkempt, a style apparently billed as "the bedroom look." That afternoon she was done up in a little hunting outfit: a hacking jacket, brown knickers, pink hose and low heels with buckles. The only hunting she did was in singles bars, bagging one-night stands as though the season were nearly over and her license about to expire. Well, wait a minute here. I can see I've been unfair about this. I don't like Pam any more than she likes me. Every time I see her, it makes me feel petty and mean—not my favorite way to experience myself. Maybe she avoids me for the same reason.

Her cubicle is near the front—a status symbol, I think. She caught sight of me and busied herself with papers and files. By the time I'd made my way over to her desk, she was on the phone. She must have been talking to a man because her manner was flirtatious. She touched herself everywhere as she talked, rolling a lock of hair around her finger, checking an earring, stroking the lapel of her jacket. She wore a series of gold necklaces and those got a workout too. Sometimes she'd rub her chin with a loop of gold chain, uttering a carefree, trilling laugh she must have practiced late at night. She glanced at me, feigning surprise, holding up a palm to indicate that I'd have to wait.

She turned away from me in her swivel chair, completing the telephone exchange with a murmured intimacy of some sort. On top of a stack of files on her desk, I could see a copy of *Cosmo*, offering articles on the G spot, cosmetic breast surgery, and social rape.

Pam hung up at long last and swiveled back, all the animation leaving her face. No point in wasting the whole show on me. "Something I can help you with, Kinsey?"

"I understand you wrote a couple of policies for Leonard and Marty Grice."

"That's right."

I smiled slightly. "Could you tell me the status of the paperwork at this point?"

Pam broke eye contact, going through another quick digital survey: earring, hair, lapel. She took up a loop of gold chain, running her index finger back and forth on it until I worried she'd saw right through the skin. She wanted to tell me Leonard Grice was none of my business, but she knew I did occasional work for California Fidelity.

"What's the problem?"

"No problem," I said. "Vera Lipton's wondering about the claim on the fire loss and I need to know if there were any other policies in effect."

"Now, wait a minute. Leonard Grice is a very dear man and

he's been through a terrible six months. If California Fidelity intends to make trouble, Vera better deal directly with me."

"Who said anything about trouble? Vera can't even process the claim until the proof of loss is in."

"That goes without saying, Kinsey," she said. "I still don't see what this has to do with you."

I could feel my smile begin to set like a pan of fudge. I leaned forward, left hand flat on the desk, right hand resting on my hip. I thought it was time to clarify our relationship.

"Not that it's any of your business, Pam, but I'm in the middle of a big investigation adjunctive to this. You don't have to cooperate, but I'm just going to turn around and present a court order to the supervisor here and somebody's going to come down on you like a ton of bricks for all the trouble it'll cause. Now is that how you want to proceed on this or what?"

Under the pancake makeup, she began to show signs of sunburn. "I hope you don't think you can intimidate me," she said.

"Absolutely not." I shut my mouth then and let her assimilate the threat. I thought it sounded pretty good.

She took up a stack of papers and rapped them on the desk, aligning the edges. "Leonard Grice was insured through California Fidelity Life and California Fidelity Casualty Insurance. He collected twenty-five hundred dollars for the life insurance and he'll get twenty-five thousand for the structural damage to the house. The contents were uninsured."

"Why only twenty-five for the house? I thought that place was worth over a hundred grand? He won't have enough money to do the repairs, will he?"

"When he bought the place in 1962, it was worth twenty-five thousand and that's what he insured it for. He never increased the coverage and he hasn't taken out any other policies. Personally, I don't see how he can do anything with the house. It's a complete loss, which I think is what's broken him."

Now that she'd told me, I felt guilty for all the macho bullshit I'd laid on her.

"Thanks. That's a big help," I said. "Uh . . . by the way, Vera wanted me to ask if you'd be interested in meeting an unattached aerospace engineer with bucks."

A wonderful look of uncertainty crossed her face: suspicion, sexual hunger, greed. Was I offering her a cookie or a flat brown turd on a plate? I knew what was going through her head. In Santa Teresa, a single man is on the market maybe ten days before someone snaps him up.

She shot me a worried look. "What's wrong with him? Why didn't you take him first?"

"I just came off a relationship," I said, "I'm in retreat." Which was true.

"Maybe I'll give Vera a buzz," she said faintly.

"Great. Thanks again for the information," I said and I gave her a little wave as I moved away from her desk. With my luck, she'd fall in love with the guy and want me to be a bridesmaid. Then I'd be stuck with one of those dumb dresses with a hunk of flounce on the hip. When I glanced back at her, she seemed to have shrunk and I felt a twinge. She wasn't so bad.

11

I ate dinner that night at Rosie's, a little place half a block down from my apartment. It's a cross between a neighborhood bar and an old-fashioned beanery, sandwiched between a Laundromat on the corner and an appliance repair shop that a man named McPherson operates out of his house. All three of these businesses have been in operation for over twenty-five years and are now, in theory, illegal, representing zoning violations of a profound and offensive sort, at least to people who live somewhere else. Every other year, some over-zealous citizen gets a bug up his butt and goes before the city council denouncing the outrage of this breach of residential integrity. In the off years, I think money changes hands.

Rosie herself is probably sixty-five, Hungarian, short, and top-heavy, a creature of muumuus and hennaed hair growing low on her forehead. She wears lipstick in a burnt-orange shade that usually exceeds the actual shape of her mouth, giving the impression that she once had a much larger set of lips. She uses a brown eyebrow pencil lavishly, making her eyes look stern and reproachful. The tip of her nose comes close to meeting her upper lip.

I sat down in my usual booth near the back. There was a mimeographed menu sheet slipped into a clear plastic cover stuck between the ketchup bottle and the napkin box. The selections were typed in pale purple like those notices they used to send home with us when we were in grade school. Most of the items were written in Hungarian; words with lots of accent marks and z's and double dots, suggesting that the dishes would be fierce and emphatic.

Rosie marched over, pad and pencil poised, her manner withdrawn. She was feeling offended about something, but I wasn't sure yet what I'd done. She snatched the menu out of my hand and put it back, writing out the order without consulting me. If you don't like the way the place is run, you go somewhere else. She finished writing and squinted at the pad, checking the results. She wouldn't quite meet my eyes.

"You didn't come in for a week so I figured you was mad at me," she said. "I bet you been eating junk, right? Don't answer that. I don't want to hear. You don't owe me an apology. You just lucky I give you something decent. Here's what you gonna get."

She consulted the pad again with a critical eye, reading the order to me then with interest as though it were news to her too.

"Green pepper salad. Fantastic. The best. I made it myself so I know it's done right. Olive oil, vinegar, little pinch of sugar. Forget the bread, I'm out. Henry didn't bring fresh today so what do I know? He could be mad at me too. How do I know what I did? Nobody tells me these things. Then I give you sour oxtail stew."

She crossed that off. "Too much grease. Is no good for you. Instead I give you tejfeles sult ponty, some nice pike I bake in cream, and if you clean you plate, I could give you deep-fried cherries if I think you deserve it, which you don't. The wine I'm gonna bring with the flatware. Is Austrian, but okay."

She marched away then, her back straight, her hair the color of dried tangerine peels. Her rudeness sometimes has an eccentric charm to it, but it's just as often simply irritating, something you have to endure if you want to eat Rosie's meals. Some nights I can't tolerate verbal abuse at the end of the day, preferring instead the impersonal mechanics of a drive-in restaurant or the peace and quiet of a peanut butter and dill pickle sandwich at home.

That night Rosie's was deserted, looking drab and not quite clean. The walls are paneled in construction-grade plywood sheets, stained dark, with a matte finish of cooking fumes and cigarette smoke. The lighting is wrong—too pale, too generalized—so that the few patrons who do wander in look sallow and unwell. A television set on the bar usually flashes colored images with no sound, and a marlin arched above it looks like it's fashioned of plaster of Paris and dusted with soot. I'm embarrassed to say how much I like the place. It will never be a tourist attraction. It will never be a singles bar. No one will ever "discover" it or award it even half a star. It will always smell like spilled beer, paprika, and hot grease. It's a place where I can eat by myself and not even have to take a book along in order to avoid unwelcome company. A man would have to worry about any woman he could pick up in a dive like this.

The front door opened and the old crone who lives across the street came in, followed by Jonah Robb, whom I'd talked to that morning in Missing Persons. I almost didn't recognize him at first in his civilian clothes. He wore jeans, a gray tweed jacket, and brown desert boots. His shirt looked new, the package folds still evident, the collar tightly starched and stiff. He carried himself like a man with a shoulder holster tucked up under his left arm. He had apparently come in to look for me because he headed straight for my table and sat down.

I said, "Hello. Have a seat."

"I heard you hung out in here," he said. He glanced around and his brows gave a little lift as though the rumor were true but hard to believe. "Does the Health Department know about this place?"

I laughed.

Rosie, coming out of the kitchen, caught sight of Jonah and stopped dead in her tracks, retreating as though she'd been yanked backward by a rope.

He looked over his shoulder to see if he'd missed something.

"What's the matter? Could she tell I was a cop? Has she got a problem with that?"

"She's checking her makeup. There's a mirror just inside the kitchen door," I said.

Rosie appeared again, simpering coquettishly as she brought my silverware and plunked it down on the table tightly bound in a paper napkin.

"You never said you was entertaining," she murmured.

"Does your friend intend to have a little bite to eat? Some liquid refreshment perhaps? Beer, wine, a mixed drink?"

"Beer sounds good," he said. "What do you have on tap?"

Rosie folded her hands and regarded me with interest. She never deals directly with a stranger so we were forced to go through this little playlet in which I interpreted as though suddenly employed by the U.N.

"You still have Mich on tap?" I asked.

"Of course. Why would I have anything else?"

I looked at Jonah and he nodded assent. "I think we'll have a Mich then. Are you eating? The food's great."

"Fine with me," he said. "What do you recommend?"

"Why don't you just double the order, Rosie? Could you do that for us?"

"Of course." She glanced at him with sly approval. "I had no idea," she said. I could feel her mentally nudge me with one elbow. I knew what her appraisal consisted of. She favored weight in men. She favored dark hair and easygoing attitudes. She moved away from the table then, artfully leaving us alone. She isn't nearly as gracious when I come in with women friends.

"What brings you here?" I said.

"Idleness. Curiosity. I did a background check on you to save us talking about all the stupid stuff."

"So we could get right down to what?" I asked.

"You think I'm on the make or something?"

"Sure," I said. "New shirt. No wedding ring. I bet your wife left you week before last and you shaved less than an hour ago. The cologne isn't even dry on the side of your neck."

He laughed. He had a harmless face and good teeth. He leaned forward on his elbows. "Here's how it went," he said. "I met her when I was thirteen and I was with her from that time to this. I think she grew up and I never could, at least not with her. I don't know what to do with myself. Actually she's been gone for a year. It just *feels* like a week. You're the first woman I've looked at since she went off."

"Where'd she go?"

"Idaho. She took the kids. Two," he said as though he knew I'd ask that next. "One girl ten, another one eight. Courtney and Ashley. I'd have named 'em something else. Sara and Diane, Patti and Jill, something like that. I don't even understand girls. I don't even know what they think about. I really love my kids, but from the day they were born it was like they were in this exclusive little club with my wife. I couldn't seem to get a membership no matter what I did."

"What was your wife's name?"

"Camilla. Shit. She ripped my heart out by the roots. I put on thirty pounds this year."

"Time to take it off," I said.

"Time to do a lot of things."

Rosie came back to the table with a beer for him and a glass of white table wine for me. Did I know this story or what? Men just out of marriages are a mess and I was a mess myself. I already knew all the pain, uncertainty and mismanaged emotions. Even Rosie sensed it wasn't going to fly. She looked at me like she couldn't figure out how I'd blown it so fast. When she left, I got back to the subject at hand.

"I'm not doing all that well myself," I said.

"So I heard. I thought we could help each other out."

"That's not how it works."

"You want to go up to the pistol range and shoot sometime?"

I laughed. I couldn't help myself. He was all over the place. "Sure. We could do that. What kind of gun do you have?"

"Colt Python with a six-inch barrel. It'll take a .38 or a .357 magnum cartridge. Usually I just wear a Trooper MK III but I had a chance to pick up the Python and I couldn't pass it up. Four hundred bucks. You've been married twice? I don't see how you could bring yourself to do that. I mean, Jesus. I thought marriage was a real commitment. Like souls, you know, fused all through eternity and shit like that."

"Four hundred bucks is a steal. How'd you pull that off?" I squinted at him. "What is it, are you Catholic or something?"

"No, just dumb I guess. I got my notions of romance out of ladies' magazines in the beauty shop my mother ran when I was growing up. The gun I got from Dave Whitaker's estate. His widow hates guns and never liked it that he got into 'em so she unloaded his collection first chance she got. I'd have paid the going rate, but she wouldn't hear of it. Do you know her? Bess Whitaker?"

I shook my head.

He glanced up then as Rosie put a plate down in front of each of us. I could tell by his look that he hadn't expected green peppers with a vinaigrette, even with little curlicues of parsley tucked here and there.

Usually Rosie waited until I tasted a dish and gave elaborate restaurant-reviewer-type raves, but this time she seemed to think better of it. As soon as she left, Jonah leaned forward.

"What is this shit?"

"Just eat."

"Kinsey, for the last ten years I been eating with kids who sit and pick all the onions and mushrooms out. I don't know how to eat if it's not made with Hamburger Helper."

"You're in for a big surprise," I said. "What have you been eating for the year since your wife left?"

"She put up all these dinners in the deep freeze. Every night I thaw one and stick it in the oven at three-fifty for an hour. I guess she went to a garage sale and bought up a bunch of those TV dinner tins with the little compartments. She wanted me to eat well-balanced meals even though she was fucking me over financially."

I lowered my fork and looked at him, trying to picture someone freezing up 365 dinners so she could bug out. This was the woman he apparently imagined mating with for life, like owls.

He was eating his first bite of pepper salad, his eyes turning inward. His facial expression suggested that the pepper was sitting in the middle of his tongue while he made chewing motions around it. I do that myself with those mashed candied sweet potatoes people insist on at Thanksgiving time. Why would anyone put a marshmallow on a vegetable? Would I put licorice on asparagus, or jelly beans on Brussels sprouts? The very idea makes my mouth purse.

Jonah nodded philosophically to himself and began to fork up the pepper salad with gusto. It must have been at least as tasty as the shit Camilla cooked for him. I pictured tray after tray of frozen tuna casserole with crushed potato chips, with maybe frozen peas in one compartment, carrot coins in the next. I bet she left him six-packs of canned fruit cocktail for dessert. He was looking at me.

He said, "What's the matter? Why do you have that look on your face?"

I shrugged. "Marriage is a mystery."

"I'll second that," he said. "By the way, how's your case shaping up?"

"Well, I'm still nosing around," I said. "Right now, I'm making a little side investigation into an unsolved murder. Her next-door neighbor was killed the same week she left."

"That doesn't sound good. What's the connection?"

"I don't know yet. Maybe none. It just struck me as an interesting sequence of events that Marty Grice was murdered and Elaine Boldt disappeared within days of it."

"Was there a positive I.D.?"

"On Marty? I have no idea. Dolan's getting really anal-retentive about that stuff. He won't tell me a thing."

"Why not take a look at the files?"

"Oh come on. He's not going to let me see the files."

"So don't ask him. Ask me. I can make copies if you tell me what you want."

"Jonah, he would fire your ass. You would never work again. You'd have to sell shoes for the rest of your life."

"Why would he have to know?"

"How could you get away with it? He knows everything."

"*Bull*shit. The files are kept over in Identification and Records. I'll bet he's got a second set in his office so he probably never even looks at the originals. I'll just wait 'til he's out and Xerox whatever you need. Then I'll put it back."

"Don't you have to sign 'em out?"

He gave me a look then like I was probably the kind of person who never parked in a red zone. Actually, for someone to whom lying comes so easily, I get anxious about vehicle codes and overdue library books. Violations of the public trust. Oh hey, once in a while I might pick a lock illegally, but not if I think there's a chance I'll get *caught*. The idea of sneaking official documents out of the police station made my stomach squeeze down like I was on the verge of getting a tetanus shot.

"Oh wow, don't do that," I said. "You can't."

"What do you mean, I 'can't.' Of course I can. What do you want to see? Autopsy? Incident report? Follow-up interviews? Lab reports?"

"That'd be great. That would really help."

I looked up guiltily. Rosie was standing there waiting to pick up our salad plates. I leaned back in the booth and waited until both had been removed. "Look, I'd never ask you to do such a thing—"

"You didn't ask. I volunteered. Quit being such a candy ass. You can turn around and do me a favor sometime."

"But Jonah, he really is a nut about department leaks. You know how he gets. Please don't put yourself in jeopardy."

"Don't sweat it. Homicide detectives are full of crap sometimes. You're not going to blow his case for him. He probably doesn't even have a case, so what's to worry about?"

After dinner, he walked me back over to my place. It was only 8:15, but I had work to do and he really seemed a bit relieved that the contact between us wasn't going to be prolonged or intimate. As soon as I heard his footsteps retreat, I turned the outside lights off, sat down at my desk with some index cards and caught up with my notes.

I checked back through the cards I'd filled out before and tacked them up on the big bulletin board above my desk. I stood there for a long time, reading card after card, hoping for a flash of enlightenment. Only one curious note emerged. I'd been very meticulous about writing down every single item I remembered from my first search of Elaine's apartment. I do that routinely almost like a little game I play with myself to test my memory. In the kitchen cabinet, she'd had some cans of cat food. 9-Lives Beef and Liver Platter, said the note. Now it seemed out of place to me. What cat?

12

At nine the next morning, I drove over to Via Madrina. Tillie didn't answer my buzz so I stood for a minute, surveying the list of tenants' names on the directory. There was a Wm. Hoover in apartment 10, right next door to Elaine's. I gave him a buzz.

The intercom came to life. "Yes?"

"Mr. Hoover? This is Kinsey Millhone. I'm a private detective here in town and I'm looking for Elaine Boldt. Would you mind if I asked you a couple of questions?"

"You mean, right this minute?"

"Well, yes, if you wouldn't mind. I stopped by to talk to the building manager, but she's not here."

I could hear a murmur of conversation and then the door buzzed at me by way of consent. I had to jump to catch it while the lock would still open. I took the elevator up a floor. Apartment 10 was just across from me when the elevator door slid open. Hoover was standing in the hall in a short blue terry-cloth robe with snags. I estimated his age at thirty-four, thirty-five. He was slight, maybe five foot six, with slim, muscular legs faintly matted with down. His dark hair was tousled and he looked as if he hadn't shaved for two days. His eyes were still baggy from sleep.

"Oh God, I woke you up," I said. "I hate to do that to people."

"No, I've been up," he said. He ran a hand across his hair, scratching the back of his head while he yawned. I had to clamp my teeth so I wouldn't yawn in response. Barefoot, he moved back into the apartment and I followed him.

"I just put some coffee on. It'll be ready in a sec. Come on in and have a seat." His voice was light and reedy.

He indicated the kitchen to the right. His apartment was

the flip image of Elaine's and my guess was that their two master bedrooms shared a wall. I glanced at the living room which, like hers, opened off the entryway and also looked down on the Grices' property next door. Where Elaine's apartment had a view of the street, this one didn't have much to recommend it—only a glimpse of the mountains off to the left, partially obscured by the two rows of Italian stone pines that grow along Via Madrina.

Hoover adjusted his short robe and sat down on a kitchen chair, crossing his legs. His knees were cute. "What's your name again? I'm sorry, I'm still half-unconscious."

"Kinsey Millhone," I said. The kitchen smelled of brewing coffee and the fumes of unbrushed teeth. His, not mine. He reached for a slim brown cigarette and lit it, hoping perhaps to mask his morning mouth with something worse. His eyes were a mild tobacco brown, his lashes sparse, face lean. He regarded me with all the boredom of a boa constrictor after a heavy meal of groundhog. The percolator gave a few last burps and subsided while he reached for two big blue-and-white mugs. One had an overall design of bunny rabbits humping. The other portrayed elephants similarly occupied. I tried not to look. The thing I've worried about for years is how dinosaurs mated, especially those great big spiny ones. Someone told me once they did it in water, which helped support all that weight, but I find it hard to believe dinosaurs were that smart. It didn't seem likely with those tiny pinched heads. I shook myself back to reality.

"What do you call yourself? William? Bill?"

"Wim," he said. He fetched a carton of milk from the refrigerator and found a spoon for the sugar bowl. I added milk to my coffee and watched with interest while he added two heaping tablespoons of sugar to his. He caught my look.

"I'm trying to gain a little weight," he said. "I know the sugar's bad for my teeth, but I've been doing up these torturous protein drinks in the morning—you know the kind—with egg and banana and wheat germ thrown in. Ugh. The aftertaste just cannot be disguised. Besides, I hate to eat before two in the afternoon so I guess I should resign myself to being thin. Anyway, that's why I load up my coffee. I figure anything's bound to help. You look a little on the Twiggy side yourself."

"I run every day and I forget to eat." I sipped my coffee, which was scented faintly with mint. It was really very good. "How well did you know Elaine?" I asked.

"We spoke when we ran into one another in the hall," he said. "We've been neighbors for years. Why do you want her? Did she run out on her bills?"

I told him briefly about her apparent absence, adding that the explanation didn't have to be sinister, but that it was puzzling nevertheless. "Do you remember when you saw her last?"

"Not really. Sometime before she went off. Christmas, I guess. No, I take that back. I did see her New Year's Eve. She said she was staying home."

"Do you happen to know if she had a cat?"

"Oh sure. Gorgeous thing. A massive gray Persian named Mingus. He was actually my cat originally, but I was hardly ever home and I thought he should have company so I gave him to her. He was just a kitten at the time. I had no idea he'd turn out to be such a beauty or I never would have given him up. I mean, I've kicked myself ever since, but what can one do? A deal's a deal."

"What was the deal?"

He shrugged indifferently. "I made her swear she'd never change his name. Charlie Mingus. After the jazz pianist. Also she had to promise not to leave him by himself, or what was the point in giving him away? I might as well have kept him myself."

Wim took a careful drag of his cigarette, resting his elbow on the kitchen table. I could hear the shower running somewhere in the back of the apartment.

"Did she take him with her to Florida every year?"

"Oh sure. Sometimes right up in the cabin if the airline had the space. She said he loved it down there, thought he owned the place." He picked up a napkin and folded it in half.

"Well, it's curious he hasn't shown up someplace."

"He's probably still with her, wherever she is."

"Did you talk to her after that murder next door?"

Wim shook his head, neatly flicking ash into the folded napkin. "I did talk to the police, or rather they talked to me. My living-room windows look right down on that house and they were interested in what I could have seen. Which was nothing, I might add. That detective was the biggest macho asshole I've ever met and I didn't appreciate his antagonistic attitude. Can I warm that up for you?"

He got up and fetched the coffee.

I nodded and he topped off both our mugs, pouring from a thermos. The sound of running water had abruptly ceased and Wim took note of it, just as I did. He went back to the sink and extinguished his cigarette by running it under the tap and then he tossed it in the trash. He got out a frying pan and took a package of bacon from the refrigerator. "I'd offer you breakfast, but I don't have enough unless you want to join me in a protein drink. I'm going to make that up in a minute, disgusting as it is. I'm doing real food for a friend of mine."

"I've got to go shortly anyway," I said, getting up.

He waved at me impatiently. "Sit down, sit down. Finish your coffee at any rate. You might as well ask whatever you want as long as you're here."

"What about a vet for the cat? Did she have someone in the neighborhood?"

Wim peeled off three strips of bacon and laid them in the pan, flipping on the gas. He leaned over, peering at the low blue flame. He had to tug his robe down in back.

He said, "There's a cat clinic around the corner on Serenata Street. She used to take Ming over in one of those cat carriers, howling like a coyote. He hated the vet."

"You have any guesses about where Elaine might be?"

"What about her sister? Maybe she's gone down to L.A. to see her."

"The sister was the one who hired me in the first place," I said. "She hasn't seen Elaine in years."

Wim looked up sharply from the bacon pan and laughed. "What a crock of shit! Who told you that? I met her up here myself not six months back."

"You met Beverly?"

"Sure," he said. He took a fork and pushed the bacon strips in the pan. He went back to the refrigerator and got out three eggs. I was starving to death just watching this stuff.

He continued chattily. "She was maybe four years younger than Elaine. Black hair, cut gamin-style, exquisite skin." He looked at me. "Am I right or am I not?"

"Sounds like the woman I met," I said. "But I wonder why she lied to me."

"I can probably guess," he said. He tore off some paper toweling and folded it, putting it near the frying pan. "They had that nasty falling-out, you know, at Christmastime. Beverly probably doesn't want the word to get out. They positively shrieked and threw things, doors slamming. Oh my God! And the language they used. It was obscene. I had no idea Elaine could swear like that, though I must say the other one was worse."

"What was it about?"

"A man, of course. What else do any of us fuss about?"

"You have any idea who it was?"

"Nope. Frankly, I suspect Elaine's one of those women who's secretly thrilled with widowhood. She gets a lot of sympathy, tons of freedom. She has all that money and no one to hassle with. Why cut some guy in on a deal like that? She's better off by herself."

"Why quarrel with Beverly if that's the case?"

"Who knows? Maybe they thought it was fun."

I finished my coffee and got up then. "I better scoot. I don't want to interrupt your breakfast, but I may want to get back to you. Are you listed in the book?"

"Of course. I do work . . . tending bar at the Edgewood Hotel near the beach. You know the place?"

"I can't afford it, but I know which one you mean."

"Pop in and visit sometime. I'm there from six until closing every night except Monday. I'll buy you a drink."

"Thanks, Wim. I'll do that. I appreciate your help. The coffee was a treat."

"Anytime," he said.

I let myself out, catching a glimpse of Wim's breakfast mate, who looked like something out of *Gentlemen's Quarterly*: sultry eyes, a perfect jawline, collarless shirt, and an Italian cashmere sweater tossed across his shoulders with the sleeves folded into a knot in front.

In the kitchen, Wim had started to sing a version of "The Man I Love." His singing voice sounded just like Marlene Dietrich's.

When I reached the lobby I ran into Tillie, who was pushing a wire cart in front of her like a stroller. It was loaded with brown paper bags.

"I feel like I go to the market twice a day," she said. "Are you here looking for me?"

"Yes, but when you weren't in, I went up and had a brief chat with Wim instead. I didn't realize Elaine Boldt had a cat."

"Oh, she's had Ming for years. I don't know why I didn't think to mention that. I wonder what she did with him?"

"You said she had some carry-on luggage that night going out to the cab. Could it have been Mingus in the cat carrier?"

"Well, it must have been. It was certainly big enough and she did take the cat with her everywhere she went. I guess he's missing too. Isn't that what you're getting at?"

"I don't know yet, but probably. Too bad he's not suffering from some rare cat disease so I could track him down through a veterinarian someplace," I said.

She shook her head. "Can't help you there. He's in good health, as far as I ever knew. He'd be easy to recognize. Big old gray long-haired thing. He must have weighed almost twenty pounds."

"Was he purebred?"

"No and she'd had him neutered early on, so he wasn't used for breeding purposes or anything like that."

"Well," I said, "I may as well start checking up on him too, since I don't have anything else at this point. Did you talk to the police yesterday?"

"Oh yes, and told 'em we thought the woman might have stolen Elaine's bills when she broke in. The officer looked at me like he thought I was nuts, but he did write it down."

"I'll tell you something else Wim brought up. He swears Elaine's sister Beverly was up here at Christmastime and got into a big fight with her. Were you aware of that?"

"No I wasn't, and Elaine never mentioned anything about it either," she said, shifting restlessly. "I've got to go in, Kinsey. I've got some sherbet that'll leak right out if I don't pop it in the freezer soon."

"All right. I'll get back to you later if I need anything else," I said. "Thanks, Tillie."

Tillie went on through the lobby, lugging her grocery cart and I went back to my car and unlocked it. I glanced over at the Grices' house as usual, my attention drawn almost irresistibly to that half-charred ruin where the murder had taken place. On impulse, I locked my car again and trotted up to the Snyders' front door. He must have spotted me through the window because the door opened just as I raised my hand to knock. He stepped out on the porch.

"I saw you coming up the walk. You're the one was here yesterday," he said. "I don't remember your name."

"Kinsey Millhone. I talked to Mr. Grice out at his sister's house yesterday. He said you had a key to his place and would let me in so I could take a look around."

"Yes, that's right. I got it here somewhere." Mr. Snyder seemed to frisk himself and then fished a key ring out of his pocket. He sorted through the keys.

"This's it," he said. He wrestled the key off the ring and handed it to me. "That's to the back door. Front's all boarded up as you can see. For a time there, they had the whole place cordovaned off 'til them fellas from the crime-scene unit could go over everything."

From the rear, I heard, "What is it, Orris? Who's that you're talking to?"

"Hold your horses! Y'old coot. I got to go," he said, his jowls atremble.

"I'll bring this back when I'm done," I said, but he was already lumbering off toward the back of the house in a snit. I thought she could hear remarkably well for someone he claimed was as deaf as a loaf of bread.

I cut across the Snyders' yard, the ivy rustling under my feet. The Grices' front lawn was dead from neglect and the sidewalk was littered with debris. It didn't look as if it had been cleaned up since the fire trucks departed, and I was crossing my fingers that the salvage crew had never gone in to clear the place out. I went around the side, passing the padlocked double doors that were slanted up against the house and led down into the basement. At the rear of the house, I climbed five crumbling steps onto a small back porch. The back door had a big glass window in the upper half and I could see into the kitchen through ruffled curtains that were dingy now and hung crookedly.

I unlocked the door and let myself in. For once, I was in luck. The floor was covered with rubble, but the furniture was still in place; kitchen table filthy, chairs knocked askew. I left the door open behind me and surveyed the room. There were dishes on the counter, shelves of canned goods visible through an open pantry door. I was feeling a faint thrill of uneasiness as I always do in situations like these.

The house smelled richly of scorched wood and there was a heavy layer of soot on everything. The kitchen walls were gray with smoke and my shoes made a gritty sound as I moved through to the hallway, crushing broken glass to a sugary consistency underfoot. As nearly as I could tell, the interior of the Grices' house was laid out like the Snyders' house next door and I could identify what I guessed was the dining room just off the kitchen, with a blackened swinging door between. This must be the counterpart to the room in the Snyders' house that Orris had now outfitted as a bedroom for his wife. There was a half-bath across the hall, just the toilet and sink. The old linoleum had blistered and buckled, showing blackened floorboards beneath. The window in the hallway was broken now, but it looked out onto a narrow walkway between the two houses and right into May Snyder's converted bedroom. I could see her clearly, lying on a hospital bed that had been cranked up to a forty-five-degree angle. She seemed to be asleep, looking small and shrunken under a white counterpane. I moved away from the window and down the hall toward the living room.

The fire had leached the color out of everything and it looked now like a black-and-white photograph. The char patterns—like dark stretches of alligator hide—covered doorframes and window sashes. The destruction became more pronounced as I moved toward the front of the house. As I passed the stairs leading to the half-story up above, I could see where the flames had chewed the treads and part of the wooden banister. The wallpaper in the stairwell was as tattered and inky as an old treasure map.

I moved on, trying to get my bearings. There was an ominous patch of missing floorboards near the front door where I imagined Marty Grice's body had been found. Flames had eaten up the walls, leaving pipes and blackened beams exposed. Across the floor here, and extending back down the hall and up the stairs, there were irregular burned trails where an accelerant of some kind had been splashed. I bypassed the gaping hole in the floor and peered into the living room, which looked as if it had been outfitted with avant-garde "works of furniture" made entirely of charcoal briquettes. Two chairs and a couch were still arranged in a conversational grouping, but the fire had gnawed the upholstery right down to the bare springs. All that remained of the coffee table was a burned frame.

I went back to the stairs and crept up with care. The fire had taken the bedroom in whimsical bites, leaving a stack of paperback books untouched while the footstool nearby had been almost completely consumed. The bed was still made, but the room had been drenched by the fire hoses and smelled now of rotting carpet fiber and soggy wallpaper, mildewed blankets, singed clothing, and clumps of insulation that had boiled out through the fire-bared lath and plaster here and there. On the bed table, there was a framèd photograph of Leonard with an appointment card for a teeth cleaning and exam tucked in the edge of the glass.

I moved the card aside, peering closely at Leonard's face. I thought about the snapshot I'd seen of Marty. Such a dumpy little thing: overweight, plastic eye-glass frames, a hairdo that looked like a wig. Leonard was much more attractive and in happier times presented a trim appearance, a rather distinguished face, graying hair, a steady gaze. His shoulders were rounded, possibly because of his back problems, but it gave the impression of something weak or apologetic in his nature. I wondered if Elaine Boldt had found him appealing. Could she have come between these two?

I put the picture back and picked my way down the stairs. As I moved along the hall toward the kitchen, I noticed a door ajar and I pushed it open gingerly. Before me yawned the basement, looking like a vast, black pit. Shit. In the interest of being thorough, I knew I'd have to check it out. I made a face to myself and went out to my car to get the flashlight out of the glove compartment.

13

The basement stairs were intact. The fire had apparently been contained before it reached this far. The damage to the rooms above seemed to be the result of some accelerant that had ensured at least a superficial combustion throughout the house. The beam from my flashlight cut through the dark, illuminating a narrow, moving path filled with things I didn't want to touch. I reached the bottom of the stairs. There wasn't a lot of headroom. The house was more than forty years old and the foundation was dank and spider-pocked. The air felt dense, like the atmosphere in a greenhouse, except that everything down here was dead, exuding that fenny perfume of old fire and old damp, abandonment and rot.

I angled the light along the joists, tracing the beams to the hole where daylight spilled down. Had the floor burned through and the body tumbled into the basement? I moved closer, craning to see better. The edges of the hole looked cut to me. Maybe the fire inspector had taken samples of the boards for lab tests. To my left, I could see the furnace, a silent squat bulge of gray, with sooty ducting extending in all directions. The floor was hard-packed dirt and cracked concrete, the entire space filled with junk. Paint cans and old window screens were stacked up under the stairs and there was an ancient galvanized sink in the corner, the pipes corroded away.

I toured the perimeter, poking the light into spaces where eight-legged creatures skittered away from me, horrified. Later I was glad I'd been such a conscientious little bun, but at the time, I only wanted to get out of there as quickly as I could. An empty house always seems to make those noises that have you wondering if an ax murderer is creeping through the premises in search of prey. I shone the flashlight over to the far wall where the stairs jutted up a short distance to the bolted double doors leading out to the side yard. Daylight slanted through the cracks but the smell of fresh air didn't sift down this far. I knew the double doors were padlocked on the outside, but the wood was old and crumbly and didn't seem that secure. From what Lily Howe had said, the burglar hadn't even bothered with breaking and entering. He'd marched right up to the front door and rung the bell. Had they struggled? Had he panicked when she opened the door and killed her instantly? The intruder might have been a woman, of course, especially if the weapon had actually been a baseball bat. Ever since Title IX, women have become more adept at the sportier side arms; death by discus, javelin, shot put, bow and arrow, hockey puck . . . the possibilities are endless, one would think.

I moved back toward the stairs shivering involuntarily with the darkness at my back. I took the steps two at a time, nearly knocking myself out when I banged into a crossbeam. I cursed soundly to myself, bursting out of the basement and into the hall again as though pursued. Something feathery caught my eye and when I realized it was a delicate centipede whiffling down my front, I did this erratic quick dance step, brushing my shirt like I'd suddenly burst into flames. God, the things I do for money, I thought savagely. I went out the back door, locking it behind me, and sat down on the porch steps. My breathing finally slowed, but it took me a few more minutes to regain my composure.

In the meantime, I had a chance to check the backyard. I don't know what I was looking for or what I thought I might find after six months. There were only overgrown bushes and weeds, a little orange tree crippled by the lack of water and covered with hard fruit turning brown because it hadn't been picked. The shed was one of those prefabricated metal jobs you can order through the Sears catalogue and put up anywhere. It was secured by a nice big fat padlock that looked sturdy enough. I crossed the yard and inspected it. It was actually a simple warded lock I thought I could open in a few minutes, but I didn't have my little double-headed pick key with me and I wasn't crazy about the idea of standing out there fiddling with a padlock in broad daylight. Better I should come back when the sun went down and find out what Grice or his nephew kept in there. Old lawn furniture was my guess, but one can never be sure.

I took the house key back to Mr. Snyder and then got in my car and headed over to the office. I let myself in and made a pot of coffee. The mail wasn't in yet and there were no messages on my machine. I opened the French doors and stood out on the balcony. Where the fuck was Elaine Boldt? And where was Elaine Boldt's pussycat? I was running out of things to do and places to look. I typed up a contract for Julia Ochsner to sign and stuck that in my out box. When the coffee was ready, I poured myself some and sat down in my swivel chair and swiveled. When in doubt, I thought, it's best to fall back on routine.

I made a long-distance telephone call to a newspaper in Boca Raton, and another call to a paper in Sarasota, placing classified ads in the personals columns of each. "Anybody knowing the whereabouts of Elaine Boldt, female, Caucasian, age 43 . . ." etc. "Please contact . . ." with my name, address, and phone number and an invitation to call collect.

That felt productive. What else? I swiveled some more and then put a call through to Mrs. Ochsner. She was on my mind anyway.

"Hello?" she said, picking up at long last. Her voice was tremulous, but held a note of anticipation, as though despite the fact she was eighty-eight, anyone might be calling and anything might come to pass. I hoped I'd always feel that way myself. At the moment, I wasn't so optimistic.

"Hi, Julia. This is Kinsey out in California."

"Just a minute, dear, and I'll turn the television down. I'm watching my program."

"You want me to call you back in a bit? I hate to interrupt."

"No, no. I'd prefer talking to you. Hold on."

Some moments passed and I heard the volume of the background noise reduced to silence. Julia was apparently creeping back to the phone as fast as she could. I waited. Finally she picked up the receiver again. "I kept the picture on," she said, out of breath, "though it just looks like one big blur from across the room. How are you?"

"Frustrated at the moment," I said. "I'm running out of things to do, but I wanted to ask you about Elaine's cat. I don't suppose you've seen Mingus in the last six months, have you?"

"Oh goodness, no. I hadn't even thought about him. If she's gone, he'd have to be missing too, I suppose."

"Well, it looks that way. The building manager here says she left that night with what looked like a cat carrier, so if she actually got to Florida, I'm assuming she'd have had him with her."

"I'd be willing to swear he never got here any more than she did, but I could check with vets and kennels in the area," Julia said. "Maybe she boarded him out for some reason."

"Could you do that? It would really save me some time. I don't know that you'll turn up anything, but at least we'll know we tried. I'm going to see if I can trace the taxicab she took and find out if she had the cat with her when she went to the airport. Did Pat Usher ever mention him?"

"Not that I recall. She's gone, you know. Moved out lock, stock, and barrel."

"Oh, really? Well, I'm not surprised, but I would like to know where she is. Could you get her forwarding address from the Makowskis? I'll call you back in a day or two, but don't you dare call Pat yourself. I don't want her to know you're involved. I may need you to do some more snooping later and I don't want your cover blown." I added, "How are things with you otherwise?"

"Oh, I'm fine, Kinsey. You needn't worry about me. I don't suppose you'd consider a partnership after we wrap this one up."

"I've had worse offers in my day," I said.

Julia laughed. "I'm going to start reading Mickey Spillane just to get in shape. I don't know a lot of rude words, you know."

"I think I've got us covered on that score. I'll talk to you later. Let me know if you come up with anything startling in the meantime. Oh—and I'm shipping you a contract for your signature. We might as well do this right."

"Roger. Over and out," she said and hung up.

I left my vintage VW in the parking lot behind the office and walked over to the Tip Top Cab Company on Delgado. The business office is located in a narrow strip of stores best noted for their liquidation sales: a constant round of discount shoes, car stereos, lunch counters, and motorcycle shops with an occasional beauty salon or a "fast-foto" establishment. It is not a desirable location. The one-way street runs the wrong way. The parking lot is too small and apparently the owner of the building, while not exacting outrageous rents, is also content to let the premises languish under worn paint and tatty carpeting.

Tip Top was jammed between a Humane Society Thrift Shop and a Big N' Tall Men's Shop with a suit in the window designed for the steroid enthusiast. The office itself was long and narrow, partitioned across the middle with a plywood wall with a door cut into it. The place was furnished like some kid's hideout, complete with two broken-down couches and a table with one short leg. There were drawings and hand-lettered signs Scotch-taped to the walls, trash piled up in one corner, dog-eared copies of *Road and Track* magazine in an irregular tier by the front door. The bucket seat from a car was propped against the far wall, tan upholstery slashed in one spot and mended with old Band-Aids covered with stars. The dispatcher was perched on a stool, leaning one elbow on a counter as littered as a workbench. He was probably twenty-five with curly black hair and a small dark mustache. He wore chinos, a pale blue T-shirt with a faded decal of the Grateful Dead, and a visor that made his hair stick up on the sides. The shortwave radio squawked incomprehensibly and he took up the mike.

"Seven-oh," he said, his eyes immediately focusing on the map of the city affixed to the wall above the counter. I saw a butt-filled ashtray, an aspirin bottle, a cardboard calendar from Our Lady of Sorrows Church, a fan belt, plastic packets of ketchup, and a big penciled note that read "F's Anybody Seen My Red Flash Lite?" Tacked to the wall the e was a list of addresses for customers who'd passed bad chec s and those in the habit of calling more than one cab to se who could get there first.

There was a short burst of squawking and th dispatcher moved a round magnet from one part of the map to another. It looked like he was playing a board game all by himself.

He rotated toward me on the stool. "Yes ma'am."

I held out my hand. "I'm Kinsey Millhone," I said. He seemed slightly disconcerted at the notion of shaking hands, but he covered himself and gamely obliged.

"Ron Coachello."

I took out my wallet and showed him my identification. "I wonder if you could check some records for me."

His eyes were very dark and bright and his look said that he could check anything he wanted if it suited him. "What's the skinny?"

I gave him the *Reader's Digest* condensed version of the tale, complete with Elaine Boldt's local address and the approximate time the taxi'd been there. "Can you go back to January ninth of this year and see if Tip Top picked up the fare? It might have been City Cab or Green Stripe. I've got some questions for the driver."

He shrugged. "Sure. It might take a day. I got that stuff at home. I don't keep it down here. Why don't I give you a call, or better yet, you buzz me back? How's that?"

The phone rang and he took a call, logging it in. Then he took up the mike and pressed the button. "Six-eight." He cocked his head, listening idly. There was static, then a squawk.

"Four-oh-two-nine Orion," he said and clicked off. I gave him my card. He glanced at it with curiosity as if he'd never known a woman with a business card before. The radio suddenly came to life again and he turned back, taking up the mike. I waved to him and he waved back over his shoulder at me.

I went through exactly the same procedure with the other two cab companies, which were fortunately within walking distance of one another. By the time I repeated the same story twice more I felt like I was suffering from a bad case of tongue flop.

When I got into the office, there was a message from Jonah Robb on my machine.

"Ah, yeah, Kinsey. This is Officer Robb on that . . . ah . . . issue we discussed. I wonder if you could give me a call sometime . . . ah . . . this afternoon and we'll find a way to get together on it. It's now Friday and it's . . . ah . . . twelve-ten P.M. Talk to you soon. Okay. Thanks." The number he left was for the police station, with the extension for Missing Persons.

I called him back, identifying myself as soon as he came on the line. "I understand you have some information for me."

"Right," he said. "You want to stop by my place later on?"

"I could do that," I said. I took down his address and we settled on 8:15, bypassing dinner. I didn't think we should get into any little domestic numbers at this point. I thanked him for his help and rang off.

I couldn't for the life of me think of anything else to do on the case that afternoon so I locked the office and headed for home. It was only 1:20 and since I'd accomplished so little at work, I felt morally obliged to be useful at my place. I washed the cup and saucer and plate that were sitting in the sink and left them in the rack to dry until I needed them again. I put a load of towels in the washer and then scoured the bathroom and kitchen sinks, took out the trash, and vacuumed a path around the furniture. Now and then, I actually move things and suck up all the woofies underneath, but today it was sufficient to have a few vacuum-cleaner tracks here and there and the apartment smelling of that peculiar cross between hot machine oil and cooked dust. I do love tidiness. When you live by yourself, you can either get all piggy or pick up as you go, which is what I prefer. There's nothing more depressing than coming home at the end of a long day to a place that looks like it's just been tossed by the mob.

I changed into my sweat pants and did three miles with

energy to burn. This was one of those rare days when the run seemed inexplicably grand.

I came home, showered, washed my hair, napped, got dressed, sneaked in a little grocery shopping, and then I sat down at my desk and worked on note cards while I drank a glass of white wine and ate a warm, sliced-hard-boiled-egg sandwich with loads of Best Food's mayo and salt, nearly swooning at the taste.

At eight, I snatched up a jacket, my handbag, and my key pick and hopped in my car, heading over to Cabana Boulevard, the wide avenue that parallels the beach. I turned right. Jonah lived in an odd little tract of houses off Primavera, maybe a mile away. I passed the marina, then Ludlow Beach, glancing to my left. Even in the gathering twilight, I could identify the big trash bin where death had almost caught up with me two weeks before. I wondered how long it would take before I could pass that area without unconsciously glancing left, without taking just that one peek at the place where I'd thought my life would end. The beach seemed to glow with the last light of day and the sky was a silver gray layered with pink and lavender, deepening to dark magenta where the near hills intersected the view. Out on the ocean, the islands retained a magical hot gold light where lingering rivulets of sunlight formed a shimmering pool.

I went up the hill, passing Sea Shore Park, turning right then into a tangle of streets across the boulevard. The proximity to the Pacific meant too much chill fog and corrosive salt air, but there was an elementary school close by. For Jonah, who had had a family to support on a cop's salary, the neighborhood was affordable, but by no means grand.

I found the street number I was looking for and pulled into the driveway. The porch light was on and the yard looked well kept. The house was a ranch-style stucco painted slate blue with dark blue trim. I guessed there would be three bedrooms with maybe a patio in back. I rang the doorbell and Jonah came to the door. He wore jeans and an L. L. Bean Oxford-cloth dress shirt with a pink pinstripe. He carried a beer bottle loosely by the neck, motioning me in with a glance at his watch.

"God, you're prompt," he said.

"Well, you're not far away. I just live at the bottom of the hill."

"I know. You want me to take that?"

He was holding his hand up for the jacket, which I shed and handed to him, along with my handbag. He tossed both unceremoniously into a chair.

For a minute neither of us could think of anything to say. He took a sip of beer. I put my hands in my back pockets. Why did this feel so awkward? It reminded me of those awful junior-high-school dates where you got driven to the movies by somebody's mother and you never knew what to talk about.

I glanced around. "Nice house," I remarked.

"Come on. I'll show you around."

I followed while he talked back over his shoulder at me.

"It was a shit heap when we first moved in. The guy'd been renting it out to these weirdos who kept a ferret in the closet and never flushed the toilet because it was against their religious beliefs. You've probably seen 'em around town. Barefoot with these red and yellow rags around their heads and outfits like something out of the Old Testament. He said they hardly ever paid their rent, but every time he came to hassle them about it, they'd start humming and hold his hand, making significant eye contact. You want some wine? I bought you some high-class stuff—no twist-off cap."

I smiled. "I'm flattered."

We detoured into the kitchen and he opened a bottle of white wine for me, pouring it into a wineglass that still had the price tag on the bottom. He grinned sheepishly when he saw it.

"All I had was plastic glasses the kids used to use in the backyard," he said. "This is the kitchen."

"I kind of figured that."

It was a nice house. I don't know what I expected, but someone had made good choices. The whole place had a stripped-down feeling: bare, gleaming wood floors, furniture with simple lines, clean surfaces. Why had Camilla left this? What else was she looking for?

He showed me three bedrooms, two baths, a deck out back and a small yard enclosed by a vine-covered stucco wall.

"I'll tell you the truth," he said. "When she walked out, I packed up all her stuff and had the Salvation Army come take it away. I wasn't going to sit around looking at her little artsy-fartsy geegaws. I kept the kids' rooms intact. Maybe she'll get tired of them like she got tired of me and send them back, but *her* stuff I don't need. She was royally irritated when she heard, but what was I supposed to do?" He shrugged, standing there holding the beer bottle by the neck.

His face was beginning to take form now that I'd seen him twice. Before, I'd only registered qualities like "bland" and "harmless." I'd been aware of the extra weight he carried, a personality made up of something nice mixed with something droll. He was direct and I responded to that, but he also had a trait I'd noticed in certain cops before: bemused self-assurance, as if he were looking at the world from a long way back but it was all okay with him. Clearly, Camilla still loomed large in his life and he smiled every time he talked about her, not with affection, but to cover his wrath. I thought he needed to go through a few more women before he got down to me.

"What is that? What's that look?" he asked.

I smiled. "Beware of dog," I said. I'm not sure if I was talking about him or me.

He smiled too, but he knew what I meant. "I got the stuff in here."

He pointed toward the dining-room table in an alcove just off the living room.

I sat down in a hot circle of light, feeling like a glutton with a napkin tucked under my chin and a knife and fork upright in each fist. Along with the reports he'd Xeroxed, he'd also managed to slip me some duplicate photographs. I was going to see the aftermath of the crime with my own eyes and I could hardly wait.

14

I read through everything quickly, just to get an overview, and then I went back and noted the details that interested me. The official version of the story, as much as I knew it, and the interviews with Leonard Grice, his sister Lily, neighbors, the fire inspector, and the first police officer on the scene more or less spelled out events in the same way I'd been told. Leonard and Marty were scheduled to go out for their traditional Tuesday-night dinner with Leonard's widowed sister, Mrs. Howe. Marty wasn't feeling well and canceled out at the last minute. Leonard and Lily went out as planned and got back to the Howes' at about nine P.M., at which point a call was put through to Marty to let her know they were home. Both Mr. Grice and his sister spoke to Marty and she finally terminated the call in order to respond to a knock at the door. According to both Lily and Leonard, they had a cup of coffee and chatted for a bit. He left at approximately ten o'clock, arriving at Via Madrina twenty-some minutes later to find that his house had burned. By then, the blaze had been brought under control and his wife's body was being removed from the partially destroyed residence. He collapsed and was revived by paramedics at the scene. Tillie Ahlberg was the one who'd spotted the smoke and she'd turned in an alarm at 9:55. Two units had responded within minutes, but the blaze was such that entry couldn't be effected through the front door. Firemen had broken in through the rear, extinguishing the fire after thirty minutes or so. The body was discovered in the entryway and removed to the morgue.

Identification had been established by full-mouth X rays supplied by Marty's local dentist and through an examination of stomach contents. She'd apparently mentioned to Leonard on the phone that she'd fixed herself some canned tomato soup and a tuna sandwich. The empty cans were found in the kitchen wastebasket. The time of death had more or less been fixed in a narrow framework between the time of the telephone call and the time the fire alarm had been turned in.

I read through the autopsy report, mentally summing up a lot of technical details. The pathologist reported no carbon granules deposited in the bronchial passages or lungs and no carbon monoxide in the blood or other tissues. It was therefore determined that she had been dead when the fire broke out. Additional lab tests had revealed no alcohol, chloroform, drugs, or poisons in the system. The cause of death was attributed to multiple skull fractures apparently caused by repeated blows with a blunt instrument. Because of the nature of the wounds, the pathologist estimated the object to be some four to five inches in width, speculating that it might have been a two-by-four wielded with great force, a baseball bat, or some kind of club, possibly metal. The murder weapon had never been found. Unless, of course, it was a big old board burned up in the fire, but there was no evidence to support that possibility.

The arson investigators didn't seem to have any doubts that fire had been deliberately set. Lab tests showed traces of kerosene in the floorboards. Charring patterns throughout the house had borne this out. They'd seen the same blackened splash marks and the same liquid trails that I'd spotted when I went through the house earlier. They'd also used some sophisticated methods of verifying the point of origin and the course the fire had taken as it burned. Leonard Grice had been questioned about the kerosene and he said he'd been storing a quantity in the basement for use in two lamps and a cooking stove that he and Marty took on camping trips, which accounted for the intruder's having had access to a flammable liquid. It looked as if the burglar had come with a weapon in hand, but without any intention of burning the place down. The fire was apparently an afterthought, a hastily concocted plan to conceal the bludgeoning of Marty Grice.

So far there was nothing to suggest that anybody knew she'd be there, so the cops were having a hard time imagining that the murder had been planned in advance.

There was no evidence that a time-delay device had been employed, which ruled out the possibility that Grice had rigged the fire before he left. Grice's nephew, Mike, had been questioned and cleared. He'd been seen by numerous impartial witnesses in a hangout called The Clockworks in downtown Santa Teresa during the critical period when experts speculated that the fire had been set. There were no other suspects and no other witnesses. Any other hard evidence including fingerprints had been destroyed by the fire. Elaine Boldt's name was on a list of persons to be interviewed and there was a note that Lieutenant Dolan had contacted her by telephone on the fifth. He'd made an appointment to see her on January 10, but she'd never appeared. According to the information I had, she'd left for Florida the night before.

One entry, appearing in the middle of a typed report, interested me considerably. According to a deputy at the police department, a call had come in at 9:06 on the night of the murder that might well have been placed by Marty Grice. The caller had been female, in a panic, and had blurted out a cry for help before the phone went dead. Since the call was placed to the police station instead of 911, the deputy had no way of getting a fix on the address from which the call had originated. She'd made a note of it, however, and when the murder came to light, she'd reported it to Dolan, who had included it in his report. He'd questioned Grice about that too. If it *was* Marty, why would she have called the station instead of dialing 911? Leonard had pointed out that he and Marty had a telephone answering machine with a rapid-dial function. She'd entered the telephone numbers of both the police department and the fire department. The answering machine was found, undamaged, on a table in the rear of the hallway with the numbers neatly printed on the index. It looked as if Marty had had some warning of the attack and had been able to reach the telephone, calling out at least part of a distress signal before she'd been killed. If she'd actually placed th call, it pinpointed the time of death at 9:06 or soon afterward.

For a moment, I harbored the fleeting hope that Leonard Grice might still be implicated. After all, as nearly as I could tell, the police had only Lily's word for the fact that he was still at her place at that time. I was speculating that he might have come home early, killed Marty, started the fire, and then parked around the block until the appropriate moment to arrive. If he and his sister were in cahoots, they could both simply maintain afterward that he'd been with her. I was out of luck on that one. Three interviews down, there was a short paragraph detailing a conversation that Dolan had had with some of Lily's neighbors who'd stopped by unexpectedly at nine P.M. to drop off a birthday present. The husband and wife both reported independently that Leonard was there and hadn't left for home until approximately ten. The time was noted because they'd been trying to persuade him to stay for a television program that came on at ten. It turned out to be a rerun and since he was anxious to get home to his wife anyway, he'd left.

Well, shit, I thought.

Now, why was this making me feel so cross? Ah, well, because I wanted Leonard Grice to be guilty of something. Murder, conspiracy to murder, accessory to murder. I was fond of the idea for tidiness' sake—for statistical purposes, if nothing else. California has over three thousand homicide victims annually, and of those, fully two-thirds are slain by friends, acquaintances, or relatives, which makes you wonder if you might be better off as a friendless orphan in this state. The point is, when a murder goes down, the chances are good that someone near and dear has had a hand in it.

I thought about that, reluctant to give it up. Could Grice have hired someone to kill his wife? It was always possible, of course, but it was hard to see what he might have gained. The police, not being ignorant buffoons, had pursued the line as well, but had come up with nothing. No moneys unaccounted for, no meetings with unsavory characters, no apparent motive, no visible benefit.

Which brought me back to Elaine Boldt. Could she have

been involved in Marty Grice's death? Most of what I'd learned about her cried out a big resounding "no." There really wasn't a hint that she'd been attached to Leonard romantically or any other way, except as an occasional bridge partner. I didn't think Marty Grice had been killed for messing up a small slam, but with bridge players one can never tell. Wim Hoover had mentioned that Elaine and Beverly had quarreled about a man at Christmastime, but it was hard to picture the two of them in an arm wrestle over Leonard Grice. I kept coming back to the same suspicion—that Elaine knew something or had seen something related to Marty's murder and had left town to avoid the scrutiny of the Santa Teresa police.

I turned my attention to the photographs, neatly disconnecting my brain. I needed to know how things had looked and I couldn't afford to react emotionally. Violent death is repellent. My first impulse, always, is to turn abruptly away, to shield my soul from the sight, but this was the only tangible record of that event and I had to see for myself. I turned a cold eye to the first black-and-white photograph. The color pictures would be worse and I thought I'd start with the "easy" ones.

Jonah cleared his throat. I looked up.

"I'm going to have to turn in," he said. "I'm beat."

"You are?" I glanced at my watch, startled. It was 10:45. I'd been sitting there for more than two hours without moving. "I'm sorry," I said. "I had no idea I'd been here that long."

"That's okay. I got up at five this morning to work out and I need some shut-eye. You can take that stuff if you like. Of course, if Dolan ever catches you with it, I'll deny everything and throw you to the wolves, but aside from that, I hope it helps."

"Thanks. It's already helped." I shoved the photographs and reports into a big manila envelope and tucked that, in turn, in my handbag.

I drove home, disturbed. Even now, there was an image of Marty's body graven behind my eyes: features blurred by charring, mouth open, lying in a circle of ash like a pile of gray confetti. The heat had caused the tendons in her arms to retract, pulling her fists up into a pugilistic pose. It was her last fight and she had lost, but I didn't think it was over yet.

I willed the image away, running back over what I'd learned to that point. One little detail still bothered me. Was it possible that May Snyder had been accurate when she talked about the bang-bang-bang of hammering that night? If so, what in the world could it have been?

I was almost home again when I remembered the shed in the Grices' backyard. I slammed the brakes on and hung a hard left, heading across town.

Via Madrina was dark, heavily overhung by Italian stone pines. There wasn't much traffic at that hour. The night sky was hazy and though the moon was full, the light that filtered down was partially blocked by the condominium next door. I parked and got a little penlight out of the glove compartment. I pulled on a pair of rubber gloves and locked my car, heading up the Grices' front walk. I cut around the side of the house, my tennis shoes making no sound at all on the concrete.

In my jacket pocket I fingered the key pick, shaped like a flattened metal mandolin. I had a set of five picks with me on a key ring and a second more elaborate set at home in a nice leather case. They'd been given to me by a nonresidential burglar who was currently serving ten months in the county jail. Last time he'd been caught, he'd hired me to keep an eye on his wife, whom he believed was misbehaving with the guy next door. Actually, she hadn't been doing anything and he was so grateful for the good news that he gave me the key picks and taught me how to use them. He'd paid me some cash too, but then it turned out he'd stolen it and he had to ask for it back when the judge ordered him to make restitution.

It was chilly and there was a frisky little breeze making breathy sounds in the pine boughs. The house behind the Grices' had canvas awnings that were snapping like sails, and the hollow sigh of dry grass gave the whole enterprise an eerie ambiance of its own. I was feeling jumpy anyway because I'd just been looking at pictures of a charbroiled corpse, and here I was, about to do a little breaking-and-entering number that could land me in jail and cause my license to be snatched away. If the next-door neighbors set up a howl and the cops arrived on the scene, what was I going to say? Why was I doing it anyway? Ah, because I wanted to know what was in this wee metal house and I couldn't figure out how else to get in.

I fixed a tiny beam of light on the bottom of the padlock. In the diagram my burglar friend had drawn of a lock like this, there is a flat, hairpin spring that latches into notches in the shackle. Usually only the tip of the key actuates the spring, so it was a question of figuring out which of my picks would spread the latch apart, releasing the mechanism. In truth, I could have tried a paper clip with a small L bent on one end but that was the shape of the first pick I used and the padlock wouldn't budge. I tried the next pick which had an H shape in the point. Nope. I tried the third, working it carefully. The lock popped open in my hand. I checked my watch. A minute and a half. I get a bit vain about these things.

The shed door made a wrenching sound when I opened it and I stood for a moment, heart thudding in my throat. I heard a motorcycle putter past in the street but I didn't pay much attention to it because I had just understood Mike's custodial relationship to his uncle's property. In the shed, along with the stack of clay pots, the hand-push lawn mower, and a weed whacker were six shelves crammed with illegal drugs: Mason jars full of reds and dexies, yellow jackets, rainbows and sopers . . . along with some fat plastic packets of grass and hashish. Well, this was all just too yummy for words. I didn't think Leonard Grice was the druggist, but I was willing to bet money his nephew had invested heavily in this little portable Rexall. I was so enamored of my discovery that I didn't know he was behind me until he let out an astonished "hey!"

I jumped back and whipped around, suppressing a shriek. I found myself face-to-face with the kid, his green eyes glowing in the dark like a cat's. He was as startled to see me as I was to see him. Fortunately, neither of us was armed or we might have had a quick duel, doing each other a lot of needless harm.

"What are you *doing*?" he said. He sounded outraged, as if he couldn't believe this was happening. His Mohawk was beginning to grow out and the wind was making it lean slightly to the left like a field of tall grass in one of those old commercials for Kotex. He had on a black leather motorcycle jacket and a rhinestone earring. His boots were knee-high and made of plastic scored to resemble cobra skin only looking more like psoriasis. It was hard to take this lad seriously, but in some odd way I did. I closed the shed door and snapped the padlock into place. What could *he* prove?

"I got curious about what you were doing back here so I thought I'd take a peek."

"You mean you just broke in?" he said. His voice had that adolescent crack left over from puberty and his cheeks were hot pink. "You can't do that!"

"Mike, sweetie, I just did," I said. "You're in big trouble."

He stared at me for a moment, his expression blank. "You gonna call the cops?"

"Shit yes!"

"But what you did is just as much against the law as this," he said. I could tell he was one of those bright boys accustomed to arguing righteously with adults.

"Oh crap," I said, "wise up. I'm not going to stand out here and argue the California penal code with you. You're dealing drugs. The cops aren't going to care what I was up to. Maybe was passing by and thought you were breaking in yourself. You're out of business, kiddo."

His eyes took on a shrewd look and he changed his tack. "Well now, wait a minute. Don't go so fast. Why can't we talk about this?"

"Sure, why not? What's to say?"

I could practically see his brain cells scurry around forming a new thought. He was no fool, but he still surprised me with the line he took. "Are you looking into Aunt Marty's death? Is that why you're here?"

Aunt Marty. Nice touch, I thought. I smiled briefly.

"Not quite, but that's close enough."

He glanced off toward the street, then down at the toe of his cobra boot. "Because I got something . . . you know, like some information about that."

"What kind of information?"

"Something I never told the cops. So maybe we could make a trade," he said. He stuck his hands in his jacket pockets looking back at me. His face was innocent, his complexion clear, the look in his eyes so pure I'd have given him my firstborn if I'd had one. The little smile that crossed his face was engaging and I wondered how much money he'd made selling dope to his high-school friends. And I wondered if he was going to end up with a bullet in his head for cheating someone higher up in the scheme of things. I was interested in what he had to say and he knew it. I had to make quick peace with my own corruption and it wasn't that hard to do. Times like this, I know I've been in the business too long.

"What kind of trade?"

"Just give me time to clear this stuff out before you tell anyone. I was about to lay off anyway because the narcs have some undercover agents at our school and I thought I'd cool it 'til the pressure's off."

We're not talking permanent reform here, folks. We're talking simple expediency, but at least the kid wasn't trying to con me . . . too much.

We looked at each other and something shifted. I knew I could rail and stomp and threaten him. I knew I could be pious and moralistic and disapproving and it wouldn't change a thing. He knew the score as well as I did and what we had to offer each other might not be a bad bet on either side.

"All right, you got it," I said.

"Let's go somewhere and talk," he said. "I'm freezin' my nuts off."

It bothered me to realize that I'd started to like him just a little bit.

126

15

We went to The Clockworks on State Street; he on his motorcycle, with me following in my car. The place is a teen hangout and looks like something out of a rock video; a long, narrow room painted charcoal gray with a high ceiling and the lighting done in pink and purple neon tubing. The whole of it resembles the interior of a clock in abstract and futuristic forms. There are mobiles looking like big black gears suspended from the ceiling, the smoke in the air moving them in slow circles. There are four small tables near the door and on the left are what look like shelves at chest height in a series of standing-room-only booths where couples can neck while drinking soda pop. The menu posted on the wall is larded with side orders like dinner salad and garlic toast that kids can snack on, paying seventy-five cents for the privilege of taking up table space for hours at a time. You can also buy two kinds of beer and a house chablis if you are old enough and have tangible proof. It was now nearly midnight and there were only two other people in the place, but the owner apparently knew Mike and his gaze slid over to me appraisingly. I tried to look like I was not Mike's date. I didn't mind a May/December romance now and then, but a seventeen-year-old is pushing it some. Also I'm not clear on the etiquette of making deals with junior dope peddlers. Who pays for the drinks? I didn't want his self-image to suffer.

"What do you want?" he asked, moving toward the counter.

"Chablis is fine," I said. He was already pulling his wallet out so I let him pay. He probably made thirty grand a year selling grass and pills. The owner looked over at me again and I waved my I.D. at him casually, indicating that he could card me, but he'd be wasting a trip across the room.

Mike came back with a plastic glass of white wine for me and a soft drink for himself. He sat down, surveying the place for narcs in disguise. He seemed strangely mature and I was having trouble dealing with the incongruity of a kid who looked like a Boy Scout and behaved like a Mafia management trainee. He turned toward me then, resting both elbows on the table. He'd taken up a sugar packet from the container on the table and he tapped it and turned it restlessly, addressing most of what he had to say to the trivia question printed on the back.

"Okay. Here's what happened," he said, "and I'm tellin' you the truth. For one thing, I didn't stash at Uncle Leonard and Aunt Marty's until after she got killed and he moved out. Once the cops got done and everything, it occurred to me the utility shed was perfect so I moved some stuff in. Anyway, I went by the house the night she got killed. . . ."

"Did she know you were coming?"

"Nuh-uh, I'm getting to that. I mean, I knew they went out on Tuesday nights and I thought they'd be gone. Like, you know, if I was hard up and needed some bucks or something, I might cruise by and pick up some loose change. They kept cash around—not a lot, but enough. Or sometimes I'd take something I could unload somewhere else. Nothing they'd miss and nobody'd ever said anything about it so I figured they hadn't tipped to it yet. Anyway what happened was I went over there that night thinking the place would be empty, but when I got there the door was open—"

"The door was standing open?"

He shook his head. "I just kind of turned the knob and it was unlocked. When I stuck my head in I knew something weird was going on. . . ."

I waited, watching him uneasily.

He cleared his throat, looking over his shoulder at the front entrance. His voice dropped.

"I think the guy was still there, you know? The light was on in the basement and I could hear someone knocking around down there and there was this rug in the hall, like an area rug that had been thrown over something. I saw a hand sticking out with blood on it. Man, I took off."

"You're pretty sure she was dead at that point?"

He nodded, hanging his head. He ran a hand along the pink center divider of hair, looking off to one side. "I should've called the cops. I knew I should, but the whole thing really freaked me out. I hate that shit. And what was I supposed to do? I couldn't tell the cops anything and I didn't want 'em looking at *me*, so I just kept my mouth shut. I mean, I couldn't see what difference it made. I didn't see who did it or anything like that."

"Do you remember anything else? A car parked out front . . ."

"I don't know. I didn't stay long. I took one look at that shit and I was gone. I could smell all these gasoline fumes or something and . . ."

He hesitated briefly. "Wait a minute, yeah, there was a brown grocery bag in the hall too. I don't know what it was doing there. I mean, I didn't know what the fuck was happening, so I just backed away real quiet and came on down here and made sure people saw me."

I took a sip of wine, running through his story. The chablis tasted like fermented grapefruit juice. "Tell me about the grocery bag. Was it empty, full, crumpled?"

"It had stuff in it, I think. I mean, I didn't see anything in particular. It was one of those brown paper bags from Alpha Beta, standing just inside the door to the right."

"Did it look like she'd been shopping? Is that what you're trying to say?"

He shrugged. "It just looked like junk, I guess. I don't know. Maybe it belonged to whoever was down in the basement."

"Too bad you didn't make an anonymous call to the cops. Maybe they could have gotten there before the place went up in smoke."

"Yeah, I know. I thought about that later and I was bummed I didn't do that, but I wasn't thinking straight."

He polished off his soft drink and rattled the ice in the cup, tilting a cube into his mouth. I could hear the ice crunching in his teeth. It sounded like a horse chewing on a bit.

"Do you remember anything else?"

"No, I guess that's it. Once I figured out what was going on, I backed out of there and hightailed it down here as fast as I could."

"You have any idea what time it was?"

"Nuh-un, not exactly. It was quarter of nine when I got here and it probably took me ten minutes on the motorcycle by the time I found a place to park and all like that. I had to walk the sucker for two blocks so nobody would hear me start it up. It was probably eight-thirty or something like that when I left Uncle Leonard's house."

I shook my head. "Not eight-thirty. You must mean nine-thirty. She wasn't killed until after nine."

He took the cup away from his mouth, looking at me with puzzlement. "She wasn't?"

"Your uncle and Mrs. Howe both say they talked to her at nine and the cops took a call they think was from your aunt at nine-oh-six."

"Well, maybe I got it wrong then because I thought it was quarter of nine when I got here. I looked at the clock when I walked in and then I turned around and asked this buddy of mine what time it was and he checked his watch."

"I'll see if I can check that out," I said. "By the way, how's Leonard related to you?"

"My dad and him are brothers. Dad's the youngest in his family."

"So Lily Howe is their sister."

"Something like that."

The purple neon tubes began to blink out in succession and the pink ones went dark after that. The owner of the place called over to the table. "Closing down in ten minutes, Mike. Sorry to break it up."

"That's okay. Thanks, man."

We got up, moving toward the back entrance. He was not much taller than I and I wondered if we looked like brother and sister or mother and son. I didn't say anything else until we got to the parking lot.

"You have any theories about who killed your aunt?"

"No, do you?"

I shook my head. "I'd get that shed cleaned out if I were you."

"Yeah, sure. That was the deal, wasn't it?"

He got on his cycle and did one of those jumps to start it up. "Hey, you know what? I don't remember your name."

I gave him my card, then got in my VW. He waited to make sure I was under way and then he roared off.

I intended to let the case sit for the weekend because I wasn't sure what else to do. Saturday morning, I went over the police reports again at home, adding note cards to my collection up on the bulletin board, but for the time being, I simply had to sit it out. Come Monday, it was possible I'd get a response from the classified ads I'd placed in the Florida papers or maybe I'd hear from the DMV in Tallahassee or Sacramento. I was still waiting for the plane ticket Julia Ochsner had mailed, hoping it would give me information of some kind. If nothing new came to light, I was going to have to start all over again and see if I could develop a few new leads. I still had local vets to check, trying to get a rundown on the cat.

I took a few minutes to do recalls on the three cab companies. The dispatcher I'd talked to at Green Stripe said he hadn't had a chance to dig through his files yet. The owner of City Cab had looked and found nothing and Ron Coachella at Tip Top wasn't in yet, but the dispatcher on duty said he'd be in shortly. So much for that.

I went down to the office. I hadn't meant to, but I couldn't help myself. I was feeling itchy and restless and dissatisfied. I don't like not succeeding at things. California Fidelity was closed for the weekend. I unlocked my door and picked up the mail that had been shoved through the slot. There was an envelope with Julia Ochsner's return address on it. I tossed it on the desk while I checked my messages. There was only one and it had apparently just come in.

"Hello, Kinsey. This is Ron Coachella over at the cab company? I got the information you want. Tip Top did pick up the fare at 2097 Via Madrina . . . let's see—on January the ninth at ten-fourteen P.M. Driver's name was Nelson Acquistapace at 555–6317. I told him you'd be in touch. I've got the trip sheet down here and you're welcome to stop by and pick up a copy so he can look at it. Twenty bucks might help his memory, if you know what I mean. Aside from that, just remember . . . 'If you want the top ride in town, call Tip Top,' " he sang and hung up.

I smiled, making a note of the driver's name and number. I put on a pot of coffee and opened the note from Julia. Her handwriting was of the old school, surprisingly firm, a clear cursive with grand flourishes and well-formed capital letters. She said she was enclosing the ticket, that the June rains were in full force, and that Charmaine Makowski had given birth to a nine-pound nine-ounce boy the night before and wanted everyone to know that she never expected to sit down again. Charmaine and Roland had not yet named the child but were accepting suggestions. Julia said that most of the appellations proffered so far were not fit to repeat. Julia thought it was a hoot. Warmest regards, said she.

I studied the ticket, which was tucked in a TWA folder. It looked like it had been generated at the Santa Teresa airport, round-trip from Santa Teresa to LAX and from LAX to Miami. All four flight coupons had been removed but the carbon remained. The ticket had been paid for by credit card. Four flight coupons torn out. Now, that was interesting. Had she come back to town at some point? If so, why had the carbon been down in Boca Raton in Pat Usher's trash? I went back to my list of travel agents, trying to figure out which one Elaine Boldt ordinarily used. I decided on Santa Teresa Travel which has an office within easy walking distance of the condominium on Via Madrina. It was just a guess, but I had to start someplace. I put in a call, but there was no answer and I assumed the agency was shut down for the weekend.

I made a list of leads to pursue on Monday. I checked the ticket again. I didn't see any indication that she'd had the cat in tow, but I wasn't sure how that worked. Did kitty cats get tickets like everybody else? I'd have to ask. There were some luggage tags still stapled to the back of the folder, but that doesn't mean much. At the airport here in town, you can pick up your bags without anybody verifying the tags. I remembered Elaine's luggage as fairly distinctive anyway, dark red leather with the designer signature writ large on the fabric trim. I'd priced that stuff once and decided to open a Keogh account instead.

I put a call through to Nelson Acquistapace, the Tip Top cab driver. He was home in bed with a head cold, but said Ron had told him what I needed. He had to pause and blow his nose twice. "Why don't you pick up the trip sheet and bring it over here? I'm on Delgado, just half a block down from Tip Top," he said. "I'll be outside around in back."

I picked up the trip sheet and arrived at his place by 9:35. I found him sitting in the backyard of a white frame bungalow tucked into a jungle of overgrown pittosporum bushes. He was lying on a hammock in a freestanding metal frame in the only patch of sunlight. The rest of the property was in deep shade, rather chilly and uninviting. He looked to be in his sixties, balding, heavyset in a dark green velour bathrobe. He had a square of pink sprigged flannel on his chest and he smelled like Vicks VapoRub. He'd set up a small metal table with his cold remedies, a box of Kleenex, an empty juice glass, and some crossword-puzzle books that I recognized.

"I know the guy who writes those puzzles," I said. "He's my landlord."

His eyebrows shot up. "This guy lives in town here? He's a whiz! He drives me up the wall with these things. Look at this one. Eighteenth-Century English Novelists and he includes all their books and their characters and everything. I had to go read Henry Fielding and Laurence Sterne and people I never even heard about just to get through the thing. It's better than a college education, I'm tellin' you. What is he, some kind of professor?"

I shook my head, feeling absurdly proud. You'd have thought Henry was a rock star the way this guy was reacting. "He used to run that little bakery at the corner of State and Purdue. He started doing the crossword puzzles when he retired."

"Is that right? You sure it's the same guy? Henry Pitts?"

I laughed. "Sure I'm sure. He tries those things out on me all the time. I don't think I've ever finished one yet."

"You tell him I want to meet him sometime. He has a very twisted sense of humor, but I like that. He did one all made up of botanical oddities, remember that? I went crazy. I was up all night. I can't believe the guy lives here in Santa Teresa. I thought he was a full professor at MIT, someplace like that."

"I'll tell him you said that. He'll be thrilled to hear he has a fan."

"You tell him to stop by here anytime. Tell him Nelson Acquistapace is at his service. He needs a cab, just call Tip Top and ask for me."

"I'll do that," I said.

"You got the trip sheet? Ron said you were looking for some lady who disappeared. Is that right?"

I took the trip sheet out of my purse and passed it over to him.

"Don't get too close, sweetheart," he said. He took a handkerchief out of his robe pocket and dusted his nose with it, honking into it before he put it back. He unfolded the sheet, holding it at arm's length to look at it. "I left my glasses inside. Which one?"

I pointed to the Via Madrina address.

"Yeah, I remember her, I think. I took her to the airport and dropped her off. I remember she was picking up that last flight from here to L.A. Where was she going, I forget now."

"Miami, Florida."

"Yeah, that's right. I remember now."

He was studying the trip sheet as though it were a pack of Tarot cards in some tricky configuration. "You know what this is?" He was tapping the paper. "You want to know why this fare is so high? Look at that. Sixteen bucks. It doesn't cost that much to go from Via Madrina to the airport. She made a stop and had me wait maybe fifteen minutes with the meter running. An intermediate stop. Now, just let me think where it was. Not far. Some place on Chapel. Okay, yeah, I got it now. That clinic down near the freeway."

"A clinic?" That took me by surprise.

"Yeah, you know. An emergency facility. For the cat. She dropped him off for some kind of emergency treatment and then she got back in the cab and we took off."

"I don't suppose you actually saw her get on the plane, did you?"

"Sure. I was done for the night. You can see for yourself from the trip sheet. She was my last fare so I went upstairs to the airport bar and had a couple beers out on the patio. I told her I was gonna be up there so she even turned around and waved at me when she was walkin' out to the plane."

"Was she alone?"

"As far as I could tell."

"Had you ever picked her up before?"

"Not me. I just moved up here from L.A. in November last year. This is paradise. I love this town."

"Well," I said, "I appreciate your help. At least, we know she got on the plane. I guess now the question is, did she ever reach Boca Raton?"

"That's where she said she was going," he said, "though I tell you somethin'. With that fur coat, I told her she ought to head someplace cold. Get some use out of it. She laughed."

I felt myself hit the pause button mentally, a quick freeze frame. It was odd, that image, and it bothered me. I pictured Elaine Boldt with her fur coat and turban, on her way to warmth and sunshine, waving back over her shoulder to the taxi driver who'd taken her to the airport. It was disturbing somehow, that last glimpse of her, and I realized that until now I hadn't really pictured that at all. I'd been weighing the possibility that she was on the run, but in my heart of hearts, I'd pictured her dead. I'd kept thinking that whoever killed Marty Grice killed her too. I just couldn't figure out why. Now the uncertainty had crept in again. Something was off, but I couldn't figure out what it was.

16

Well, at least now I had a tiny mission in life. When I left Nelson, he was taking his temperature with a digital thermometer, confessing sheepishly a secret addiction to gadgets like that. I wished him a speedy recovery and hopped in my car, circling back around to Chapel.

The veterinary clinic is a small box of glass and cinderblock painted the color of window putty and tucked into the dead end formed when Highway 101 was cut through. I love that whole series of dead-end streets—relics of the town as it used to be, a refreshing departure from the pervading Spanish look. The small frame houses in that neighborhood are actually Victorian cottages built for the working class, with hand-turned porch rails, exotic trim, wooden shutters, and peaked roofs. They look like shabby antiques now, but it's still possible to imagine a day when they were newly constructed and covered with fresh paint, the full-grown trees no more than slender saplings planted in the midst of newly seeded lawns. The town then must have been dirt roads and carriages. I'm not above wishing more of it remained.

I parked in the lot behind the clinic and went in through the back door. I could hear dogs barking hoarsely somewhere in the rear; shrill cries for mercy, freedom, and relief. There were only two animals in the waiting room, both bored-looking cats who had formed themselves into bolster pillows. Their humans spoke to them in what was apparently cat-English, using high-pitched voices that made my own head hurt. Now and then when some dog set up a howl in the back, one or the other of the cats would appear to smile faintly.

There must have been two vets working because both cats got called at the same time and were carted off down the hall, leaving me alone with the receptionist behind the counter. She was in her late twenties, blue-eyed, pale, with an Alice-in-Wonderland blue ribbon across her straight blond hair. Her name tag read "Emily."

"May I help you?"

She spoke as though she'd never progressed beyond the age of six; a breathy, wispy tone, softly modulated, perhaps especially cultivated to soothe distressed beasts. Occasionally I run into women who talk like that and it's always puzzling, this perpetual girlhood in a world where the rest of us are struggling to grow up.

Dealing with her made me feel like a linebacker. "I wonder if you could give me some information."

"Well, I'll try," she whispered. Her voice was sweet and musical, her manner submissive.

I was going to show her the photostat of my P.I. license but I worried that it would seem brutal and coarse. I decided to hold off on that and whip it out if I had to turn the screws.

"Back in January, a woman brought a cat into the clinic for some kind of emergency treatment and I want to find out if she ever came back to pick it up."

"I can check our records if you like. Can you tell me the name, please?"

"Well, the woman's name was Elaine Boldt. The cat was Mingus. It would have been the night of January ninth."

Two patches of mild pink appeared on her cheeks and she licked her lips, staring at me fixedly. I wondered if she'd sold the cat to a vivisectionist.

"What happened?" I asked. "Do you know which one I'm talking about?"

"Well yes, I know which one. He was here for *weeks*," she said. Her speech had taken on a nasal cast, coming out through her nostrils now as though by ventriloquist. She wasn't exactly whining, but it was the tone of voice I've heard kids use in department stores when their moms accuse them of misbehavior and threaten to jerk their arms off. It was clear she was feeling defensive about something, but I wasn't sure quite what. She reached for a small tin box and walked her fingers through a file of index cards. She pulled out the record, snapping it onto the counter top self-righteously.

"She only paid three weeks' board and care and she never responded to any of our postcards or calls, so in February the doctor said we'd have to make other arrangements because our space is so limited." She was really working herself into a snit here.

"Emily," I said patiently. "Is that your name, or somebody else's tag?"

"It's Emily."

"I really don't care where the cat is. I just need to know if the woman came back."

"Oh. No, she didn't."

"What happened to the cat? I'm just curious."

She stared at me for a moment, her chin coming up. She brushed her hair back across her shoulder with a flip of her hand. "I adopted him. He's really a fabulous cat and I just couldn't turn him over to the pound."

"That's fine. Hey, that's great. I've heard he was terrific and I'm glad you found a place for him. Enjoy. I will take your secret with me to the grave. If the woman shows up, though, would you let me know?" I put my card on the counter. She read it and nodded without another word.

"Thanks."

I went back to the office. I thought I better give Julia Ochsner a call and tell her I'd located the cat, thus saving her an unnecessary canvas of Boca kennels and vets. I left my car in the parking lot out back and came up the rear stairs. When I reached my office there was a man standing in the corridor, scribbling a message on a scrap of paper.

"Can I help you?"

"I don't know. Are you Kinsey Millhone?" His smile seemed superior and his attitude amused, as though he had a piece of information too precious to share.

"Yes."

"I'm Aubrey Danziger."

It took me a second to compute the name. "Beverly's husband?"

"Right," he said and then gave a little laugh in the back of his throat. So far, I didn't think either one of us had much cause for merriment. He was tall, maybe six foot two, with a smooth, thin face. He had very dark hair, lank, looking as if it would be silky to the touch, brown eyes, an arrogant mouth. He was wearing a pale gray three-piece suit. He looked like a riverboat gambler, a dandy, a "swell," if such persons exist in this day and age.

"What can I do for you?"

I put my key in the lock, opened the door, and went in. He followed, surveying the premises with the sort of look that told me he was pricing the furniture, calculating my overhead, estimating my quarterly taxes, and wondering why his wife hadn't hired a high-class outfit.

I sat down behind my desk and watched him while he took a seat and crossed his legs. Nice, sharp crease in the pants, nice narrow ankle, Italian leather pumps with a narrow polished toe. I caught sight of his snow-white shirt cuff, his initials—AND—in a pale blue monogram, hand-done no doubt. He was smiling at me faintly, watching me watch him. He took a flat cigarette case out of his inside jacket pocket and extracted a slim, black cigarette that he tamped on the case and then stuck in his mouth, flicking a lighter that shot out a jet of fire I thought might set his hair ablaze. He had elegant hands and his fingernails were beautifully manicured, with clear polish on each tip. I confess I was sore amazed at the sight, amazed by the scent of him that was wafting across the desk at me; probably one of those men's designer aftershaves called Rogue or Magnum. He studied the ember on his cigarette and then fixed me with a look. His eyes reminded me of hard clay, flat brown with no warmth and no energy.

I didn't offer him coffee. I pushed the ashtray toward him as I'd done with his wife. The smoke from his cigarette smelled like a smothered campfire and I knew it would linger long after he'd driven back to Los Angeles.

"Beverly got your letter," he said. "She was upset. I thought maybe I should drive up here and have a chat."

"Why didn't she come herself?" I said. "She can talk."

That amused him. "Beverly doesn't care for scenes. She asked me to handle it for her."

"I'm not crazy about scenes myself, but I don't see the problem here. She asked me to look for her sister. I'm doing that. She wanted to dictate the terms and I decided I should work for someone else."

"No, no, no. You misunderstood. She didn't want to terminate the relationship. She simply didn't want you to go to Missing Persons with it."

"But I disagreed with her. And I didn't think it was nice to take her money when I was ignoring her advice." I tried a noncommittal smile on him, swiveling slightly in my chair. "Was there something else?" I asked. I felt certain he was angling around for something. He didn't have to drive ninety miles for this.

He shifted in his chair, trying a friendlier tone. "I can tell we've gotten off on the wrong foot here," he said. "I'd like to know what you've found out about my sister-in-law. If I've pissed you off, I'd like to apologize. Oh. And you might be interested in this."

He took a folded paper from his jacket pocket and passed it across the desk to me. For a moment, I thought it was going to be an address or a telephone number, some scrap of information that might really help. It was a check for the $246.19 Beverly owed me. He made it seem like some kind of bribe and I didn't like that. I took the money anyway. I knew the difference whether he did or not.

"I sent Beverly a copy of my report two days ago. If you want to know what I've come up with, why not ask her?"

"I've read the report. I'd like to know what you've found out since then if you're willing to share that."

"Well, I'm not. I don't mean to sound surly about this, but any information I have belongs to my current employer and that's confidential. I'll tell you this much. I did go to the cops and they're circulating a description of her, but that's only been a couple of days and so far they haven't come up with anything. You want to answer a question for me?"

"Not really," he said, but he laughed. I was beginning to realize that his manner was probably born of discomfort, so I plowed ahead anyway.

"Beverly told me she hadn't seen her sister for three years, but a neighbor of Elaine's claims she was not only up here at Christmas, but the two had a knock-down-drag-out fight. Is that true?"

"Well, yeah, probably." His tone was softening and he seemed less aloof. He took a final drag of his cigarette and pinched the ember loose from the end. "To tell you the truth, I've been concerned that Beverly's somehow involved in this."

"How so?"

He'd stopped looking at me now. He rolled the tag end of his cigarette between his fingers until nothing was left but a small pile of tobacco shreds and a scrap of black paper. "She's got a drinking problem. She's had it for some time, though you'd probably never guess. She's one of those people who might not have a drink for six months, then . . . boom, she's off on a three-day drunk. Sometimes a binge lasts longer than that. I think that's what happened in December." He looked at me then and most of the pomposity had dropped away. This was a man in pain.

"Do you know what they quarreled about?"

"I have a fair idea."

"Was it you?" I asked.

He focused on me suddenly, with the first real life in his eyes. "What made you say that?"

"The neighbor said they probably quarreled about a man. You were the only one I knew about. You want to buy me lunch?"

We went to a cocktail lounge called Jay's just around the corner. It's very dark, with massive art deco booths in pale gray leather and black onyx tables that look like small free-form pools. The surface on them is so shiny you can almost see your reflection, like some kind of commercial for liquid

141

dishwashing detergent. The walls are padded with gray suede and the carpet underfoot is tricked out with matting so thick you feel as if you're walking on sand. The whole place comes close to a sensory-deprivation tank, dim and hushed, but the drinks are huge and the bartender puts together incredible hot pastrami sandwiches on rye. I can't afford the place myself, but it felt like the perfect setting for Aubrey Danziger. He looked like he could pay the tab.

"What sort of work do you do?" I asked when we were seated.

Before he could answer, the waitress appeared. I suggested two pastrami sandwiches and two martinis. That look of secret amusement returned to his face, but he agreed with a careless shrug. I didn't think he was accustomed to women ordering for him, but there didn't seem to be any harmful side effects. I felt like this was my show and I wanted to work the lights. I knew we'd get blasted, but I thought it might take the high gloss off the man and humanize him some.

When the waitress left, he answered my question. "I don't work," he said, "I own things. I put together real-estate syndicates. We buy land and put up office buildings and shopping malls, sometimes condominiums." He paused, as though he could have said a lot more, but had decided that much would suffice. He took out his cigarette case again and held it out to me. I declined and he lit another slim black cigarette.

He tilted his head. "What'd I do that pissed you off? That happens to me all the time." The superior smile was back but this time I didn't take offense. Maybe that's just the way his face worked.

"You seem arrogant and you're way too slick," I said. "You keep smiling like you know something I don't."

"I've had a lot of money for a long time, so I feel slick. Actually, it amuses me to think about a girl detective. That's half the reason I drove up here."

"What's the other half?"

He hesitated, debating whether to say it. He took a long drag of his cigarette. "I don't trust Beverly's account of what went on. She's devious and she manipulates. I like to double-check."

"Are you talking about her transactions with me or hers with Elaine?"

"Oh, I know about her transactions with Elaine. She can't stand Elaine. She also can't leave her alone. Have you ever hated anybody that way?"

I smiled slightly. "Not recently. I guess I have in my day."

"It's like Bev has to know about Elaine and if she hears something good, it pisses her off. And if she hears something bad, she's satisfied, but it's never enough."

"What was she doing up here at Christmastime?"

The martinis arrived and Aubrey took a long sip of his before he answered. Mine was silky and cold with that whisper of vermouth that makes me shudder automatically. I always eat the olive early because it blends so nicely with the taste of gin.

He caught sight of the shiver. "I can leave the room if you want to be alone with that."

I laughed. "I can't help it. I never drink these things, but Jesus Lord, what a rush. I can already feel the hangover forming."

"Hell, it's Saturday. Take the day off. I didn't think I'd catch you in your office at all. I was going to leave you a note and then nose around seeing if I could find out something about Elaine myself."

"I take it you're as puzzled as everybody else about where she might be."

He shook his head slightly. "I think she's dead. I think Bev killed her."

That got my attention at any rate. "Why would she do that?"

Again, the long hesitation. He looked off across the room, checking the premises, doing some kind of mental arithmetic as though in placing a dollar value on his surroundings, he'd know where he stood. His eyes slid back to me and the smile hovered on his mouth. "She found out I'd had an affair with Elaine. It was my own damn fault. The IRS is auditing my tax returns from three years back and, like a fool, I asked Beverly to dig up some canceled checks and credit-card receipts. She figured out I'd been in Cozumel right at the same time Elaine went down there after Max died. I'd told her I was off on a business trip.

"Anyway, I got home from the office that day and she flew at me in such a rage it's a wonder I got out alive. Of course, she'd been drinking. Any excuse to sock down the sauce. She took a pair of kitchen shears and stabbed me right in the neck. Caught me right here. Just above the collarbone. The only thing that saved me was my collar and tie and maybe the fact that I have my shirts done with heavy starch."

He laughed, shaking his head uncomfortably at the recollection. "When that didn't work, she got me in the arm. Fourteen stitches. I bled all over the place. When she drinks, it's like Jekyll and Hyde. When she doesn't drink, she's not too bad . . . bitchy and hard as nails, but she isn't nuts."

"How'd you get involved with Elaine? What was that about?"

"Oh hell, I don't know. It was stupid on my part. I guess I'd had the hots for her for years. She's a beautiful woman. She does tend to be self-involved and self-indulgent but that only made her harder to resist. Her husband had just died and she was a mess. What started out as brotherly concern turned into unbridled lust, like something off the back of a paperback novel. I've strayed before, but never like that. I don't shit in my own Post Toasties as the old saying goes. This time I blew it."

"How long did it last?"

"Until she disappeared. Bev isn't aware of that. I told her it was over after six weeks and she bought it because that's what she wanted to believe."

"And she found out about it this past Christmas?"

He nodded and then caught the waitress' attention, glancing over at me. "You ready for another one?"

"Sure."

He held up two fingers like a victory sign and the waitress moved over to the bar. "Yeah, she found out right about then. She tore into me and then jumped straight in the car and drove up here. I got a call through to Elaine to warn her, so we could at least get our stories straight, but I'm not really sure what was said between them. I didn't talk to her after that and I never saw her again."

"What'd she say when you told her?"

"Well, she wasn't crazy about the idea that Bev knew, but there wasn't anything she could do about it. She said she'd handle it."

The martinis arrived, along with the sandwiches, and we stopped talking for a while in order to eat. He was opening up a whole new possibility and I had a lot of questions to ask.

17

"What's your theory about what went on?" I asked when we'd finished lunch. "I mean, as nearly as I can tell, Elaine was in Santa Teresa until the night of January ninth. That was a Monday. I've tracked her from her apartment to the airport and I've got a witness who saw her get on the plane. I've got someone else who claims she arrived in Miami and drove up through Fort Lauderdale to Boca. Now, this person swears she was in Boca briefly and then took off again and was last heard from in Sarasota where she's supposedly staying with friends. I have a hard time believing that last bit, but it's what I've been told. When could Beverly have killed her and where?"

"Maybe she followed her to Florida. She was off on one of her benders just after New Year's. She was gone for ten days and came home a mess. I'd never seen her so bad. She wouldn't say a word about where she'd been or what had happened. I had a business deal I had to close in New York that week so I got her settled and then I took off. I was out of town until the following Friday. She could have been anywhere while I was gone. Suppose she followed Elaine to Florida and killed her the first chance she had? She flies home afterward and who's the wiser?"

"I can't believe you're serious," I said. "Do you have any evidence? Do you have anything that links Beverly even superficially with Elaine's disappearance?"

He shook his head. "Look, I know I'm fishing here and I could be completely off base. I hope like hell I am. I probably shouldn't have said anything. . . ."

I could feel myself getting restless, trying to make sense of what he had said. "Why would Beverly have hired me if she'd killed Elaine?"

"Maybe she wanted to make it look good. The business

bout the cousin's estate was legitimate. The notice arrives in he mail and now what's she going to do? Suppose she knows Elaine is strolling along the bottom of the ocean in a pair of concrete shoes. She has to go through the motions, doesn't he? She can't ignore the situation because somebody's going o wonder why she doesn't show more concern. So she drives up here and hires you."

I looked at him skeptically. "Only then she panics when I ay I'm going to the police."

"Right. And then she figures she better cover for that so he talks to me."

I finished my martini, thinking about what he'd said. It was ery elaborate and I didn't like that. Still, I had to concede hat it was possible. I made concentric circles on the tabletop vith the bottom of my glass. I was thinking about the break-n at Tillie's place. "Where was she Wednesday night?"

He drew a blank. "I don't know. What do you mean?"

"I'm wondering where she was Wednesday night and early Thursday morning of this week. Was she with you?"

He frowned. "No. I flew to Atlanta Monday night and came ack yesterday. What's the deal?"

I thought I should keep the details to myself for the time eing. I shrugged. "There was an incident up here. Did you all her from Atlanta on either of those days?"

"I didn't call her at all. We used to do that when I was off n business trips. Talk back and forth long-distance. Now it's relief to be away." He took a sip of his drink, watching me bove the rim of the glass. "You don't believe any of this, do ou?"

"It doesn't make any difference what I believe," I said. "I'm rying to find out what's true. So far it's all speculation."

He shook his head. "I know I don't have any concrete proof, ut I felt like I had to tell someone. It's been bugging the shit ut of me."

"I'll tell you what's bugging me," I said. "How can you live ith someone you suspect of murder?"

He stared down at the table for a moment and the smile hen it came was tainted with the old arrogance. I thought he was going to answer me, but the silence stretched and finally he simply lit another cigarette and signaled for the check.

I called Jonah in the middle of the afternoon. The encounter with Aubrey Danziger had depressed me, and the two martinis at lunch had left me with a nagging pain between the eyes. I needed air and sunshine and activity.

"You want to go up to the firing range and shoot?" I said when Jonah got on the line.

"Where are you?"

"I'm at the office, but I'm on my way home to pick up some ammo."

"Swing by and pick me up too," he said.

I smiled when I hung up the phone. Good.

The clouds hung above the mountains like puffs of white smoke left in the wake of a giant old-fashioned choochoo train. We took the old road up through the pass, my VW making high-pitched complaints until I shifted from third gear to second and finally into first. The road twisted up through sage and mountain lilac. As we approached, the dark green of the distant vegetation separated into discreet shrubs clinging obstinately to the slopes. There were very few trees. Steep expanses of California buckwheat were visible on the right, interspersed with the bright little orange faces of monkey flower and the hot pink of prickly phlox. The poison oak was thriving, its lush growth almost overwhelming the silvery leaves of the mugwort which grew alongside it and is its antidote.

As we reached the summit, I glanced to my left. The elevation here was about twenty-five hundred feet and the ocean seemed to hover in the distance like a gray haze blending into the gray of the sky. The coastline stretched as far as the eye could see and the town of Santa Teresa looked as insubstantial as an aerial photo. From this perspective, the mountain ridge seemed to plunge into the Pacific, appearing again in four rugged peaks that formed the offshore islands. The sun up here was hot and the volatile oils, exuded by the underbrush ented the still air with camphor. There were occasional manzanita trees along the slope, still stripped down to spare, misshapen black forms by the fire that had swept through two years back. Everything that grows up here longs to burn; seed pods broken only by intense heat, germinating then when the rains come again. It's not a cycle that concedes much to human intervention.

The narrow road to the firing range veered off to the left just at the mountain's crest, climbing at an angle through huge sandstone boulders that looked as light and fake as a movie set. I pulled into the dirt and gravel parking area and Jonah and I got out of the car, taking guns and ammo from the backseat. I don't think we'd exchanged six words the entire thirty-minute trip, but the silence was restful.

We paid our fees and tucked little wads of foam in our ears to muffle the sound. I had also brought along a headset, like earmuffs, for additional protection. My hearing had already sustained some damage that I was hoping wasn't going to be permanent. With the plugs in place, I could hear the air going in and out of my own nose, a phenomenon I didn't pay much attention to ordinarily. I liked the quiet. At the core of it, I could hear my own heart, like someone thumping on a plaster wall two floors below.

We moved up to the range, roof overhead like a carport extending fifteen feet on either side of us. Only one man was shooting and he had an H&K .45 competition pistol that Jonah coveted the minute he laid eyes on it. The two of them talked about the adjustable trigger and adjustable sights while I inserted eight rounds of reloads into the magazine of my little gun. I inherited this no-brand semiautomatic from the very proper maiden aunt who raised me after my parents died. She'd taught me to knit and crochet when I was six, and when I was eight, she'd brought me up here and taught me to target-shoot, bracing my arms on a wooden ironing board that she kept in the trunk of her car. I had fallen in love with the smell of gunpowder when I first came to live with her. I'd sit out on her concrete porch steps with a strip of caps and a hammer, patiently banging away until each snapped out its load of perfume. The porch steps would be littered afterward with bits of red paper and gray spots of burned powder the size of the buckle holes in a belt. I guess she decided after two years of my incessant hammering that she might as well school me in the real thing.

Jonah had brought both his Colts and I fired a few rounds from each, but they felt like too much gun for me. The walnut grip on the Trooper handled like a big hunk of petrified wood and the four-inch barrel made sighting a bitch. The gun bucked in my hand like that quick, automatic kick when a doctor taps on your knee, and each time the gun bucked a whiff of gun powder blew back at me. I did slightly better with the Python but it was still a distinct and familiar treat when I took up my .32 again, like holding hands with an old friend.

At five, we packed up our gear and headed over to the old stagecoach tavern, tucked into a shady hollow not far from the range. We had beer and bread and baked beans and talked about nothing in particular.

"How's your case going?" he asked me. "You turned up anything yet?"

I shook my head. "I've got some things I may want to talk to you about at some point, but not for now."

"You sound bummed out," he said.

I smiled. "I always do this to myself. I want quick results. If I don't get things wrapped up in two days, I get depressed. What about you? Are you okay?"

He shrugged. "I miss my kids. I used to spend Saturdays with them. It was nice you called. Gave me something to do besides mope."

"Yeah, you can watch *me* mope," I said.

He patted my hand on the table and squeezed it lightly. The gesture was brief and compassionate and I squeezed back.

I dropped him off at his place again at 7:30 or so and went home. I was tired of worrying about Elaine Boldt so I sat on the couch and cleaned my gun, taking in the smell of oil, finding it restful to dismantle and wipe and put it all back together again. After that, I stripped my clothes off and rapped up in my quilt, reading a book about fingerprint mechanics until I fell asleep.

Monday morning, I stopped by Santa Teresa Travel on my way into the office and talked to an agent named Lupe who looked like an interesting mix of Chicano and black, slim as a cat. She was in her twenties, with tawny skin and dark frizzy hair with a faint golden cast, cut close to the shape of her head. She wore small rectangular glasses and a smart navy blue pantsuit with a striped tie. I showed her the ticket carbon and told her what I was looking for. My guess was correct. Elaine had been a regular client of theirs for the past several years, though Lupe seemed puzzled by the carbon. She pulled the glasses down low on her nose and looked at me. Her eyes were a flat gold, like a lemur's, and it gave her face an exotic quality. Puffy mouth, small straight nose. She had fingernails that were long and curved and looked as tough as horn. Maybe she had been some kind of burrowing creature in another life. She pushed the glasses back into place again thoughtfully.

"Well, I don't know what to think," she said. "She always bought her tickets through us, but this one was purchased at the airport." She touched at one corner of the carbon, turning the ticket around so I could see the face of it. It reminded me of those teachers in grade school who somehow managed to read a picture book while holding it forward and to one side. "These numbers indicate that it was generated by the airline and paid for by credit card."

"What kind of credit card?"

"American Express. She usually uses that for travel, but I tell you what's odd. She'd made reservations for . . . wait a minute. Let me check." Lupe typed some numbers into her computer terminal, nails tap-dancing across the keys. The computer fired out line after line of green print-like tracers. She studied the screen.

"She was scheduled to fly out of LAX, first class, on February third, with a return 3 August and those tickets were paid for."

"I hear she left on the spur of the moment," I said. "If she set up the reservations over the weekend, she'd have had to go through the airlines, wouldn't she?"

"Sure, but she wouldn't just forget about the tickets she had. Hold on a sec and I'll see if she ever picked 'em up. She could have traded 'em in."

She got up and moved over to the file cabinet on the far wall, sorting through her files. She pulled out a packet and handed it to me. It was a set of tickets and an itinerary, tucked into a travel folder from the agency. Elaine's name was neatly typed across the front.

"That's a thousand dollars' worth of tickets," Lupe said. "You'd think she'd have called us and had 'em cashed in when she got to Boea."

I felt a chill. "I'm not sure she got there," I said. I sat for a full minute with the unused tickets in my hand. What was this? I reached into my purse and pulled out the original TWA folder Julia Ochsner had mailed to me. On the back flap there were the four luggage tags sequentially numbered and still stapled firmly in place. Lupe was watching me.

I was thinking about my own quick flight to Miami, getting off the plane at 4:45 in the morning, passing the glass-fronted cases where abandoned suitcases were stacked.

"I want you to call Miami International for me," I said slowly. "Let's put in a claim for lost baggage and see if we come up with anything."

"You lost some bags?"

"Yeah, four of 'em. Red leather with gray fabric bindings. Hard-sided, graduated sizes, and my guess is that one is a hanging bag. These are the tags for them." I pushed the folder across the desk, and she wrote the numbers down.

I gave her my business card and she said she'd be in touch as soon as she heard anything.

"One more question," I said. "Was that flight she took non-stop?"

Lupe glanced at the carbon and shook her head. "That's the red-eye. She'd have had a layover and a change of planes in St. Louis."

"Thanks."

When I got to the office, the message light on my answering machine was blinking. I pressed the playback button.

It was my punker friend, Mike. "Hey, Kinsey? Oh shit, a machine. Well never mind. I'll call you back, okay? Oh. This is Mike and there's just something I want to talk to you about, but I have a class right now. Anyway, I'll call back later. Okay? Bye."

I made a note. The timer on the machine indicated that he'd called at 7:42 A.M. Maybe he'd try again at noon. I wished he'd left me a number.

I put in a call to Jonah and told him about Elaine's stopover. "Could you circulate a description of her through the St. Louis police?"

"Sure. You think that's where she is?"

"I hope."

I intended to sit and chat with him, but I didn't have the chance. There was a quick knock and my office door flew open. Beverly Danziger stood on the threshold and she looked pissed off. I told Jonah I'd get back to him and hung up, turning my attention to Beverly.

18

"You goddamn bitch!" She slammed the door behind her, eyes flashing.

I'm not real fond of being addressed like that. I could feel the heat rise in my cheeks, my temper climbing automatically. I wondered if she was going to challenge me to hand-to-hand combat. I gave her a slow smile just to show her I wasn't impressed with the histrionics.

"What's the problem, Beverly?" I sounded like a smart aleck even to myself and I thought I better cast about for something to smite her with if she came flying across the desk at me. All I spotted was an unsharpened pencil and a Rolodex.

She put her hands on her hips. "What the fuck did you contact Aubrey for? How dare you! How fucking *dare* you!!"

"I didn't contact Aubrey. He got in touch with me."

"I hired you. *I* did. You had no right to talk to him and no right to discuss my business behind my own back! You know what I'm going to do? I'm going to sue you for this!"

I wasn't worried she'd sue me. I was worried she'd pull a pair of scissors out of her purse and cut me up like patches for a quilt.

By now, she was leaning over my desk, stabbing a pointed index finger into my face. Shout lines appeared to come out of her mouth as in a cartoon. She thrust her chin forward, cheeks pink, bubbles collecting in the corner of her mouth. I wanted to slap the shit out of her, but I didn't think it'd be smart. She was beginning to hyperventilate, chest heaving. And then her mouth began to tremble and the fiery blue eyes filled with tears. She sobbed once. She dropped her handbag and put both hands to her face like a little kid. Was this woman nuts or what?

"Sit down," I said. "Have a cigarette. What's going on?"

I glanced down at the ashtray. Aubrey's telltale pile of shredded tobacco and a scrap of black paper were still sitting in my ashtray. Discreetly, I removed it, tipping the contents into my trash. She sat down abruptly, her anger gone, some deep-seated grief having taken its place. I'm sorry to report myself unmoved. I can be a coldhearted little thing.

While she wept, I made coffee. My office door opened a crack and Vera peered in, making eye contact. She'd apparently heard the ruckus and wanted to make sure I was all right. I lifted my eyebrows in a quick facial shrug and she disappeared. Beverly fished out a Kleenex and pinched it across the bridge of her nose, pressing her eyes as though to extract the last few tears. Her porcelain complexion was now mottled and her glossy black hair had taken on a stringy look, like a fur muff left out in the rain.

"I'm sorry," she breathed, "I know I shouldn't have done that. He's making me crazy. He's driving me absolutely insane. He's such a son of a bitch. I just hate his *guts!*"

"Take it easy, Beverly. You want some coffee?"

She nodded. She got a compact out of her bag and checked her eye makeup, mopping up a run of mascara with Kleenex folded over her finger. Then she tucked the compact away and blew her nose without making a sound. It was just a sort of squeezing process. She opened her bag again and searched for her cigarettes and matches. Her hands were shaking, but the minute she got her cigarette lighted, all the tension seemed to leave her body. She inhaled deeply as though she were taking in ether before surgery. I wish cigarettes felt that good to me. Every time I've had a drag, my mouth has tasted like a cross between charred sticks and spoiled eggs. It's made my breath smell about that good too, I'm sure. My office was now looking like the fog had rolled in.

She began to shake her head hopelessly. "You have no idea what I've been through," she said.

"Look," I said, "just to set the record straight—"

"I know you didn't do anything. It's not your fault." Her eyes filled with tears briefly. "I should be used to it by now, I guess."

"Used to what?"

She began to fold the Kleenex in her lap. She recited slowly, fighting for control, sentences punctuated with silences and little humming noises when the weeping closed off her throat. "He . . . um . . . goes around to people. And he tells them . . . um . . . that I drink and sometimes he claims I'm a nymphomaniac or he says I'm undergoing shock treatments. Whatever occurs to him. Whatever he thinks will do the most harm."

I wasn't sure what to do with this. He *had* told me she was an alcoholic. He'd told me she went off on three-day toots. He'd told me she attacked him with a pair of scissors and had possibly murdered her sister in revenge for an affair he was having with her. Now here she sat, sobbing her tiny heart out, claiming that he was the perpetrator of this weird pathological stuff. Which of them was I to believe? She composed herself, giving her nose the old silent squeeze. She looked at me, the whites of her eyes now tinted with pink.

"Didn't he tell you something like that?" she asked.

"I think he was just concerned about Elaine," I said, trying to hedge until I could decide what to do. "We really didn't discuss anything personal so don't worry about that. How did you find out he'd been up here?"

"Something came up in conversation," she said. "I don't even remember what. That's how he handles these things. He gives me these *clues*. He leaves the evidence around and waits for me to discover it. And if I don't stumble across it accidentally, he points me right to it and then sits back and pretends to be contrite and amazed."

I was just about to say, "Like his affair with Elaine," but it suddenly occurred to me that it might not even be true, or if true, that she might not actually know about it. "Like what for example?" I said.

"He had an affair with Elaine. He was fucking around with my only sister. God, I can't believe he did that to me. I didn't doubt *she'd* do it. She was always jealous. She'd take anything she could. But *him*. I felt like such a fool. He was off balling her the minute Max died and I was such a dunce I didn't figure it out for years! It took me *years*."

She did one of those bubbling laughs, filled more with hysteria than mirth. "Poor Aubrey. He must have been at his wit's end trying to get me to pick up on that. He finally cooked up this absurd tale about the IRS auditing his taxes. I told him the accountant could take care of it, but he said Harvey wanted us to go through the canceled checks and credit-card receipts. So like a dodo I did it and there it was."

"Why don't you leave?" I asked. "I don't understand why you stay in a relationship like that." I always say the same thing. Every time I hear a tale like this. Drunkenness, beatings, infidelity, and verbal abuse. I just don't get it. Why do people put up with it? I had said it to Aubrey so I figured I might as well say it to her too. The marriage was a mess and regardless of where the truth lay, these two people were miserable. Was misery the point?

"Oh, I don't know. Part of it's the money, I guess," she said.

"Screw the money. This is a community-property state."

"That's what I mean," she said. "He'll walk away with half of everything I have and it just seems so unfair."

I looked at her blankly. "The money's yours?"

"Well of course it's mine," she said, and then her expression changed. "He told you it was his, didn't he?"

I shrugged uncomfortably. "More or less. He told me he put together real-estate syndicates."

She was startled for an instant and then she laughed.

She started to cough, patting her chest. She stubbed out her cigarette, pecking it in the bottom of the ashtray. Smoke was streaming out of her nostrils as though her brain had caught fire. She was shaking her head, smile fading. "Sorry, but that's a new one on me. I should have guessed. What else did he say?"

I held a hand up in protest. "Hey," I said. "Enough. I don't want to play this game. I don't know what your problems are and I don't care. . . ."

"You're right, you're right. God, we must seem like lunatics to you. I'm sorry you got sucked in. It's not your concern. It's mine. How much do I owe you for your time?" She was rooting through her handbag for her checkbook and her famous rosewood pen-and-pencil set.

I could feel my temper on the rise again.

"I don't want any money from you. Don't be absurd. Why don't you give me some straight answers for a change?"

She blinked at me, the china blue eyes glazing over like ice on a pond. "About what?"

"Elaine's neighbor claims you were up here at Christmas and the two of you had a big fight. You told me you hadn't seen her for years. Now which is it?"

She stalled, reaching for another cigarette so she'd have time to frame a reply.

I headed her off. "Come on, Beverly. Just tell me the truth. Were you up here or not?"

She took out a packet of matches and removed a match, scratching it repeatedly across the packet without effect. She tossed that one, a dud apparently, into the ashtray and took out a second match. This time, she managed to light her cigarette. "I did come up," she said carefully. She tapped the lighted cigarette on the lip of the ashtray as though to remove an ash when there was none yet.

I was going to scream if she did any more shit with that cigarette. "Did you quarrel with her or didn't you?"

She switched to her officious tone, mouth going all prim. "Kinsey, I had just found out about the affair. Of course we quarreled. That's exactly what Aubrey had in mind, I'm sure. What would you have done?"

"What difference does it make? I'm not married to him so who gives a damn what I'd have done! I want to know why you lied to me."

She stared at the desk, her face taking on a stubborn look.

I tried another tack. "Why'd you call me off? Why wouldn't you let me contact the police?"

She smoked for a moment and I thought at first she didn't intend to answer that question either. "I was worried he'd done something."

I stared at her.

She caught my look and leaned forward earnestly.

"He's crazy. He is a truly crazy man and I was worried that he'd . . . I don't know . . . I suppose I was worried he'd killed her."

"All the more reason to call the police. Isn't it?"

"You don't understand. I couldn't turn the police loose on this. That's why I hired you in the first place. When this whole business came up about the will, I didn't think anything of it. It was such a minor matter. I just assumed she'd signed the paper and sent it to the attorney. And then when I realized no one had heard from her, it occurred to me that something might be wrong. I don't even know what I thought it was."

"But when I mentioned she might be dead, the penny dropped, right?" I sounded bored. I sounded contemptuous too.

She shifted uncomfortably. "Before that. I guess I'd just never really put it in words until you said it and then I realized I better reassess the situation before I agreed to anything."

"What makes you think Aubrey's involved?"

"That day . . . when I drove up here and Elaine and I had words . . . she told me then that the affair had been going on for years. She'd finally figured out that Aubrey was a psychopath and she was trying to break it off." She paused and the blue eyes came up to mine. "You don't understand about Aubrey yet. You don't know what he's like. You just don't *leave* him. You just don't break it off. I've threatened to do that myself. Don't think it hasn't occurred to me. But I'd never make it. I don't know what he'd do, but I'd never get away from him. Never. He'd follow me to the ends of the earth and bring me back, only then he'd really make me pay."

"Bev, I've got to tell you I'm having trouble with this," I said.

"That's because you fell for it. He came waltzing up here and he laid a number on you. He conned you good and now you can't bear to admit you've been had. He's done it before. He does it to everyone. The man is certifiably insane. He was in Camarillo for years until Reagan became governor. Remember that? He cut the state budget and turned them all out in the streets. Aubrey Danziger came home at that point and my life has been hell ever since."

I picked up a pencil and tapped on the edge of the desk, then tossed it aside. "I'll tell you the truth. I want to find Elaine. That's all I want to do. I'm like a terrier pup. Somebody tells me to do something and it gets done. I'll worry the damn thing to death. I'm going to find out what happened to her and where she's been all these months. And you better hope it doesn't lead back to you."

She got up. She picked up her bag and leaned on my desk. "And you better hope it doesn't lead back to Aubrey, my dear!" she spat.

And then she was gone, leaving behind her the faint aura of whiskey that I'd just caught on her breath.

I hauled out my typewriter and wrote a detailed report for Julia, itemizing expenses for the last couple of days. I needed time to assimilate what Beverly had told me about Aubrey. It was like the paradox of the jungle tribes where one always lies and the other always tells the truth. How could one ever determine which was which? Aubrey had told me Beverly was Mr. Hyde when she drank. She had told me he was certifiably mad, but she'd apparently been drinking when she said so. I hadn't the faintest idea which of them was on the level and I wasn't sure how to find out. I didn't even know if it mattered. Was Elaine Boldt really dead? It had certainly crossed my mind more than once, but I hadn't imagined that Beverly or Aubrey might be at the heart of it. I'd been looking in the opposite direction, assuming somehow that Elaine's disappearance was linked to the murder of Marty Grice. Now I'd have to go back and take another look.

I went home at lunchtime and did a run. I knew I was just treading water at this point, but in some ways I had to wait it out. Something would break. Some piece of information would come to light. In the meantime, I was feeling tense and I needed to work that off. The run was a bad one and that put me in a foul mood. I picked up a stitch in my side at the end of the first mile. I thought I could shake it. I tried digging my fingers in, bending at the waist, thinking that if it was a muscle cramp it might ease. No deal. Then I tried expelling breath after breath, again bending from the waist. The pain was no worse, but it didn't go away either. Finally, I slowed to a walk until it subsided, but the minute I started to jog again, my side seized up, stopping me in my tracks. I'd reached the turnaround by then, but running seemed futile so I walked the entire mile and a half back to my place, cursing to myself. I hadn't even broken a sweat, and my frustration, instead of dissipating, had doubled.

I showered and dressed again. I didn't want to go back to the office, but I forced myself. I was going to have to start all over again, go back to the beginning and cast a new set of lines in the water to see if I could get a bite somewhere. I had just about used up my whole bag of tricks, but there had to be something else.

When I let myself into the office, I saw the message light blinking on my machine. I opened the French doors to let some air in and then punched playback.

"Hi, Kinsey. This is Lupe, over at Santa Teresa Travel. It looks like you hit the jackpot on that luggage trace. I put a call through to Baggage Claim at TWA and had the agent check it out. The four bags were sitting right there. He said he could put 'em on a plane this afternoon if you like. Could you call me back and let me know what you want to do?"

I snapped the machine off and shook both fists in the air, mouthing "All riiight!" to myself with a big grin. I put a call through to Jonah first and told him what was going on. I was jazzed. It was the first good news I'd had since I tracked down the cat. "What should I do, Jonah? Am I going to need some kind of court order to open those bags?"

"Screw that. Look, you have the claim tags, don't you?"

"Sure, I've got 'em right here."

"Then go down to Florida and pick up the bags."

"Why not just have them flown out?"

"Suppose she's *in* one," he said.

That certainly conjured up an image I didn't like. I could

161

feel myself squirm. "Don't you think someone would have *noticed* by now? You know, an odor . . . something dripping out the side?"

"Hey, we found a body once had been in the trunk of a car for six months. Someone had shoved a high heel down some whore's throat and she ended up mummified. Don't ask me how or why, but she didn't decompose at all. She just dried up. She looked like a big leather doll."

"Maybe I'll get on a plane," I said.

By ten o'clock that night, I was back in the air again.

19

It was drizzling and the temperature was already in the seventies at 4:56 A.M. EST when we touched down. It was still dark outside, but the airport was filled with the flat light and artificial chill of a space station orbiting a hundred and ten miles out. Dawn travelers walked purposefully down deserted corridors while doors shushed open and shut automatically and the paging system seemed to drone on and on without hope of response. For all I knew, the whole operation was mechanical, running itself at that hour without any help from humankind.

The TWA baggage-service office didn't open until nine, so I had time to kill. I hadn't brought any luggage of my own, just a big canvas bag where I keep a toothbrush and all the odds and ends of ordinary life, including clean underpants. I never go anywhere without a toothbrush and clean underpants. I went into the women's room to freshen up. I washed my face and ran my wet fingers through my hair, noting how sallow my skin looked with the fluorescent lights overhead. There was a woman behind me, changing the diaper on one of those oversized babies who looks like a solemn adult with flushed cheeks. The child kept his eyes pinned on me gravely while his mother attended to him. Sometimes cats look at me that way, as though we're foreign agents sending silent signals to one another in an out of the way meeting place.

I paused at a stand and picked up a newspaper. There was a coffee shop open and I bought scrambled eggs, bacon, toast, and juice, taking my time about breakfast while I read a human-interest story about a man who'd left all his money to a myna bird. I can't cope with the front section before seven A.M.

At quarter to nine, having walked the airport from end to end twice, I stationed myself near Baggage Claim with a portable cart I'd rented for a buck. I could see Elaine's bags, neatly lined up at one end of the locked glass-fronted cabinets. It looked as if someone had hauled them out from the bottom of the pile in readiness. Finally, a middle-aged man in a TWA uniform, with a big set of jangling keys, unlocked the small cubicle and started turning on lights. It looked like the opening curtain of a one-act play with a modest set.

I presented myself and the baggage-claim tags and then followed him out to the storage cabinets and waited while he extracted the suitcases and stacked them on the cart. I expected him to ask for identification, but apparently he didn't care who I was. Maybe abandoned bags are like litters of unwanted kittens. He was just grateful to have someone take them off his hands.

When the Penny-Car Rental desk opened, I rented a compact car. I had given Julia a call the night before so she knew I was flying in. All I needed to do now was find the highway again and drive north. Once outside, I pushed the cart toward the slot where the rental car was parked. The drizzle settled on my skin like a layer of silk. The morning air was hot and close, smelling of rain and jet exhaust. I loaded the bags in the trunk of the car and headed toward Boca. It wasn't until I reached the condominium parking lot, unloading the suitcases one by one, that I realized all four were locked and had no key. Well, how very cute. Maybe Julia would have a plan. I lugged them over to the elevator and went up to the third floor, hauling them to Julia's front door in two trips.

I knocked and waited a long interval while Julia thumped her way to the front door with her cane, calling encouragement.

"I'm coming. Don't give up. Six more feet to go and I'm bearing down hard."

On my side of the door, I smiled, peering over at Elaine's apartment. There was no sign of life. Even the welcome mat had been taken inside or thrown out, leaving a square of fine sand that had filtered through the bristles.

Julia's door opened. The dowager's hump sat between her shoulder blades like a weight, forcing her to bend with its

rden. She seemed to be staring at my waist, tilting her head
dandelion fuzz to one side so she could peer up at me. Her
in seemed as sheer as rubber, pulled over her hands like
rgical gloves. I could see veins and broken capillaries, her
uckles as knotted as rope. Age was making her transparent,
ushing her from both ends like a can of soda pop.

"Well, Kinsey! I knew that was you. I've been awake since
this morning, looking forward to this. Come on in."

She hobbled to one side, making way for me. I set the four
itcases inside the door and closed it after me. She tapped
e with her cane. "I recognize those."

"Unfortunately, they're locked."

Each of the four bags apparently had a combination lock,
e numbers arranged on a dial embedded in the metal catch.
"We'll have to do some detective work," she said with sat-
action. "You want coffee first? How was your flight?"

"I'd love some," I said. "The flight wasn't bad."

Julia's apartment was crowded with antiques: a peculiar mix
Victorian pieces and Oriental furnishings. There was a
ge carved cherry sideboard with a marble top, a black
rsehair sofa, an intricate ivory screen, jade figures, a plat-
rm rocker, two cinnabar lamps, Persian rugs, a pier-glass
irror in a dark mahogany frame, a piano with a fringed
awl across the top, lace curtains, wall hangings of embroi-
red silk. A big portable television set with a twenty-five-inch
reen loomed on the far side of the room surrounded by
mily photographs in heavy silver frames. The television set
s turned off, its blank gray face oddly compelling in a room
filled with memorabilia. The only sound in the apartment
s the steady ticking of a grandfather clock that sounded
e someone tapping on Formica with a set of drumsticks.

I moved out to the kitchen, poured coffee for us both, and
rried it back to the living room, the cups rattling slightly in
e saucers like the tremor of a minor California earthquake.
re these family antiques? Some of the pieces are beautiful."

Julia smiled, waggling her cane. "I'm the last person alive
my family so I've inherited all this by default. I was the
ungest in a family of eleven children and my mother said

I was fractious. She always swore I'd never get a thing, but I just kept my mouth shut and waited it out. Sure enough, she died, my father died. I had eight sisters and two brothers and they all died. Little by little, it all drifted down to me, though I hardly have a place to put anything at this point. Eventually you have to give it all away. You start with a ten-room house and finally you find yourself stranded in a nursing home with space for one night table and a candlestick. Not that I intend to let that happen to me."

"You've got a ways to go yet anyway from what I can see."

"Well, I hope so. I'm going to hold out as long as I can and then I'll lock and bar the door and do myself in, if nature doesn't take me first. I'm hoping I'll die in my bed one night. It's the bed I was born in and I think it'd be nice to end up there. Have you a large family?"

"No, just me. I was raised by an aunt, but she died ten years ago."

"Well then, we're in the same boat. Restful, isn't it?"

"That's one way to put it," I said.

"I came from a family of shriekers and face slappers. They all threw things. Glasses, plates, tables, chairs, anything that came to hand. The air was always filled with flying missiles—objects rocketing from one end of the room to the other with howls on contact. This was mostly girls, you know, but all of us had deadly aim. I had a sister knock me out of my high chair once with a grapefruit thrown like a curve ball, oatmeal flying everywhere. Eulalie, her name was. Now that I look back on it, I see we were common as mud, but effective. We all got what we wanted in life and no one ever accused us of being helpless or fainthearted. Well now. Let's tackle those bags. If worse comes to worst, we can always hurl them off the balcony. I'm sure they'll open when they hit the pavement down below."

We approached the problem as though it were a code to be broken. Julia's theory, which proved to be correct, was that Elaine would have come up with a combination of numbers she already had in her life somewhere. Her street address, zip code, telephone number, social security, birthdate. Each

f us chose one group of digits and started to work on separate
ags. I hit it the third time around with the last four numbers
n her social-security card. All four suitcases were coded with
he same number, which simplified the task.

We opened them on the living-room floor. They were filled
ith exactly what one would expect: clothing, cosmetics, cos-
ame jewelry, shampoo, deodorant, slippers, bathing suit, but
acked in a jumble the way they do in movies when the wife
caves the husband in the middle of a vicious snit. The hangers
ere still on the hanging clothes, garments folded over and
unched in, with the shoes tossed on top. It looked as if draw-
rs had been turned upside down and emptied into the largest
f the bags. Julia had hobbled over to the rocker and she sat
ere now, propping herself up with her cane as though she
ere an unwieldy plant. I sat down on the horsehair sofa,
aring at the suitcases. I looked at Julia uneasily.

"I don't like this," I said. "From what I know of Elaine, she
as almost compulsively neat. You should have seen the way
ae left her place . . . everything just so . . . clean, tidy, tucked
. Does she strike you as the type who'd pack this way?"

"Not unless she were in a fearful hurry," Julia said.

"Well actually, she might have been, but I still don't think
ae'd pack like this."

"What's on your mind? What do you think it means?"

I told her about the double set of plane tickets and the
yover in St. Louis and any other facts I thought might per-
in. It was nice to have someone to try ideas on. Julia was
right and she liked to pick at knots the same way I did.

"I'm not convinced she ever got here," I said. "We only
ave Pat Usher's word for it anyway and neither of us set
auch store by that. Maybe she got off the plane in St. Louis
r some reason."

"Without her luggage? And you said she left her passport
ehind too, so what could she have done with herself?"

"Well, she did have that lynx coat," I said, "which she could
ave pawned or sold." I had one of those little nagging thoughts
n the subject, but I couldn't bring it into focus for the mo-
ent.

Julia waved dismissively. "I don't believe she'd sell her coat, Kinsey. Why would she do that? She has lots of money. Stocks, bonds, mutual funds. She wouldn't need to pawn anything."

I chewed on that one. She was right, of course. "I keep wondering if she's dead. The luggage got here, but maybe she never made it. Maybe she's in a morgue somewhere with a tag on her toe."

"You think someone lured her off the plane and killed her?"

I wagged my head back and forth, not wholly convinced. "I don't know. It's possible. It's also possible she never made the trip at all."

"I thought you told me someone saw her get on the plane. The cab driver you talked about."

"That wasn't really a positive identification. I mean, a cab driver picks up a fare and the woman claims she's Elaine Boldt. He never saw her before in his life, so who knows? He just takes her word for it, like we all do. How do you know I'm Kinsey Millhone? Because I say I am. Someone might have posed as her just to establish a trail."

"What for?"

"Well now, *that* I don't know. We've got a couple of women who might have pulled it off. Her sister Beverly for one."

"And Pat Usher for another," Julia said.

"Pat did benefit from Elaine's being off the scene. She get a rent-free condo in Boca for months."

"That's the first time I ever heard of anyone murdered for room and board," she said tartly.

I smiled. I knew we were floundering, but maybe we'd stumble onto something. I could have used a break at that point. "Did Pat ever leave that forwarding address she promised?"

Julia shook her head. "Charmaine says she left one, but it was humbug. She packed and took off the same day you were here and nobody's seen her since."

"Oh shit. I knew she'd do that."

"Well, it wasn't anything you could have prevented," she said charitably.

I leaned my head back against the sofa frame, playing mind games. "It could have been Beverly too, you know. Maybe Bev bumped her off in the ladies' room at the St. Louis airport."

"Or killed her in Santa Teresa and impersonated her from that point on. Maybe she was the one who packed the bags and took the plane."

"Try it the other way," I said. "Think about Pat. I mean, what if Pat Usher were a stranger to Elaine, just someone she met on the plane. Maybe they started talking and Pat realized—" I dropped that idea when I saw the expression on Julia's face. "It does sound pretty lame," I said.

"Oh, well—no harm done in speculating. Maybe Pat knew her in Santa Teresa and followed her from there."

I ran that around in my head. "Well, yeah. I guess it could be. Tillie says she heard from Elaine—at least, she assumed it was Elaine—by postcard until March, but I guess somebody could have faked that too."

I filled her in on my conversations with Aubrey and Beverly and right in the middle of it, my memory kicked in; one of those wonderful little mental jolts, like a quick electrical shock when a plug's gone bad. "Oh wait. I just remembered something. Elaine got a bill from some furrier here in Boca. What if we could track him down and find out if he's seen the coat? That might give us a lead."

"What furrier? We have quite a few."

"I'd have to check with Tillie. Can I make a call to California? If we can track down the coat, maybe we can get a line on her."

Julia wagged the cane toward the telephone. Within minutes, I'd gotten Tillie on the line and told her what I needed.

"Well, you know that bill got stolen along with the rest, but I just got another one. Hold on and I'll see what it says." She put the receiver down and went to fetch the mail.

She got back on the line. "She's being dunned. It's a second overdue notice from a place called Jacques—seventy-six dollars for storage and two hundred dollars for having the coat recut. Wonder why she'd do that? There's a little happy face

169

drawn by hand: 'Thanks for your business'—followed by a sad face: 'Hope the delay in payment is just an oversight.' A few more bills have come in too. Let me see what those look like."

I could hear Tillie ripping open envelopes on her end of the line.

"Oops. Well, these are all overdue. It looks like she's run up a lot of charges. Let's see. Oh my. Visa, MasterCard. The last date on these is about ten days ago, but I guess that was just the end of the billing period. They're asking her not to use her cards until she's paid the balances down."

"Does it indicate where she was when the purchases were made? Was she in Florida somewhere?"

"Yes, it looks like Boca Raton and Miami for the most part, but you can check them yourself when you get back. Now that I've had the locks changed, they should be safe."

"Thanks, Tillie. Can you give me the furrier's address?"

I made a note of it and got directions from Julia. I left her and went back down to the parking lot. The sky was an ominous gray and thunder rumbled in the distance like movers rolling a piano down a wooden ramp. It was hot and still, the light a harsh white, making the grass turn phosphorescent green. I was hoping I could take care of business before the downpour caught up with me.

Jacques was located in the middle of an elegant shopping plaza, shaded with latticework overhead and planted with delicate birches in big pale blue urns. Tiny Italian lights had been threaded through the branches, and in the prestorm gloom they twinkled like an early Christmas. The storefronts were done in a dove-gray granite and the pigeons strutting across the pavement looked as if they'd been placed there purely for their decorative effect. Even the sound they made was refined, a low, churring murmur that rode on the morning air like cash being riffled in a merchant's hands.

The window display at Jacques had been artfully done. A golden sable coat had been tossed carelessly across a dune of fine white sand against a sky-blue backdrop. Tufts of sea oats were growing on the crest of the sand and a hermit crab had crossed the surface, leaving a narrow track that looked like an embroidery stitch. It was like a little moment frozen in time: a woman—someone reckless and rich—had come down to the shore, had shrugged aside this luscious fur so that she could plunge naked into the sea—or perhaps she was making love to someone on the far side of the dune. Standing there, I could have sworn I saw the grasses bending in a nonexistent wind and I could almost smell the trail of perfume she'd left in her wake.

I pushed the door open and went in. If I'd had money and believed in wearing furry creatures on my back, I'd have laid down thousands in that place.

20

The interior was done in muted blues with a glittering chandelier dominating the high-ceilinged space. Chamber music echoed through the room as though there might be a string quartet sawing away somewhere out of sight. Chippendale chairs were arranged in gracious conversational groupings and massive gilt-edged mirrors lined the walls. The only detail that spoiled an otherwise perfect eighteenth-century drawing-room was the little camera up in one corner monitoring my every move. I wasn't sure why. There wasn't a fur in sight and the furniture was probably nailed to the floor. I shoved my hands down in my back pockets just to show I knew how to behave myself. I caught sight of my reflection. There I stood in that rococo setting, in faded jeans and a tank top, looking like something deposited in error by a time machine. I flexed, wondering if I should start lifting weights again. The bicep made my right arm look like a snake that had recently eaten something very small, like a wad of socks.

"Yes?"

I turned around. The man who stood there looked as out of place as I did. He was huge, maybe three hundred pounds, wearing a caftan that made him look like a pop-open tent with a built-in aluminum frame. He was in his sixties with a face that needed to be taken up. His eyelids drooped and he had a sagging mouth and a big double chin. What was left of his hair had slipped down around his ears. I wasn't certain, but I thought he made a rude noise under his skirt.

"I'd like to talk to you about a past-due account," I said.

"I got a bookkeeper handles that. She's out."

"Someone left a twelve-thousand-dollar lynx coat here to be cleaned and recut. She never paid her bill."

"So?"

This guy didn't have to get by on good looks alone. He was gracious too.

"Is Jacques here?" I asked.

"That's who you're talking to. I'm Jack. Who are you?"

"Kinsey Millhone," I said. I took out a card and handed it to him. "I'm a private investigator from California."

"No fooling," he said. He stared at the card and then at me. He glanced around suspiciously like this might be a "Candid Camera" gag. "What do you want with me?"

"I'm looking for information about the woman who brought the coat in."

"You got a subpoena?"

"No."

"You got the money she owes?"

"No."

"Then what are you bothering me for? I don't have time for this. I got work to do."

"Mind if I talk to you while you do it?"

He stared at me. His breathing made that wheezing sound that fat people sometimes make. "Yeah, sure. Why not? Suit yourself."

I followed him into the big cluttered back room, taking in his scent. He smelled like something that spent the winter in a cave.

"How long have you been cutting fur?" I asked.

He turned and looked at me as if I were speaking in tongues.

"Since I was ten," he said finally. "My father cut fur and his father before him."

He indicated a stool and I sat, setting my big canvas handbag at my feet. There was a long worktable to my right, with coarse brown-paper pattern laid out on it. The right front portion of a mink coat had been put together and he was apparently still working on it. The wall on the left was lined with hanging paper patterns and there were various quite ancient-looking sewing machines to my right. Every available surface was covered with pelts, scraps, unfinished coats, books, magazines, boxes, catalogues. Two dress forms stood side by side, like twins posing self-consciously for a photograph. The place reminded me of a shoe-repair shop, all leather smell and machinery and the feel of craftsmanship. He took up the coat and examined it closely, then reached for a cutting device with a nasty curved blade. He glanced up at me. His eyes were the same shade of brown as the mink.

"So what do you want to know?"

"You remember the woman?"

"I know the coat. Naturally, I remember the woman who brought it in. Mrs. Boldt, right?"

"That's right. Can you tell me when you saw her last?"

He dropped his gaze back to the fur. He made a cut. He crossed to one of the machines, motioning me to follow. He sat down on a stool and began to sew. I could see now that what had looked at first like an old-fashioned Singer was actually a machine especially designed for the stitching of fur. He lined up the two cut pieces vertically, fur-side in, and caught them in the grip of two flat metal disks, like large silver dollars set rim to rim. The machine whipped the leather edges together with an overhand stitch while he deftly tucked the fur out of the way so it wouldn't get caught in the seam. The whole maneuver took about ten seconds. He spread the seam, smoothing it with his thumb on the backside. There were maybe sixty similar cuts in the leather, a quarter-inch apart. I wanted to ask him what he was doing, but I didn't want to distract him.

"She came in in March and said she wanted to sell the coat."

"How'd you know it was really hers?"

"Because I asked for some identification and the bill of sale." The irritable tone was back, but I ignored it.

"Did she say why she was selling it?"

"Said she was bored with it. She wanted mink, maybe blond, so I offered her credit against something in the store, but she said she wanted the cash, so I told her I'd see what I could do. I wasn't that anxious to pay cash for a used coat. Ordinarily, I don't deal in secondhand fur. There's no market for it here and it's a pain in the ass."

"I take it you made an exception for her."

"Well yeah, I did. The thing is, this lynx coat was in perfec

174

condition and my wife's been after me to get her one for years. She's already got five coats, but when this one came in, I thought . . . what the hell? Make the old broad happy. What's it to me? Mrs. Boldt and I haggled and I finally got the coat for five thousand, which was a good deal for both of us, especially since I got the matching hat. I told her she'd have to pay to have the coat cleaned and recut."

"Why recut?"

"My wife is on the down side of five feet. She's four foot eleven, if you want her exact height, but don't ever tell her I told you that. She considers it some kind of birth defect. You ever noticed that? Short women get that way. From the time they're teen-agers, they start wearing funny shoes, trying to look like tall people when they're not. Know what she finally did? Learned to roller skate. She said it was the only time she really felt like a real human being. Anyway, I thought I'd give her this lynx. Gorgeous. You know the coat?"

I shook my head. "I've never seen it."

"Hey, come on. You ought to take a look. I've got it right back here. I haven't cut it yet."

He moved toward the rear and I trotted obediently behind. He opened the massive metal door to his vault. Cold air wafted out as though from a meat locker. There were fur coats hanging on both sides in double racks, sleeves almost touching, like hundreds of women lined up with their backs to us. He moved down the aisle checking coats as he went, wheezing from the effort. He really needed to lose some weight. His breathing sounded like someone sitting down on a leather couch and it couldn't connote good health.

He took a fur down off the top rack and we moved back out of the cold-storage room, the door shutting behind us with a clang. He held Elaine Boldt's coat up for me to inspect. The lynx was two shades—white and gray in a luscious blend, with the pelts arranged so that each panel ended in a tapering point at the hem. He must have guessed from the look on my face that I'd never seen a coat that expensive close up.

"Here. Try it on," he said.

I hesitated for a moment and then eased into the coat. I

pulled it around me and looked at myself in the mirror. The coat hung almost to my shins, the shoulders protruding like protection pads for some strange new sport.

"I look like the Abominable Snowman," I said.

"You look great," he said. He looked from me to the image in the mirror. "So we take it in a little bit. Shorten the sleeves. Or maybe you'd look better in fox if this doesn't suit."

I laughed. "On my income, I think it's high-class to have a sweatshirt with a zipper up the front." I took the coat off and handed it to him, getting back to the subject. "Why'd you pay her for the coat before she paid you? Why not deduct your costs from the five grand and give her a check for the balance?"

"The bookkeeper wanted it the other way. Don't ask me why. Anyhow, it's not going to cost that much to clean the coat, and the alterations I'm doing myself, so what's it to me? I got a good deal. Adele probably bugged her for payment as a matter of course, but I can't get that upset over the whole thing."

While he returned the coat to cold storage, I went over to my bag and took out the Polaroid picture of Elaine and Marty that Tillie Ahlberg had given me.

When he came back out, I showed it to him. "Is this the woman you dealt with?"

He glanced at it briefly and gave it back.

"Nuh-un. I never saw either one of those women before in my life," he said.

"What did she look like?"

"How do I know? I only saw her once."

"Young, old? Short, tall? Fat, thin?"

"Yeah, about like that. She was middle-aged and she had blondish hair. And she wore a muumuu and chain-smoked. I wouldn't let her come back here because I don't like the smoke around my skins."

"What kind of identification did she have?"

"You know. The usual stuff. Driver's license. Check guarantee card. Credit cards. You gonna tell me the coat was stolen? Because I don't want to hear it."

"I don't think 'stolen' quite covers it," I said. "I suspect someone's been borrowing Elaine Boldt's identity. I'm just not sure where she is in the meantime. If I were you, I'd leave the coat intact until we figure out what's going on."

My last glimpse of him, he was pulling unhappily at the wattles on his neck and he didn't offer to accompany me to the door.

I went out into the oppressive Florida humidity. The cloud cover felt like a premature twilight and the first of several big raindrops had begun to splatter against the hot pavement. I scurried to my car, half-ducking as though I could avoid getting wet by shrinking myself to half my size. I thought about Jack's description of the woman who'd called herself Elaine Boldt. He'd seen the snapshot of Elaine and he'd sworn it wasn't her. It had to be Pat Usher as nearly as I could tell. I ran back through my encounter with her: her attitude of wary amusement, the questions about Elaine she'd fielded, the mixture of lies and truth she'd told. Had she simply stepped into someone else's shoes? She'd been staying in Elaine's condominium, but how had she acquired the lynx coat if not from Elaine? If she was the one running up charges on Elaine's credit cards, she had to be sure somehow that Elaine wouldn't catch her at it. It seemed to me she could only pull that off if she knew Elaine was dead, which had been my suspicion for days now anyway. There might be some other explanation, I supposed, but nothing that tied everything together so neatly.

The rain was coming down hard now, the windshield wipers on my rental car flapping back and forth like metronomes, doing little more than smearing the windshield with a thin film of grime. I found a phone booth and placed a credit-card call to Jonah at the Santa Teresa P.D. The connection was bad and we could barely hear each other over the static on the line, but I did manage to holler out what I needed, asking him if he'd expedite the request form I'd sent to the DMV in Tallahassee. A driver's license was the one thing Pat Usher would have had to come up with, since Elaine had none, but it wouldn't have been that hard to falsify. All she had to do was apply in Elaine Boldt's name, pass the test, and wait for the license to arrive in the mail. In some states, you could walk out of the Department of Motor Vehicles with license in hand within minutes of taking the test—at least for a renewal. I wasn't sure what the procedure was in Florida. Jonah said he'd put a call through to Tallahassee and get back to me. I expected to be in Santa Teresa again by the next day, so I said I'd call him when I got in.

In the meantime, I drove back to the condominium and had a brief chat with Roland Makowski, the building manager, who confirmed what I'd already heard through Julia. Pat Usher had departed, bag and baggage, the same day I'd spoken to her. She'd dutifully left a forwarding address—some motel down near the beach—but when Roland had tried to get in touch, he'd found out it didn't exist. I asked him why he'd wanted to contact her. He said she'd taken a dump in the swimming pool as a parting gesture and then scrawled her name across the concrete in spray paint.

"She did what?" I asked.

"You heard right," he said. "She left a turd the size of a Polish sausage floating right in the pool. I had to have the whole thing drained and sanitized and I got people who still won't go in. That woman is demented and you know what pissed her off? I told her she couldn't hang her towels over the balcony rail! You should have seen her reaction. She was in such a rage her eyes rolled back in her head and she started to pant. She scared the hell out of me. She's *sick*."

I blinked at him. "She panted?"

"She was almost foaming at the mouth."

I thought about Tillie's night visitor. "I think we better take a look at Elaine's apartment," I said flatly.

The stench came at us like a wall the minute the door was opened. The destruction was systematic and complete. There was fecal matter smeared everywhere and the couch and chairs had been slashed with murderous intent. It was clear that she'd gone about it quietly. Unlike Tillie's apartment, no glass had been broken and no furniture overturned. What she'd done instead was to open all the canned goods and pour the ontents on the carpeting. She'd ground in crackers and dried asta, jams, spices, coffee, vinegar, soups, moldering fruit, dding contributions from her own intestinal tract. The whole ck stew had been sitting there for days and the Florida heat ad humidity had cooked the mess to a boiling foment of angus and rot. The packages of once frozen meat that she'd rn open and tossed into the thick of it were full of a wiggling fe of their own that I didn't care to inspect. Big flies buzzed round malevolently, their glittering fluorescent heads like eacons.

Roland was speechless at first and when I turned he had ars in his eyes. "Well, we're never going to get this cleaned p," he said.

"Don't do it yourselves," I said automatically. "Hire some-e else. Maybe your insurance will cover it. In the meantime, u better call the cops."

He nodded and swallowed hard while he backed out the oor so that I was left to search the apartment by myself. I ad to be very careful where I put my feet and I made a little ental note never to chide Pat Usher for anything. As far as was concerned, she could hang her towels anyplace she eased.

21

With the cops on the way, I didn't have much time. I picke
my way through the apartment, gingerly opening drawe
with a hankie across my fingertips out of respect for later
prints. I did a superficial run-through and came up with noth
ing, which didn't surprise me. She'd stripped the place. A
of the drawers and closets were empty. She hadn't left so muc
as a tube of toothpaste behind. By now, she could be anyplac
but I had a feeling I knew where she was. I suspected she
used the last two flight coupons for a return trip to San
Teresa.

I closed the place up again and went next door to tell Jul
what was going on. It was two-thirty in the afternoon and
had a four o'clock plane to catch with almost an hour
driving just to get to the airport. The sky was miraculous
clear again, the air smelling damp and sweet, sidewalks stean
ing. I loaded Elaine's suitcases back in the rental car and to
off, promising to call Julia as soon as I learned anything ne
This case was going to break for me. I could feel it in
bones. I'd been on it a week now and I had smoked Pat Ush
out of hiding. I wasn't sure what she'd done to Elaine or wl
but she was on the run now and I wasn't far behind. We we
circling right back to Santa Teresa where the whole thing h
begun.

When I reached the airport in Miami, I returned the ren
car and picked up my seat assignment at the TWA count
checking the four bags through to Santa Teresa. I got on
plane with six minutes to spare. I was beginning to feel a lo
level anxiety, the sort of sensation you experience when y
know you're having major surgery in a week. There was
immediate danger, but my mind kept leaping into the
certain future with a churning dread. Pat Usher and I we

n a collision course and I wasn't sure I could handle the
mpact.

With the three-hour time difference, I felt like I got back to
California roughly one hour after I left Florida and my body
ad trouble dealing with that. I had to wait an hour at LAX
o catch the short hop to Santa Teresa, but even so it was only
even in the evening when I got home, toting Elaine's bags
ith me like a packhorse. It was still light outside, but I was
xhausted. I'd never eaten lunch and all I'd had on the plane
ere some square things wrapped in cellophane that I was
lmost too tired to pick open. It was one of those lurching
ights with sudden inexplicable drops in altitude that make
apping tough. Most of us were too worried about how they'd
ollect and identify all the body parts once we'd crashed and
urned. Some woman behind me had two kids of the whining
nd screeching sort and she spent most of the flight having
ong ineffectual chats with them about their behavior. "Kyle,
oney, 'member Mommy told you she didn't want you to bite
rett because that hurts Brett. Now, how would you like it if
Aommy bit you?" I thought a quick chop in the ear would
o a long way toward parent effectiveness training, but she
ever consulted me.

At any rate, when I got home, I headed straight for the
uch and fell asleep, still in my clothes. Which is why it took
e until morning to figure out that somebody had been in
y apartment searching discreetly for God knows what. I got
p at eight and did a run, came home, showered, and dressed.
sat down at my desk and started to unlock the top drawer.
's a standard-issue office desk with a lock on the top drawer
at controls the bank of drawers to the right. Somebody had
parently slipped a knife blade into the lock and jimmied it
en. The realization that someone had been there made the
pe of my neck feel like I'd just applied an ice pack.

I pushed back from the desk and got up, turning abruptly
 that I could survey the room. I checked the front door,
t there was no indication that anyone had tampered with
e double-key dead bolt. It was possible that someone had

made a duplicate of the key, though, and I'd have to have the lock replaced. I've never worried about security, and don't run around doing tricky things to assure that my domain is inviolate—no talcum powder on the floor near the entranceway, no single strands of hair affixed across the window crack. I resented the fact I was going to have to deal with this break-in, surrendering a sense of safety I'd always taken for granted. I checked the windows, moving carefully around the perimeter of the room. Nothing. I went into the bathroom and examined the window there. Someone had used a glass cutter to make a small square opening just above the lock. Electrical tape had evidently been used to eliminate any sound of breaking glass. Where the strips of tape had been peeled off, I could still see remnants of adhesive. The aluminum screen was skewed in one corner. It had probably been popped out and then put back. The job had been cleverly done, set up in such a way that I might not have discovered it for weeks. The hole was large enough to allow someone to unlock the window, sliding it up to permit ingress and egress. There's curtain at that window and with the panels in place, the small hole in the glass wasn't even visible.

I went back into the other room and did a thorough search. Nothing seemed to be missing. I could see that someone had eased sly fingers between my folded clothes in the chest of drawers, had deftly gone through the files, leaving everything much as it had been, but with faint disarrangements here and there. I hated it. I hated the cunning and the care with which it had all been done, the satisfaction somebody must have felt at pulling it off. And what was the point? For the life of me I couldn't see that anything was gone. I didn't own anything of value and the files themselves were not worth much. Most of the ones I kept at home had been closed out anyway and my notes on Elaine Boldt were at the office. What else did I have that someone might want? What worried me too was the suspicion that this might be Pat Usher's handiwork. Somehow she seemed much more dangerous if, along with savagery, she was also capable of craftiness and stealth.

I called a locksmith and made an appointment to have her

come out later in the day to change all the locks. I could replace the window glass myself. I did some quick measurements and then headed out to the street. Fortunately, no one had broken into my car, but I didn't like the idea that someone might try that too. I took my .32 out of the glove compartment and tucked it into the waistband of my jeans at the small of my back. I was going to have to lock it in my office file cabinet and leave it there for the time being. I was relatively certain that my office was secure. Since I'm on the second floor with a balcony right out in plain view, I didn't think anyone would risk a break-in from that vantage point. The building is kept locked at night and the door from the hallway is solid oak two inches thick with a double-key dead bolt that could only be reached if the lock itself were cored out with a power saw. Still, I was feeling apprehensive when I pulled into the parking lot behind the office and I ended up taking the back stairs two at a time. I didn't relax until I unlocked the office door and saw for myself that no one had been there.

I put the gun away and took out the file on Elaine Boldt. I typed up additional notes, bringing everything up to date. Inwardly, I was still fuming that someone had been in my apartment. I should have called the police and reported it, but I didn't want to stop for that. I tried to concentrate on the matter at hand. I had a lot of unanswered questions and wasn't even sure which ones mattered at this point. Why, for instance, had Pat Usher closed up shop so abruptly in Boca after my first trip down there? I had to guess that once he knew I was looking for Elaine, she'd had to scuttle her plans. I was assuming, of course, that she'd headed to Santa Teresa and that it was she who'd broken into Tillie's apartment and stolen that stack of bills. But to what end? The bills had continued to arrive and if pertinent information might be gleaned from inspecting them, all we had to do was wait for the next batch.

Then I had Mike's account of what he saw on the night of his aunt's murder. I still wasn't sure how that fit in, if indeed it did. The fact remained that his estimate of the time of Marty Grice's death differed by thirty minutes from the time her husband and sister-in-law claimed they'd spoken to her. Were Leonard and Lily in cahoots?

There was still the minor matter of May Snyder next door who'd reported the sound of hammering at the Grices' house that night. Orris swore she was deaf and had it all confused with something else, but I wasn't quite willing to write her off like that.

When the phone rang, I jumped, snatching up the receiver automatically. It was Jonah. He didn't even bother to identify himself. All he said was, "I've got a response from the DMV in Tallahassee. You want to take a look?"

"I'll be right there," I said and hung up, heading out.

Jonah was waiting for me in the small reception area as I came into the police station and he walked me through the locked doors to the corridor leading back to Missing Persons.

"How'd you get the information so fast?" I asked. He held the gate open for me and I passed into the bullpen, where he had his desk.

He smiled faintly. "That's why cops are so much better a this business than private eyes," he said. "We've got access t information you can't even touch."

"Listen, *I* was the one who put in the original request! It' public record. I can't get it as fast as you can, but I was o the right track and you know it."

"Don't get so hot," he said, "I was just ragging you."

"Very cute. Lemme see it," I said, holding my hand ou He passed me a computer print-out, a magnetic image of driver's license issued to Elaine Boldt in January, with th Florida condominium address. I stared at the picture of th woman staring back at me and uttered a quick, involuntar "ah!" I knew the face. It was Pat Usher: same green eye same tawny hair. There were a few glaring differences. I' seen her after an automobile accident, when her face was sti a bit bruised and swollen. The resemblance was clear enough though. Hot damn.

"I got her," I said. "Hey wow, I got her!"

"Got who?"

"I don't really know yet. She calls herself Pat Usher, but se probably made that up. I'll bet you money Elaine Boldt dead. Pat had to know that or she never would have had se nerve to apply for a driver's license in Elaine Boldt's name. se's been living in Elaine's apartment ever since she disap- eared. She's used her credit cards and probably helped her- elf to any bank accounts. Shit. Let's run a check on her through CIC. Can we do that?" The National Crime Information enter might well turn up identification on Pat Usher in sec- ds.

"Computer's down. I just tried. I'm surprised you didn't k me to do that before."

"Jonah, I didn't have the right data before. I had a name t no numerical identifier. Now I've got a birthdate. Can I ave a copy of this?"

"That's yours," he said mildly. "I've got one for my files. hat makes you think the birthdate is legitimate?"

"I'm just crossing my fingers on that. Even if she faked a me, it'd make sense for her to use her own birthdate. She ight be forced to fabricate a lot of other stuff so why falsify is? She's smart. She wouldn't work harder than she had to." I studied the print-out, turning it toward the light. "Look that. They marked the box that says 'corrective lenses.' errific. She has to wear glasses when she drives. It's great, n't it? Look at all the information we have. Height, weight. od, she looks tired in this picture. And look how fat she is. heck the *bags* underneath her eyes. Oh boy, you should've eard her when I talked to her down there. So *smug*. . . ."

He'd perched himself up on the edge of the desk and he as smiling at me, apparently amused by my excitement. "Well, m glad I could help," he said. "I'm gonna be out of town r a couple of days so it's lucky that came through when it d."

For the first time, I really focused on his face. His smile as slightly fixed and his posture had a self-conscious quality. ou're taking some time off?" I asked.

"Well yeah, something like that. Camilla's got a problem with one of the kids and I thought I better go straighten it out. It's no big deal, but you know how it is."

I looked at him, computing backward from what he'd said. Camilla had called and snapped her fingers. He was taking off like a shot. The kids, my foot. "What's going on?" I said.

He gestured casually and told me some long tale about bed-wetting and nightmares and visits to a child psychiatrist who'd recommended a session with the whole family. I said, uh-huh, uh-huh, not even tuning into which girl it was. I'd forgotten what their names were. Oh yeah, Courtney and something.

"I'll be back on Saturday and I'll give you a buzz. Maybe we can go back up and shoot some," he said and smiled again.

"Great. That'd be fun," I said, smiling back. I almost suggested that he bring a blowup of Camilla for a target, but I kept my mouth shut. I felt a tiny little moment of regret, which amazed me no end. I hadn't even gone to bed with this man . . . hadn't even *thought* of it. (Well, hardly.) But I'd forgotten what it's like with married men, how married they are even when the ex is somewhere else . . . *especially* when the ex is somewhere else. I didn't think she'd filed papers yet, which made the whole thing much simpler. He was running out of frozen dinners anyway, and by now she'd probably figured out how slim the choices were out there in Singlesland.

I suddenly felt myself growing self-conscious too. "Well, better get on with this. Thanks a lot. You've been a big help."

"Hey, anytime," he said. "Spillman's gonna be on the desk while I'm gone if you need anything. I'll brief him so he knows the scoop, but I want you to take care of yourself." He pointed a finger at me as though it were a gun.

"Don't worry about it. I don't take chances if I don't have to," I said. "I hope things work out up north. I'll talk to you when you get back."

"Absolutely. Let's do that. Good luck."

"Same to you. Tell the kids I said hi."

That was dumb. I'd never met them and I couldn't think what the other one's name was in any event. Sarah?

I pushed through the gate.

"Hey, Kinsey?"

I looked back.

"Where's that hat of yours? I liked that. You should wear it all the time."

I smiled and waved and went on out. I didn't need advice on how to dress.

22

It was midmorning and I was suddenly starving to death. I left my car in front of the police station where it was parked and walked over to a little hole-in-the-wall called The Egg and I. I ordered my standard breakfast of bacon, scrambled eggs, toast, jelly, and orange juice, with coffee throughout. It's the only meal I'm consistently fond of as it contains every element I crave: caffeine, salt, sugar, cholesterol, and fat. How can one resist? In California, with all the health nuts around, the very act of eating such a meal is regarded as a suicide attempt.

I read the paper while I ate, catching up on local events. I had just gotten down to the second piece of rye toast when Pam Sharkey walked in with Daryl Hobbs, the manager at Lambeth and Creek. She caught sight of me and I waved. I didn't give it everything I had. It was a casual offhand wave to indicate that I was a good joe and wasn't going to lord it over her just because I bested her last time we met. Her expression faltered and she broke off eye contact, passing my table without a word. The snub was so pronounced that even Daryl seemed embarrassed. I was puzzled, but not cut to the quick, shrugging to myself philosophically. Maybe the aerospace engineer had turned out to be a jerk.

When I finished breakfast, I paid the check and retrieved my car, popping over to the office to drop off the data I'd picked up from Jonah. I was unlocking my office door when Vera stepped out into the corridor from California Fidelity.

"Can I talk to you?" she said.

"Sure. Come on in." I pushed the office door open and she followed me in. "How are you?" I said, thinking this was a social call. She tucked a strand of auburn hair behind her ear, ooking at me through the big pale blue-tinted lenses that made her eyes seem large and grave.

"Uh, listen. Just a word to the wise," she said uncomfortably. "All hell's broken loose over that Leonard Grice business."

I blinked at her. "Like what?"

"Pam Sharkey must have called him after you talked to her. I don't know what she' said to him, but he's all up in arms. He's hired an attorney who fired off a letter to CFI threatening to sue us within an inch of our lives. We're talking millions."

"For what?"

"They're claiming slander, defamation of character, breach of contract, harassment. Andy's livid. He says he had no idea you were involved. He says you weren't authorized by California Fidelity or anybody else to go out there and ask questions . . . blah, blah, blah. You know how Andy gets when he's on his high horse. He wants to see you the minute you come in."

"What *is* this? Leonard Grice hasn't even filed a claim!"

"Guess again. He submitted forms first thing Monday morning and he wants his money right now. The lawsuit was filed on top of that. Andy's over there processing papers as fast as he can and he's pissed. He's told Mac he thinks we should terminate the whole arrangement with you after the jeopardy you put us in. The rest of us think he's being a complete horse's ass, but I thought you should know what's going on."

"What's the total on the claim itself?"

"Twenty-five grand for the fire damage. That's the face value on the homeowner's policy and he has his losses itemized down to the penny. The life insurance isn't at issue. I think he's already collected some dinky little policy on her life—twenty-five hundred—and our records show he was paid that months ago. Kinsey, he's out for bear and you're it. Andy's looking for someone to point a finger at so Mac doesn't point a finger at him."

"Shit," I said. I couldn't think of anything else to say. The last thing in the world I needed right now was a dressing down by Andy Montycka, the CFI claims manager. Andy's in his forties, conservative and insecure, a man whose prime obsessions are biting his fingernails and not making waves.

"You want me to tell him you haven't come in?" she asked.

"Yeah, do that for me, if you would. Just let me check my phone messages and I'll disappear," I said. I unlocked the file and took out the folder on Elaine Boldt, looking back at Vera. "I'll tell you something, Vera. This is hot. Leonard Grice has had six months to file a claim, but he hasn't lifted a finger. Now, all of a sudden, he's putting pressure on the insurance company to pay off. I'd like to know what prompted him."

"Hey, I gotta scoot before they come looking for me," Vera said. "Just don't cross Andy's path today or you'll pay for it."

I thanked her for the warning and told her I'd be in touch. She eased out into the hallway again, closing the door behind her. Belatedly, I felt my cheeks flush and my heart begin to thump. I got sent down to the principal's office once in first grade for passing notes in class and I've never recovered from the horror of it. I was guilty as charged, but I'd never been in trouble in my life. There I was, a timid little child with skinny legs, so stricken with fear that I left the school and went home in tears. My aunt marched me right back and read everybody out while I sat on a little wooden chair in the hall and prayed for death. It's hard to keep passing myself off as a grown-up when a piece of me is still six years old and utterly at the mercy of authority.

A glance at my answering machine showed no messages. I locked up again and went down the front way so that I could avoid passing the glass double doors of California Fidelity. I got back in my car and drove over to Elaine's old condominium. I wanted to have a brief talk with Tillie and let her know what was happening. I was turning right on Via Madrina when I glanced in the rearview mirror and realized there was some guy on a motorcycle roaring right up my tailpipe. I eased over slightly to let him pass and glanced back again. He was beeping away at me frantically. What had I done, run over his dog? I pulled over to the curb and he pulled up behind me, turning his bike off and booting his kickstand into place. He was wearing a shiny black jumpsuit, black gloves and boots, and a black helmet with a smoky face guard. I got out of my car and walked back toward him, watching him peel his helmet off as he approached. Oh hell, it was Mike. I should have guessed. The pink of his Mohawk seemed to be fading and I wondered whether he did his touch-ups with Rit dye, food coloring, or cooked beets. He was irked.

"God, I been honking at you for blocks! How come you never called me back? I left a message on your machine on Monday," he said.

"Sorry. I didn't realize it was you back there. I thought you said you were going to call *me*."

"Well, I tried to, but I kept getting your machine so I gave up. Where were you?"

"Out of town. I just got back last night. Why? What's happening?"

He pulled his motorcycle gloves off and tucked them in his helmet, which he cradled in the crook of his arm. "I think my Uncle Leonard has a girl friend. I just thought you might like to know."

"Oh really? How'd you find out about that?"

"I was moving that . . . uh . . . stash out of the shed at his old place and I saw him go into the building next door."

"The condo?"

"Well yeah, I guess that's what it is. That big apartment building."

"When was this?"

"Sunday night. That's why I called you so early Monday morning. At first, I wasn't sure it was him. I kind of *thought* it was his car pulling up out front but it was almost dark and I couldn't see that good. I figured he was coming over to the house for something and I was shovin' shit in my duffel bag like crazy. Man, I didn't know how I was going to explain what I was up to. Finally I was in such a panic, I whipped into the shed and pulled the door shut and watched through the crack. He ended up going over there instead."

"What makes you think he has a girl friend, though?"

"Because I saw him with her. I didn't have anything else

to do, so I went across the street and hid behind a tree and waited until they came out. He was only in there five or ten minutes and then the lights went out, second floor left. Pretty soon they came out and shoved some stuff in the trunk and got in the car."

"Did you get a good look at her?"

"Not really. It was hard to see 'em from where I was and they were walking kind of fast. Then when they got in the car they were all over each other. He nearly jumped her bones right there in the front seat. It was kind of weird. I mean, you usually don't see people that age making out, you know what I mean? And anyway, I never thought about him like that. I figured he was just some old dried-out fart who couldn't even get it up. I didn't think he had it in him."

"Mike, the man is probably fifty-two years old. Would you knock that off! What did she look like? Had you ever seen her before?"

Mike held his hand up to his chin. "She came up to about here on him. I noticed that. She had her hair tied back with a scarf—like a babushka or whatever you call 'em. I don't think I'd seen her before. I mean, it wasn't like I thought, Oh yeah, there's old what's-her-face or anything like that. She was just some babe."

"Look, do me a favor. Go find a pencil and paper and write all this down while it's fresh in your mind. Make a note of the date and time and anything else you remember. You don't have to say what you were doing around here. You can always claim you came over to check on the house or something. Will you do that?"

"Okay, sure. What are you going to do?"

"I haven't made that part up yet," I said.

I got back in my car, and five minutes later I was being buzzed through from the lobby to Tillie's apartment.

She was waiting for me at the door and I followed her into the living room. She was wearing a pair of spectacles low on her nose and she peered at me over the rims. She took a seat in the rocker and picked up some needlework. It looked like a hunk of upholstery fabric printed with a scene of mountains and forest, deer grazing here and there, a stream gushing down through some rocks. She had wads of cotton and she was shoving them into the back of the cloth with a crochet hook. The deer were puffed out into three dimensions, surrounded by stitching, to produce a quilted effect.

"What *is* that?" I asked, sitting down. "Are you stuffing it?"

She smiled faintly. She'd finally let her new permanent wave have its way and her head was a nest of tight, frizzy curls the color of apricots. "That's right, I am. It's called trapunto. When I finish, I'll have it blocked and framed. I do it for the church bazaar in the fall. This cotton I save out of the tops of pill bottles, so next time you open some Tylenol or cold caps, you keep the packing for me. Sit down. I haven't seen you for days. What have you been up to?"

I gave her a summary of events since Friday, which was when I had seen her last. I did some censoring. I told her how I'd found the cat, but deleted the stash of drugs Mike kept in the shed next door. I told her about Aubrey Danziger and my confrontation later with Beverly, the suitcases, the trip to Florida, the threatened lawsuit, and Mike's tale about Leonard Grice having a girl friend upstairs. That made her take her glasses off and click the stems against the frames.

"I don't believe it," she said flatly. "Mike must have been high."

"Well, of course he was high, Tillie, but a little grass isn't going to make him hallucinate."

"Then he's inventing it."

"I'm just telling you what he told me," I said.

"Well, who in the world could it be? I'd be willing to guarantee Leonard wasn't having an affair with any tenant of mine! And from his description, it would have been Elaine's apartment, and that's simply impossible."

"Oh come on, Tillie. Don't be naïve. It's the perfect setup. Why couldn't he have a woman over here?"

"Because there's no one in the building who fits that description."

"What about the woman in apartment 6? The one you thought might be up early the day your place got broken into."

"She's seventy-five."

"But you have lots of other tenants."

"Young married couples. Kinsey, I have more single *men* who'd go for Leonard than I do single women."

"I'd buy that too. What about Elaine? Why couldn't it be her?"

Tillie shook her head stubbornly.

"What about yourself?"

Tillie laughed and patted herself on the chest. "Well, I'm flattered. I'd like to believe I'm still capable of hip-grinding out on the street, but he's not exactly my type. Besides, Mike knows me. He'd have recognized me even in the dark."

I conceded that one. I truly couldn't picture Tillie in a liplock with Leonard Grice. It just didn't parse.

"What *about* Elaine?" I persisted. "What if she and Leonard had a thing going and decided to eliminate his wife? She does the deed while he's off at his sister's place that night. She takes off for Florida a few days later and then lays low for the next six months, waiting for him to get his affairs in order so they can run away together into the sunset. Once they realize I'm on to something, they step up the pace so they can blow town."

Tillie stared at me for a long time. "Then who is Pat Usher?"

I shrugged again. "Maybe they enlisted her help and she's covering for them."

"But who broke in here and why? I thought you were convinced Pat Usher did that."

I could feel myself getting exasperated. "I don't have all the answers, Tillie! I'm just telling you it's possible that he had some little tootsie stashed over here. Maybe it *was* Pat."

She didn't say a word. She just put her glasses back on and started stuffing the mountain with cotton, making it bulge like Mount St. Helens before it blew.

"Can I have the key to the apartment upstairs?"

"Of course," she said. "I'll go too."

She put down her needlework and went over to the sec-

etary, taking a set of keys out of the drawer. She handed me
bunch of bills while she was at it and I stuffed them in the
ack pocket of my jeans. It reminded me vaguely of some-
ning, but I couldn't think what.

She locked her apartment and we headed for the elevator.
"You haven't heard anyone walking around overhead?"

She looked back at me. "Not at all, but this place is well
uilt and someone could be upstairs without my hearing them.
ou really believe he was keeping someone up there?"

"It does make sense," I said. "With Elaine off the scene, it's
perfect little love nest. Maybe Pat Usher found a way to get
. I'm sure she's somewhere here in town. If she had access
Elaine's place in Florida, why not this one too? By the way,
vere you here Sunday night?"

She shook her head. "I was at a church social and didn't
et home until shortly after ten."

The elevator door opened at the second floor and Tillie
noved down the corridor to the left, talking to me over her
houlder. She reached Elaine's front door and turned the key
n the lock.

"I can't believe anyone's been here," she said as we went
n.

She was wrong, of course. Wim Hoover, the tenant from
umber 10, was sprawled in the entryway with a bullet hole
ust behind his right ear. The air smelled of stale cigarette
moke and the fetid perfume wafting up from his souring
lesh. He'd been dead for at least three days.

Tillie paled and went down to her place to call the police.

23

As is my usual habit, I did a quick tour of the place whil
Tillie called the cops. I had cautioned her to keep my nam
out of it because I didn't want to have to stop and take on
of Lieutenant Dolan's famous pop quizzes. I was already i
trouble with California Fidelity and I couldn't take on Dola
as well. The place smelled so foul that I didn't think Tilli
would have any trouble explaining what had brought her u
here to investigate.

I didn't have to be Sherlock Holmes to figure out that Pa
Usher had been in residence. She'd made no attempt to dis
guise her presence. The gauzy float I'd seen her wear in Boc
Raton was now tossed carelessly across Elaine's unmade bec
She'd apparently helped herself to whatever suited her—foo
clothing, cosmetics. There were dirty dishes everywhere, ash
trays filled to the brim, trash spilling out of the brown pape
bag with its neatly cuffed top. The crime-scene unit was goin
to have a ball with this place, but what interested me was th
den. All the desk drawers had been opened, the content
scattered furiously, file folders ripped in half. It looked lik
Pat Usher's usual rage and impatience. I wondered what she'
been looking for and whether she'd found it. I didn't touc
a thing. It had been maybe five minutes since Tillie wen
downstairs and I thought I better scram. I didn't want to b
anywhere in the neighborhood when the black-and-white
came screaming into view.

I paused in the foyer and looked down at Wim. He wa
lying facedown, one hand tucked under his cheek as thoug
he meant to nap. His flesh was swollen, the skin darkening
the bullet hole as tidy as the eyelet for a shoelace. The gu
was probably a .22—not a lethal weapon as a rule, but let
slug ricochet around inside a human skull and it could turi

brains into scrambled eggs in no time flat. Poor Wim. I wondered why she'd killed him. There wasn't any doubt in my mind it was Pat. Had she killed Marty Grice as well? The autopsy hadn't shown any gunshot wounds, only the repeated blows of an unidentified blunt instrument. What was the weapon, and where?

I went down on the elevator and left the building without talking to Tillie again. I unlocked my car and got in, suddenly aware of the crackle of paper in my jeans pocket. I pulled out the bunch of bills Tillie had given me and let out an involuntary "ooohh." It had just dawned on me what Pat Usher might have been looking for upstairs. Elaine's passport. I had come across it myself the second time I searched the place and I'd stuck it in the back pocket of my jeans. I couldn't remember taking it into the office, so it must be somewhere in my apartment. Had Pat broken in to look for it? If she'd found it, she was probably already on a plane headed into the great beyond. On the other hand, Leonard hadn't collected his insurance money yet, so maybe the two of them were still somewhere in town.

I started the car and pulled out, determined to clear the neighborhood before the cops showed up. I was thinking hard. Pat and Leonard must have eliminated Marty first, then disposed of Elaine Boldt, maybe because she'd guessed what was going on. In any event, it must have opened up a whole new possibility. They had now gained entrance to her properties and all of her bank accounts, helping themselves to her credit while Leonard waited the requisite six months for Marty's estate to clear. The payoff there probably wasn't large, but add it to Elaine Boldt's assets and the profits began to mount. Once Leonard had acquired sole possession of the property on Via Madrina, he could sell it off for a hundred and fifteen thousand. The lot was probably worth more with the house gone anyway. In the meantime, all he had to do was pose as the grief-stricken spouse, feigning disinterest in the proceeds. Not only did he garner sympathy, but he deflected attention from his true motivation, which was monetary from the get-go. The scheme might have gone off without a hitch except that Beverly Danziger showed up, needing a routine signature on a minor document. Pat's claim about Elaine being off in Sarasota with friends simply wouldn't bear up under close scrutiny because Elaine's whereabouts couldn't really be accounted for. But how was I going to prove any of this? I was speculating like crazy, probably making a few wrong guesses here and there, but even if I had it right on the nose, I'd have to come up with some kind of concrete evidence to take to the police.

In the meantime, Leonard had effectively blocked my path, putting me in check at least where the insurance company was concerned. I didn't dare go back and question *him* again and I knew I'd better be careful about any inquiries I made in the world at large. Any line I pursued was going to be interpreted as slander, harassment, or defamation from his point of view. What had I gotten myself into? Leonard Grice and Pat Usher would have to stonewall my investigation or the whole operation would come tumbling down around their ears.

I stopped off at the hardware store to pick up a pane of glass and then went back to my place. I had to find Elaine's passport. I checked the trash bags, behind couch cushions, under furniture, and all the other niches where I tend to tuck odds and ends. I didn't remember filing it and it hadn't occurred to me to hide it. I knew I hadn't thrown it out, which meant it had to be here somewhere. I kept standing there, doing a 360 degree turn, surveying every corner of the room—desk top, bookcase, coffee table, the small counter that separates the kitchenette.

I went out to the car and looked in the glove compartment, map pocket, down behind the seat, sun visor, briefcase, jacket pocket—shit. I went back into my apartment and started all over again. Where had I put the damn thing? It *might* be at the office. I decided to try there after CF had closed up and Andy Montycka had gone home. God, what did he know anyway? I was beginning to unravel the knots and I only hoped I could finish before he got nervous and paid off the claim.

I checked my watch. It was a little after one and I had the locksmith coming at four. I sat down at my desk and hauled out my file on Elaine Boldt. Maybe there was something I'd overlooked. I baited my hook and started to cast about randomly. I felt like I'd been through my notes a hundred times and I couldn't believe anything new would surface. I went back and read every report I had. I tacked all my index cards to the bulletin board, first in order, then haphazardly just to see if any contradictions would appear. I reread all the material Jonah had photocopied from the homicide files and I studied glossy eight-by-tens of the murder scene until I knew every detail by heart. How had Marty been killed? A "blunt instrument" could mean just about anything.

A lot of things were bothering me—minor questions buzzing around at the back of my brain like a swarm of gnats. I had begun to believe that if Elaine was dead, she'd been killed fairly early on. I had no proof yet but I suspected that Pat Usher had masqueraded as Elaine and had staged that whole bogus departure for Florida as a sleight of hand, laying a false trail to create the illusion that Elaine was alive and well and on her way out of town when, in fact, she was already dead. But if she'd been killed in Santa Teresa, where was the body? Disposing of a corpse is no mean feat. Fling one in the ocean and it swells up and floats right back. Toss it in the bushes and a jogger will stumble across it by six A.M. What else do you do with one? You bury it. Maybe the body was concealed in the Grices' basement. I remembered the floor down there—cracked concrete and hard-packed dirt—and I thought, now that might explain why Leonard had never had the salvage crew come in. When I'd first searched the Grices' house I'd just been grateful for my good luck, but even at the time it had seemed almost too good to be true. Maybe Leonard didn't want the demolition experts knocking around down there.

Pat Usher bothered me too. Jonah hadn't had a chance to run a check on her through the National Crime Information Center because the computer had been down. By now he'd left for Idaho, but maybe I could have Spillman run the name for me to see what he could come up with. I didn't think Pat

Usher was her real name, but it might show up as an alias— *if* she had a criminal record, which was uncertain at this point. I took out a legal pad and made myself a note. Maybe with some judicious backtracking, I could figure out who she was and how she'd gotten involved with Leonard Grice.

I sorted through the new stack of Elaine's bills that Tillie had given me, tossing out the few pieces of junk mail. I came across an appointment reminder from a dentist in the neighborhood and tossed that aside. Elaine Boldt didn't drive and I knew she patronized businesses within walking distance of her condominium. I remembered in the first batch of bills I'd seen, there was a bill from the same dentist. John Pickett D.D.S., Inc. Where else had I run into him? I leafed back through the material from the homicide file, running my eye down each page. Ah. No wonder the name rang a bell. He was the dentist who supplied the full mouth X-rays used to identify Marty Grice. There was a knock at the door and I looked up, startled. It was already four o'clock.

I glanced out through the little fish-eye peephole and opened the door. The locksmith was young, maybe twenty-two. She flashed me a smile that featured nice white teeth.

"Oh hi," she said, "I'm Becky. Is this the right place? I tried up front and the old guy said I probably wanted you."

"Yes, that's right," I said, "come on in."

She was taller than I and very thin, with long bare arms and blue jeans that hung on her narrow hips. She had a carpenter's belt slung around her waist, a hammer hanging down like a gun in a holster. Her fair hair was cut short with a boyish cowlick across the front. Freckles, blue eyes, pale lashes, no makeup, all the gawkiness of an adolescent. She had an athlete's no-nonsense good looks and she smelled of Ivory soap.

I moved toward the bathroom. "The window's in here. I want some kind of heavy-duty hardware installed that can't be breached."

Her eyes lit up when she saw the cut in the glass. "Gee, not bad. Slick job, huh. You want to put new locks on the other windows or just this?"

"I want new locks on everything including my desk. Can you rekey the dead bolt?"

"Sure. I can do anything you want. If you got glass, I'll glaze the window for you too. I love doing things like that."

I left her to install the heavy-duty hardware. Belatedly, I snatched up several articles of dirty clothing strewn about my living room. There's nothing like an outsider's idle glance to make you conscious of your own environment. I chucked two beach towels, a sweatshirt, and a dark cotton sundress on top of some other stuff in the washing machine. I tend to use my washer as a dirty-clothes hamper anyway since I'm pinched for space. I tossed in a cup of detergent. I cranked the dial around to permanent press, just to keep the cycle short, and was on the verge of popping the door shut again when I spotted Elaine's passport poking up out of the back pocket of a pair of blue jeans. I think I must have hooted my surprise because Becky stuck her head out of the bathroom door.

"Did you call me?"

"No, that's all right. I just found something I'd been looking for."

"Oh. Okay. Good for you." She went back to work. I put the passport at the back of my bottom desk drawer and locked it. Thank God I have the passport, I thought. Thank God it had turned up. It was like a talisman, a good omen. Cheered, I decided I might as well type up my notes, so I hauled out my little portable typewriter and set it up. I could hear Becky bumping around with the window, and after a few minutes, she stuck her head out of the bathroom again.

"Hey, Kinsey? This thing is all gimmicked up. You want me to fix it?"

"Sure, why not?" I said. "If you get the window to work right, I've got some other things you can take care of too."

"Hey, great," she said and disappeared again.

I could hear a big wrenching noise as she pried the window frame away. It was worrisome. All that pep and enthusiasm. I thought I heard something crack.

"Don't worry about the noise," she called out. "I saw my dad do this once and it's a snap."

After a moment, she passed through the room, tiptoein elaborately, finger to her lips. "Sorry to disturb your work. have to go out to the truck and get some line. You go righ ahead," she murmured. She was speaking in a hoarse whispe as though it would be less intrusive if she used a softer tone

I rolled my eyes heavenward and went on typing. Thre minutes later, she came back to the front door and tapped. had to get up to let her in. She apologized again briefly an went back into the bathroom where she settled in. I did cover letter for Julia and caught up with my accounting. Beck was in the other room going bang-bang-bang with her trust hammer.

After a few minutes, she appeared again. "All done. Wan to come try it?"

"Just a minute," I said. I finished typing the envelope an got up, moving into the bathroom. I wondered if this wa what it felt like to have a little kid around the house. Noise interruptions, the constant bid for attention. Even the averag mother amazes me. God, what fortitude.

"Look at this," she said happily. She raised the window Before, it had been like lifting a fifty-pound weight. It woul stick midway and then shriek, flying up unexpectedly, glas nearly cracking as it whacked into the frame. To lower th window, I practically had to hang by my hands, humping down inch by inch. Most of the time I just left it shut. No it slid up without a hitch.

She stepped back so I could try it. I reached over and lowere it, apparently unprepared for the improvement because th window dropped so fast, it made the window weights thum against the studs in the wall.

Becky laughed. "I told you it worked."

I was staring from her to the window frame. Two ideas ha popped into my head simultaneously. I was thinking abou Dr. Pickett and the dental X rays and about May Snyder claim that she heard someone going bang-bang-bang the nigl Marty died.

"I have to go someplace," I said. "Are you nearly done?"

She laughed again; that uneasy, false merriment that bu

les out when you think you're dealing with someone who's
me unhinged. "Well, no. I thought you said you had other
ings you wanted me to do."

"Tomorrow. Or maybe the next day," I said. I was moving
er toward the door, reaching for my handbag.

Becky allowed herself to be pushed along.

"Did I say something?" she asked.

"We'll talk about it tomorrow," I said. "I really appreciate
our help."

I drove back to Elaine Boldt's neighborhood and circled
e block, looking for Dr. Pickett's office on Arbol. I'd seen
before; one of those one-story clapboard cottages once so
revalent in the neighborhood. Most of them had been con-
rted into branch offices for real-estate companies and an-
ques stores that looked like someone's tiny, crowded living
ace with a sign hung out front.

Dr. Pickett had paved over some flowerbeds to create a little
arking lot. There was only one car out back: a 1972 Buick
ith a vanity plate that read: FALS TTH. I pulled in beside it
d locked my car, moving around the front and up to the
orch. The sign on the door said PLEASE WALK IN, so I did.

The interior felt distinctly like my old grade school: var-
shed wood floors and the smell of vegetable soup. I could
ar someone clattering around out in the kitchen. There was
radio on out there, tuned to a country-music station. A
arred wooden desk was angled across the entry hall with a
tle bell and a sign that said PLEASE RING FOR SERVICE. I tapped
the bell.

To my right was a waiting room with Danish-modern plastic
uches and low tables done in wood laminate. The magazines
re lined up precisely, but I suspected the subscriptions had
n out. I spotted an issue of *Life* with "Starlet Janice Rule"
the front. A partition had been put up between the re-
ption area and Dr. Pickett's examining room. Through the
en door, I caught sight of an old-fashioned dental chair
th a black plastic seat and a white porcelain spitting sink.
he instrument tray was round and apparently swiveled on
metal arm. The surface was protected with white paper, like

a placemat, and the instruments were lined up on it like some
thing out of a dental museum. I was certainly thrilled that
didn't need my teeth cleaned right then.

To my left, along the wall, were some battered wooden fil
cabinets. Unattended. I could hear the devil call out to me
Dutifully, I rang the bell again, but the country music waile
right on. I knew the tune and the lyrics routinely broke m
heart.

There were little brass frames on the front of each fil
cabinet into which hand-lettered white cards had been slipped
A–C read the first. D–F read the next. You can't lock thos
old files, you know. Well, sometimes you can, but not these
I was going to have to go through such a long song and danc
too, I thought. And I might be on the wrong track, whic
would just waste everybody's time including my own. I onl
hesitated because the courts are real fussy about the integri
of evidence. You're not supposed to run around stealing in
formation that you later hope to offer up as "Prosecution
Exhibits A & B." The cops are supposed to acquire all tha
stuff, tag it, initial it, and keep meticulous records about who
had access to it and where it's been. Chain of evidence, i
called. I mean, I read all this stuff and I know.

I called "Yoo-Hoo!" and waited, wondering if "yoo-hoo
like "mama" and "dada," was one of those phrases that cro
up in most languages. If nobody responded in the next te
seconds, I was going to cheat.

24

Mrs. Dr. Pickett appeared. At least, I assumed it was she. She was stout, with a big round face, rimless glasses, and a soft pug nose. The dress she wore was a navy blue nylon jersey with a print of tiny white arrows flying off in all directions. Her hair was pulled up to the top of her head and secured with a rubber band, curls cascading as though from a little fountain. She had on a wide white apron with a bib front and she smoothed the lap of the fabric down self-consciously.

"Well now, I thought I heard someone out here, but I don't believe I know your name," she said. Her voice was honeyed, tinted with faint southern overtones.

I had one split second in which to decide whether to tell the truth. I held my hand out and gave her my name. "I'm a private detective," I said.

"Is that right?" she said, wide-eyed. "What in the world can I do for you?"

"Well, I'm not sure yet." I said, "Are you Mrs. Pickett?"

"Yes, I am," she said. "I hope you're not investigatin' John." Her voice rode up and down musically, infused with drama.

I shook my head. "I'm looking into the death of a woman who lived here in the neighborhood. . . ."

"And I bet you're talkin' about Marty Grice."

"That's right," I said.

"Aw, and wadn't that the awfullest thing? I can't tell you how upset I was when I heard about that. Nice woman like her to meet up with such a fate. But now idn't that just the way."

"Terrible," I said.

"And you know what? They never did catch whoever did it."

"She was a patient of Dr. Pickett's, wasn't she?"

"She sure was. And a sweeter person you couldn't hope to meet. You know, she used to stop in here all the time. She'd set right there and we'd have us a chat. When my arthritis was actin' up, she'd help out with the phones and what not. I never saw John so upset as when we had to go out there and identify the remains. I don't believe he slept for a week."

"Was he the one who took the dental X rays during the autopsy?"

"The pathologist did that. John hand carried the X-rays he'd done in the office and they compared 'em right on the spot. There wasn't any doubt, of course. It was just a formality, is what they told us. He'd taken those X-rays not six weeks before she died. I felt so sorry for that husband of hers I just thought I'd choke. We went over to the funeral too, you know, and I made the awfullest fool of myself that ever was. Cried like a baby and John did too. Oh, but now he's the one you'll want to talk to, I'm sure. This is his day off, but he should be home soon. He's out runnin' some errands. You can wait if you like or come back later on."

"You can probably help me as well as he could," I said.

"Well, I'll do what I can," she said dubiously. "I'm no expert but I've assisted him all our married life. He's often said I could probably fill a tooth as well as he could, but now I don't like that Novocain. I won't fool with needles. It makes my hands turn to ice and I get all goose-bumpy on my arms." She rubbed her arms, giving a mock shiver to illustrate how upsetting it was. "Anyway, you go on and ask what you want. I don't mean to interrupt."

"I understand Dr. Pickett had a patient named Elaine Boldt," I said. "Could you check your records and tell me when she came in last?"

"The name sounds familiar, but I can't say I know her offhand. She wouldn't be anyone regular, I will say that, because I'd know her if she'd been here more than once." She leaned closer to me. "I don't suppose you're allowed to tell me how this applies," she said in a confidential tone.

"No, I'm not," I said, "but they were friends. Mrs. Boldt lived right next door to Mrs. Grice."

Mrs. Pickett nodded slightly, giving her eyebrows a lift as though she got the drift and wouldn't repeat a word of it. She went over to the file cabinets and pulled open the top drawer. I was right next to her. I wondered if she'd mind my looking over her shoulder, but she didn't seem to object. The drawer was packed so tightly she could barely squeeze her fingers in. She started reciting the names on the tags.

"Let's see. Bassage, Berlin, Bewley, Bevis . . . Uh oh, looka here now. That's out of place," she said. She switched the two files around and started where she'd left off. "Birch, Black-mar, Blount. I have Boles. Is that the name you gave?"

"No, Boldt," I said. "B-o-l-d-t. I know you billed her once and I just saw a reminder for a six-month checkup."

"I believe you're right. I wrote that recall card myself and I remember now. Via Madrina, wadn't it?" She looked back into the file drawer, checking a few folders forward and a few folders back. "I bet you for some reason he's got that on his desk," she said. "You come on in here and we'll take a look."

I followed her down a short hallway and into a small office on the left that had probably once been a powder room. Dr. Pickett's desk was stacked with files and his wife put her hands on her hips as though she'd never laid eyes on such a sight.

"Oh my stars. Now if that's not a mess." She began to check through the nearest pile.

"Why would he have it on his desk?" I asked.

"We might have had a request for dental records is all I can think of," she said. "Sometimes patients transfer out of state."

"You want me to help?"

"I sure do, hon. This might take all day at this rate."

I pitched in, riffling through the stack nearest me, then rechecking the pile she'd done to make sure she hadn't over-looked anything. There was no Elaine Boldt.

"I got one more place," she said. She held a finger up and marched us back to the front desk where she opened the top desk drawer and reached for a small gray metal file box. "This is the recall file. If she got a notice, she'd be in this box. I don't guess she gave any hint when she might have been in."

"Nope," I said. "I'd guess December, though, if she just got a six months' notice."

Mrs. Pickett gave me an appreciative glance. "Good point. I guess that's why you're a detective instead of me. All right, let's see what December looks like." She sorted through about fifteen cards. Already, I was worried about Dr. Pickett's annual income if he saw fewer patients than one a day.

"Light month," I remarked, watching her.

"He's semiretired," she said, absorbed in her hunt. "He still takes care of these old people in the neighborhood, but he tries to limit his practice. He's got varicose veins worse than me and his doctor doesn't want him on his feet all day. We get out and walk every chance we get. Keeps the circulation up. Here it is." She held an index card up, handing it to me with a mixture of triumph and relief. They might be near retirement age, but the office was still well run.

I studied the card. All it had on it was Elaine Boldt's name and address and the date she'd been in. December 28. Was I on the right track? I turned the notion over in my mind.

"Marty Grice would have come in first," I said, "and then recommended Dr. Pickett to Elaine."

"That's not hard to verify," Mrs. Pickett said. "See? On the back of the card, I have that line says 'referred by' and here's Mrs. Grice's name sure enough. Actually, we do that so if folks skip out on their bill, we have some way to trace back."

"Could I see Marty's chart?" I asked.

"Well, I don't see why not."

She went back to the file cabinet and pulled a slim folder out of the drawer marked G–I and passed it to me. Marty's name was neatly typed across the tag on the top. I opened the file. There were three sheets inside. The first was a medical questionnaire, asking for information about medications, known allergies, and past illnesses. Marty had completed the form and signed it, automatically authorizing "all necessary dental services." The second was a dental history inquiring about root canals, bleeding gums, occasional bad breath, and grinding or clenching of teeth. The third sheet contained information about treatment actually rendered, with a line drawing of the top and bottom rows of teeth laid out like a Mercator projection, current fillings marked in ball-point pen. Marty's name was neatly typed on the top line. Below were Dr. Pickett's brief handwritten notes. A routine visit. She'd had her teeth cleaned. There were apparently no dental caries. X-rays had been done and she was scheduled to return in June. I stared at it for a long time, running the whole sequence of events through my head. Everything seemed to be in order except for the date: December 28. I moved over to the window and held the chart to the light. I could feel a chill smile forming because somehow I'd known it would come down like that. I just hadn't believed I would actually find the proof. Yet here it was. Someone had neatly whited out the name originally typed in and typed Marty's name right over it. I ran my finger across the top line, feeling for the name typed underneath as though it were done in Braille. Elaine Boldt's name was visible as a faint imprint under the name Marty Grice. The last few pieces were falling into place. I was certain hers were the charred remains recovered from the Grices' house that night. I closed my eyes. It suddenly seemed very strange. I'd been tracking Elaine for ten days without realizing I'd already seen her in a photograph in the homicide file, burned beyond recognition. Marty Grice was alive and I suspected that she and Pat Usher were one and the same. There were details to nail down yet, but I had a very good idea how the murder had been set up.

"Are you feelin' all right?"

"I'm fine," I said briefly.

"Did you want to talk to John?"

"Not right now, but at some point, yes. You've been a big help, Mrs. Pickett. Thanks."

"Well, I don't know what I did, but you're certainly welcome."

I shook her hand, dimly aware of the mystified gaze that followed me as I left. I got in my car and sat there, trying to figure out what to do next. Jesus, how had they assured that the stomach contents would match? That must have been a slick one. The autopsy report indicated the blood type was

O-positive, the most common type, so that was easy enough.
Marty and Elaine were close in height. It wasn't as though the
murder victim was completely unknown. Everyone assumed
it was Marty, and the dental X rays had simply been used to
confirm her identity. There was no reason to imagine that the
dead woman was anyone else. Leonard and his sister had
talked to her on the phone at nine and Lily claimed Marty
had hung up to go answer the door. The call to the police
station was a little flourish someone thought up for effect.
Mike was right about the time. At 8:30 that night, there was
a woman's body wrapped up in a rug. It just wasn't his aunt.
Elaine must have been bludgeoned to death sometime earlier,
with enough of her jaw and teeth left intact to make identification possible. So many things were suddenly falling into
place. Wim Hoover must have recognized Marty going in or
out of Elaine's apartment. Marty or Leonard apparently got
to him before he got to a phone.

I started the car and pulled out of the lot, turning left. I
headed over to the police station and parked out front in a
fifteen-minute green zone across the street. Once inside the
station, I stopped at the counter on the left. Beyond the counter
there was a doorway leading back into the squad room.

Some cop in plainclothes I'd never laid eyes on spotted me
standing there as he passed the door. He paused.

"You need some help?"

"I'm looking for Lieutenant Dolan."

"Let me check. I was just back there and I didn't see him."

He disappeared. I waited, glancing over my shoulder into
Identification and Records. The black clerk was the only one
there and she was typing away like crazy. I kept going back
over it in my mind. It was so clear now how it all fit. Marty
Grice had gone to Florida and lived in Elaine's apartment. It
wasn't hard to figure out what she'd done. Lost some weight.
Had her hair restyled and dyed. No one down there knew
her from Adam so it wasn't as if she had to hide. She probably
just got herself spiffed up once she had Elaine's bucks to do
it with. I thought back to my encounter with her: the bruised,
puffy face, the tape across her nose. She hadn't been in any

automobile accident. She'd had cosmetic surgery—a new face to go along with her new identity. She'd told me herself that she was "retired" and didn't expect to work another day in her life. She and Leonard had fallen on hard times and there sat Elaine Boldt with money to burn and a tendency to indulge herself. How Marty must have seethed at the sight. Murder had been an equalizing force, with grand larceny providing a pension fund after the fact. Now all she had to do was wait until Leonard freed up and the two were set. It was Dolan's case. If the murder weapon turned up, I thought he'd have enough evidence to act on. For now, at least I could tell him what was happening. I didn't think it was smart to keep it to myself.

The plainclothesman returned. "He's gone for the day. Is there something I can help you with?"

"Gone?" I said. I bit back my customary expletive but inside my head, I was saying, "Shit!"

"I'll be in touch first thing in the morning."

"Sure. You want to leave him a note?"

I took one of my cards out and gave it to him. "Just tell him I'll stop by and fill him in."

"Will do," he said.

I went back to my car and took off. I had a theory about where the murder weapon was, but I wanted to talk to Lily Howe first. If she'd figured out what was going on, she'd be in danger. I glanced down at my watch. It was 6:15. I spotted a pay phone at a gas station and pulled in. My heart had begun to thud with dread. I didn't want Mike in jeopardy. If he realized his aunt was alive, he'd be in trouble too. Hell, we all were. My hands were trembling as I paged through the telephone book, feverishly scanning for the other Grice listings. I found a Horace Grice on Anaconda, which looked like a good bet, and then had to scramble around in the bottom of my handbag for twenty cents. I dialed, holding my breath while the phone rang once, twice, four times, six. I let twelve rings go by and then I put the receiver back. I ripped the page out of the phone book and shoved it into my bag, hoping I'd have an opportunity to call again.

I got back in my car and headed out to Lily Howe's place. Where were Leonard and Marty at this point? Could they have skipped or was it possible they were still together somewhere in town—at Lily Howe's perhaps? I missed Caroline Avenue and had to circle back, peering at house numbers as I passed. I spotted the Howes' residence and slowed, much to the annoyance of the people in the car behind me. I drove on by and did a turnaround in a driveway six doors down. As I pulled in to the curb to park, my heart gave a lurch. Leonard and his lady friend had just pulled into Lily's drive.

I slouched down in my seat abruptly, banging one knee on the dashboard. Oh jeez, that hurt! I eased up slightly, peering over the edge of the steering wheel. They apparently hadn't paid any attention to me because they were both getting out of the car, moving toward Lily's front door with nary a backward glance. They knocked and she opened the door for them without any exclamation of surprise, horror, shock, or dismay. I wondered how long she'd known that Marty was alive. Had she been in league with them from the beginning? I watched the house uneasily. As long as Leonard was there, I was reasonably certain that Lily was safe, but I didn't think Marty would be at all inclined to leave Lily Howe alive when the went off. I was going to have to do a little hovering over Lily Howe, playing guardian angel to her whether she knew it or not.

25

at there while an incredibly painful, probably permanent
:uise formed on my knee, trying to figure out what I should
 next. I didn't want to leave the scene now that I had the
:my in range. There wasn't a public phone within miles,
:d who was I going to call anyway? I thought about getting
 of the car and creeping up to the house, but I've never
:d very good results with that sort of thing. There are never
:dows open where you want them to be. On the few oc-
:ions when I've managed to eavesdrop, the subject matter
 always been irrelevant. People just don't sit around ver-
:izing the pertinent details of recent crimes. Peer over a
:dowsill and chances are you're going to watch the villains
 y Crazy Eights. I've never seen anyone dismember the body
:divvy up the bank heist. I decided to stay in my car and
:t.

There's nothing as conspicuous as someone sitting alone in
:arked car in a residential neighborhood. With any luck,
:ne worried homeowner would spot me and call the cops
:d then I could have a nice chat with someone in uniform.
:ntally, I organized a condensed version of the murder plot
:I could tell it succinctly when the time came. The house
: quiet. An hour and forty-five minutes passed and the
:hering darkness gradually reduced visibility to mush. Lights
:nouses all up and down the street came on, including Lily
:we's. Somebody sprayed the neighborhood with barbecue
:ogne. I was hungry and I wanted to take a leak and I
:ıldn't decide if I should risk squatting down behind some-
:'s bush. I don't feel I suffer from penis envy, but in mo-
:nts like this, I do yearn for the anatomical advantages.
:At 9:23, Lily's front door opened and Leonard and Marty
:ne out. I leaned forward, squinting. There weren't any

lingering farewells. The two of them got in the car, slamm
the doors, and backed out of the drive. I waited until th
car had disappeared and then approached the house. T
porch light had gone off. I knocked. There was a moment
silence and then I heard the chain slide into place. Lily h
read all the manuals on rape prevention. Good for her.

"Who is it?" came the muffled voice from inside.

I reduced my voice to a whisper. "It's me. I forgot
handbag."

The burglar chain slid back and Lily opened the doo
crack. I pushed forward so fast, the door almost broke
nose. There was a clunk and she cried out, but by then
closed the door behind me again.

"We have to talk," I said.

She had a hand to her face and tears had risen in her ey
not because of any damage I'd done, but because she w
upset to begin with. "She said she'd kill me if I said anythin

"She's going to kill you anyway, you twit. What do y
think—she's going to walk off and leave you around to s
the beans? Did she tell you what she did to Wim Hoover? :
put a bullet right behind his ear. You're dog meat. You de
stand a chance."

Lily paled. A sob broke the surface like a bubble of air fr
the bottom of a pond, but then she seemed to collect hers
She closed her eyes and shook her head, like a prisoner fa
with the rack. She didn't care what I did to her, she was
going to talk.

"God damn it! Tell me what's going on!"

Her expression hardened and I got a sudden glimpse
what she must have been like as a kid. Leonard's sister kr
how to deal with bullies like me. She became stubborn, passi
a defensive stance she'd apparently perfected over the ye
as a way of warding off attack. She simply withdrew, pull
in on herself like a mollusk. She must have been threaten
routinely as a child with everything from tetanus shots if
didn't wash her hands every time she peed, to police arr
if she didn't look both ways before she crossed the stre
Instead of learning the rules, she'd learned to disappear.

To my amazement, she crossed to one of the turquoise
chairs and sat down without another word. She picked up the
remote control and flicked the television on, moving through
the channels until she found a sitcom she liked. She was going
to tune me out. I went over to the chair and hunkered beside
her, talking earnestly while she kept her face to the screen.
She watched intently as a buxom platinum blonde in a tank
top proceeded to put together a birthday cake.

"Mrs. Howe, I'm not sure you understand what's going on
here. Your sister-in-law has killed two people and no one
seems to be aware of it but us."

Flour puffed up in a big cloud, obscuring the blonde's baby
face. Befuddled, she'd apparently used baking powder *and*
yeast, causing the dry flour to explode. The laugh track was
cranked up to "hilarious." Oh that gal! Wasn't she a screech?
Lily smiled faintly, reminded perhaps of baking disasters of
her own.

I touched her arm. "We're running out of time, Lil, because
you know what? I think Marty Grice is going to double back and
kill us too. She'll have to."

No response. Maybe what I said had no more reality for
her than this bimbo with the birthday cake. She was cracking
eggs now, getting splatted in the face with yolks. Simple laws
of nature were being violated here and she was the butt of
the joke. In walked the husband. His mouth fell open at the
mess she'd made. New paroxysms of laughter erupted. I wondered if anything in the real world had ever struck me with
such force.

I said, "Where did they go just now? Are they leaving town?"
Lily laughed aloud. The blonde had turned the mixing bowl
upside down on her husband's head. She showed *him*. A few
bars of the show's dizzy theme song played and the station
cut away to the commercial. I reached over and pressed the
volume button, extinguishing the sound. In silence, a dog
bounded across the linoleum with a can of chopped liver in
pursuit.

"Hey," I said, "Leonard's in trouble. Are you going to help
me or not?"

She glanced over at me, and I saw her lips move. I lean(e)
closer.

"Excuse me. What?"

The strain was showing in her face and her eyes seem(e)
unfocused. She watched me with all the concentration of (a)
drunk, dependent and out of control. "Leonard never hu(rt)
anyone," she said. "He had no idea what she was doing 'til (it)
was too late."

I thought about Mike's report of Leonard's passion for (his)
wife. I didn't see him as an innocent victim in all of this, b(ut)
I kept my big mouth shut. "As long as he knows anythin(g)
he's in danger. If you'll tell me where they're going, I can g(et)
him out of it."

She spoke in a whisper. "Just to Los Angeles 'til the ne(w)
passport for Marty comes through, and then they're flying (to)
South America." Her eyes filled with tears. "I might never s(ee)
him again," she said. "And we were always so close. I ca(n't)
turn him in. I can't betray him, don't you see?"

"You're trying to do what's best for him, Lily. He'll und(er)
stand."

"It's been awful. It's been a nightmare. When you show(ed)
up, I thought he'd die of fright. He nearly had a heart atta(ck)
and that's when she came back. She thinks you took Elain(e's)
passport and she's furious at the delay. He's afraid of h(er.)
He's always been frightened by the fits she throws. . . ."

"Of course he has. I'm afraid of her myself. She's nuts. (Do)
they have the bags in the car with them?"

She was breaking down now, caving in. The notion of Le(on)
ard's desertion caused too much pain and the image of pack(ed)
suitcases cracked her heart. It was all too much. What diff(er)
ence did any of it make now that he was leaving her?

"They've gone off to pack," she said. Her voice came (in)
in a gasp and her nose had started to run. "That's where th(ey)
went. The motel out by the pass and then the house. Th(ey)
fought about it, but she wouldn't leave it behind, becaus(e it)
was evidence."

"Leave what?"

"The . . . uh . . . you know. . . ."

"The murder weapon?"

Lily nodded and nodded again. I didn't think she could stop. It was as if the cords in her neck had come loose and her head was destined to wag indefinitely. She looked like one of those bobble-head dogs people have perched up in the back windows of their cars.

"Lily, listen to me. I want you to call the police. Go to a neighbor's house and stay there until somebody comes. Do you understand? Come on. Do you need anything? A sweater, a handbag?" I wanted to scream at her to hurry, but I didn't dare.

She was looking at me with washed-out, worried blue eyes, her gaze as trusting as a dog's. I got her to her feet and flipped the TV off, and then bundled her out the front. I scanned the street, but there was no one in sight. I couldn't believe Leonard would let Marty hurt her, but we all knew who was in charge. In some ways I felt as if I was wasting time, but I had to make sure Lily Howe was safe. We went up to the first house that showed a light, a cedar-shingle place two doors down.

I rang the bell. Some man opened the door and I pushed her forward, explaining that there was trouble and she needed some help. I urged Lily to call the cops and then I left. I wasn't sure if she'd do it or not.

I got in my car and squealed out, burning rubber as I skidded around the corner two blocks down. I drove tensely, sliding through stop signs, bypassing traffic any way I could. I had to get to the house before they did. I got stuck at a light and used the time to paw through my glove compartment, looking for the flashlight. I pulled it out and checked the batteries. They seemed fine. The signal changed to green and I took off again.

Belatedly, I realized my gun was still locked in the file cabinet at the office. I nearly slammed the brakes on and went back for it, but I didn't have time. If they went to the motel first, packed, checked out, and loaded the car up, I might have time to get to the murder weapon before they did. If they beat me to the punch, I was going to head straight for

Tillie's and call the police. I had no intention of taking on Marty Grice all by myself.

I could feel a big rush of adrenaline and my neurons fired up, completing a circuit with a joyous leap. An answer to an old question popped into my head and I suddenly knew how they'd maneuvered the stomach contents. Marty had stolen Elaine's kitchen trash. It wasn't any more complicated than that. The brown grocery bag Mike had seen in the hall was Elaine Boldt's garbage, containing the empty tuna can and the soup can that comprised her supper that night. Marty had had hours to set it up and I could visualize the scenario as though I had powers of clairvoyance. Leonard went out to dinner with Lily and Marty gave Elaine a call, inviting her over on some casual pretext. Elaine stopped by and at some point was bashed in the face until dead. Marty took the key and went over to Elaine's as soon as it was dark. She retrieved the kitchen garbage and took it back to her house, leaving it in the hall for a minute while she went down to the basement for the kerosene. That's when Mike had appeared, opening the front door and closing it again when he realized that something was desperately wrong. Marty finished dousing the place with kerosene and sat back to wait for Leonard's prearranged call at nine, reporting by phone what Elaine had eaten so he could later mention it to the police. A tuna sandwich and tomato soup. Maybe Marty stuck the leftovers on her own refrigerator shelf so it would all tally up and look legitimate. Marty set the fire and then slipped over to Elaine's where she holed up in comfort until her flight to Florida the following Monday night. My guess was that she'd dyed her hair before she left and I suspected that the fine clump of gray-brown hair I'd seen in Elaine's bathroom wastebasket during my initial search was, in fact, additional evidence that Marty Grice had been there.

I reached the Grices' house and pulled up across the street, taking a moment to study the house and yard. In the darkness the fire damage was hidden, but the place still exuded that aura of ruin and abandonment. There was no sign of the car

ut front. No lights anywhere in the house. No pedestrians
n the street.

I took the keys from the ignition and got out of the car,
eaving the door ajar. I wanted to be able to ease back in and
ake off without a lot of fumbling around, if it came to that.
opened the trunk and took out the tools I thought I'd need.
s soon as I determined that nobody was coming, I crossed
he street and cut through the Grices' side yard.

I moved quietly along the walk, surveying windows as I
assed. Most of the windows at the front of the house had
een broken out by the fire and boarded back up again, but
here were two near the back of the house that were still intact.
chose one and jimmied it open. It was pitch-black, and the
eighborhood was quiet except for crickets chirring in the
rass. I knew I should give myself an escape route, but I
ouldn't take the chance. If the two of them showed up, they'd
pot any open windows or doors. I'd just have to work fast
nd hope my guess about the murder weapon was correct. I
idn't have time for mistakes.

I climbed into the kitchen and pulled the window shut. The
oor crackled with broken glass as I passed through. My flash-
ght streaked across blackened doorframes, smoke-tinged walls,
to a hallway dense with shadow. I held my breath, listening.
he silence was flat, one-dimensional. The electricity was turned
ff and I missed the soft hum of machinery. No refrigerator,
o furnace, no wall clock, no water heater ticking from the
ther room. Some vague phrase about the silence of the tomb
ame to mind, but I pushed it away.

I moved forward, startled as a shard of glass popped un-
erfoot. Was someone moving around upstairs? I swung the
ght across the ceiling, half expecting footsteps to appear up
ere like visible dents. The imagination has primitive, car-
oonlike qualities, as any child can testify. I moved again.
here was some illumination farther on, a pale light spilling
from the house next door. I paused at the window that
oked directly into the living room across the way. Mr. Snyder
as watching a television show, images flickering silently. The

only other window on this side of the house was a small one
just off the kitchen near the rear. I had a theory now about
the banging May Snyder heard that night and I was about to
test it out. I glanced toward the room where she slept, but it
was already dark. I wondered if that's what old age is about—
sleeping longer and longer hours until one day you simply
don't bother to wake.

I ran my fingers along the window frame, shining the light
across the fire-warped paint, a shriveled and puckered white
like dead skin. I could see where the wood had been damaged
before. I could see where it had been secured with nails again.
bang-bang-bang. I propped the flashlight on the window sill.
It took me a few minutes to get the flashlight angled properly
so I could see what I was doing and still have both hands free
to work. I edged the narrow curve of the crowbar into the
window frame and pried it loose with a crack so deafening it
made my heart skip. I believed Elaine had been killed with a
sash weight that had been tucked back in the window frame
and nailed into place. The notion had come to me in one of
those flashes of insight when I heard the weights in my own
bathroom window thump dully against the studs.

It was nice. It had a certain domestic tidiness about it that
Marty must have liked. If the house had burned down entirely
that night, then who would ever have figured it out? The
bulldozers would have mowed down what was left of the house,
rubble loaded into high-siders, hauled off to the dump. Even
now, even as it was, who was going to know? In a way, she
was foolish to come back for it. Why not just leave it where
it was? She was being pushed into a panic, probably anxious
to tie up loose ends so that she could feel safe wherever she
went. They might catch her, but what could they prove? The
murder weapon probably had her prints all over it. Maybe it
still bore strands of Elaine's hair or fragments of broken teeth
and bones, microscopic particles of flesh. I wondered what
she planned to do with the grisly thing. Bury it somewhere
perhaps . . . toss it off the end of a pier. I jammed a big screwdriver into the tight crack between the framing and the strip
of wood that held it in place. Window parts must have names.

I thought, but I didn't know what they were. I was just imitating Becky's carpentry. The result was the same. I had the frame dismantled, exposing both sets of weights, the cord connecting them, and the pulleys that regulated the raising and lowering of the sash. I hauled both sets into view, four weights all together, careful not to touch anything. Shit, prints weren't going to show up on these things. The metal was covered with a thin film of sawdust and grime. Moisture in the wall had generated so much rust that any latent prints had probably been obliterated now. It wasn't going to help that six months had passed. Flecks of dried blood would still show up on a microscopic exam, but I wasn't sure what else. I shone the flashlight along the sash. At the tip were two glinting blond hairs caught in a knot of dark brown. I could feel my lips purse with distaste.

I eased a small plastic Baggie over the tip and secured it with tape. I advanced the blade in the utility knife I'd brought with me and slashed through the cords, clanging the weights together inadvertently as I lowered them into a big plastic bag. Lieutenant Dolan and his trusty crime-scene crew would have fits if they saw me manhandling evidence this way, but I didn't have any choice. I tossed the utility knife in the plastic bag along with the rest of my tools, plastic rustling with my every move—which is why I didn't hear Leonard and Marty until they had already reached the back steps.

26

The key rattled in the lock and my head whipped up. Fear shot through me like a jolt of electricity and my heart started thudding so hard it made my whole neck pulse. My single advantage was that I knew about them before they knew about me. I snatched up the flashlight, tucking the plastic-wrapped packet of weights under my arm. I was already on the move, assessing my options with a brain that felt slow and cold, as though plunged in an icy surf. My temptation was to head up to the second floor, but I scotched the impulse. There was no cover up there and no access to the roof.

I eased to my left, toward the kitchen, my hearing opened to the full. I could pick up low conversational tones out there. They were probably trying to get their bearings just shining a flashlight here and there. If Marty hadn't been in the house since the night of the fire, she might be reacting to the damage, momentarily repelled as I had been by the charring, decay, and ruin. They hadn't figured it out yet, but soon they would. The minute they saw that window frame, they'd start looking for me.

The basement door was ajar, a vertical black slot against the gloom of the hallway. I allowed myself one flicker of light from the flashlight and slipped through the crack, descending as quickly as I could without making noise. I knew the slanted basement doors leading out to the side yard were padlocked shut, but at least I'd find someplace to hide down there. I hoped.

Down I went, pausing at the bottom of the stairs so that I could orient myself. Above me, I heard the snap and crunch of footsteps. It was pitch-bloody-black where I was. It felt like the darkness was lying on the surface of my eyes, a thick, black mask that no light could penetrate. I had to risk the flashlight again. Even after so short a time, I felt myself recoil from the glare, turning my head abruptly to shield my eyes. I blinked, willing my eyes to adapt. Oh God, how was I going to get out of this?

I did a quick search, raking the beam in a 360-degree arc. I had to hide the sash weights and there wasn't much time. They might catch me, but I didn't want them to get their hands on the murder weapon, which is exactly what they'd come to fetch. I crossed to the furnace which stood massive and dead, looking somehow as ominous as a tank down there. I eased the door open and shoved the weights in, jamming the packet down between the outer wall and the housing for the gas jets. The hinge gave a harsh shriek as I pushed the door shut. I froze, glancing up automatically, as though I might make a visual assessment of how far the sound had carried.

Silence overhead. They had to be in the hall by now, had to have seen the damage I'd left. Now they were listening for me as I listened for them. In the dark of an old house like this, sound can be as deceptive as the voice of a ventriloquist.

Frantically, I scanned for someplace to hide. Every nook and cranny I spotted was too small or too shallow to do me any good. Overhead, a floorboard creaked. It wasn't going to take them long. There were two of them. They'd split up. One would go upstairs and one would come down.

I cut left, tiptoeing across the basement to the short concrete stairwell that led to the outside world. I crouched and crept upward, squeezing into the narrow space at the top. My hunched back was right up against the wood doors, my legs drawn up under me. With the electricity shut down in the house, they'd be forced to search by flashlight and maybe they'd miss me. I hoped I'd be hard to spot wedged up in here, but I couldn't be sure. In the meantime, the only thing that separated me from freedom was that slanted expanse of wood at my back. I could smell the damp night air through the cracks. The sweet scent of the jasmine near the house blended unpleasantly with the musk of soot and old paint. My heart was pounding in my chest, anxiety flying through me with such force that my lungs hurt. I held the flashlight like a club and stilled my breathing to some infinitesimal sibilance.

I became aware of a hard knot pressing into my thigh. Car keys. I shifted my weight, extending my right leg with care, reluctant to allow so much as a whisper of tennis shoe on gritty concrete step. I placed the flashlight ever so carefully on the stair below me and inched the keys out, holding onto the bunch to prevent their jingling together. Attached to my key ring was a small ornamental metal disk, maybe the size of a fifty-cent piece with no rim, the closest thing to a tool I had access to at this point. I thought with longing of the utility knife, the crowbar, and hammer wrapped in plastic and wedged down in the furnace along with the weights. I ran my left hand up along the wood just above my head, feeling for the hinge. It was shaped like an airplane wing, maybe six inches long, and flat. The screws protruded unevenly, some loosened with age, some gone.

I tried using the edge of the disk like a screwdriver, but the heads of the screws had been painted over and the groove was too shallow now to afford any leverage. I hunched, pushing up. I sensed a little give. Hands shaking with hope, I sorted through the keys, picking out the VW key, which was longer than the rest. I eased it between the hinge and the wood and applied a slight pressure. The hinge yielded a bit. If I could work a little slack into the hinge, maybe the door could be forced up and wrenched free. I pried at it, pressing my lips tight to keep from wheezing with the effort.

I paused. All I could hear was my own breathing, labored now as I struggled to loosen the hinge. The wood was pine, old and rotting and soft. I shifted my weight again, trying to give myself more room to work. The basement door creaked.

I heard the soft scratch of a shoe on the basement stair.

And then I heard the panting and I knew who it was. Slowly I turned my head to the right. I could see the dim yellow glow from a flashlight, one of those big jobs the size of a lunchbox, throwing out a wide square beam of light. The batteries were weak, washing back only pale illumination. Even so, I recognized the woman I'd met in Florida. Pat Usher . . . Marty

Grice. She wasn't looking good. The tawny hair seemed lifeless and her eyes were in deep shadow, cheekbones exaggerated by the angle of the light. She swung the beam to the far wall. I held my breath, wondering if there was any chance whatever she'd bypass my hiding place. She moved out of my line of sight for a moment. I didn't dare move. The tension made my bones ache. I could feel my legs start to shake, that uncontrollable trembling made up of stress and muscle cramp and the need to move. It was the drive toward flight turned inward, my body locked in place with no hope of relief. The flashlight beam made a slow turn in my direction, illuminating item by item everything in its path. She was going to pick me up any second and I did the only thing I could. I launched myself upward like a surfacing whale, pushing the locked doors with such force that they nearly sprung apart. I simply didn't have enough purchase and she was too quick. I strained, shoving upward again.

She must have crossed the room like a shot. My upward motion had taken me almost into an upright position, the doors bulging outward with a cracking sound. My feet were snatched out from under me and I went down, cracking my head on the concrete step. Her flashlight had careened off to one side, its fading beam aimed ineffectually now at the wall, the light as pointless as a television picture after sign-off. In the thick dark of the basement, there was just enough illumination to work to my disadvantage.

I scrambled sideways, pushing to my feet again. She flew at me, nearly climbing my frame, her arms locked around my head. I staggered backward, thrown off-balance by the sudden weight. I tried to heave her sideways, skinning her off by bashing with her into the stairs. She was on me like an octopus—tentacles, suckers, and ravaging mouth. I was going down. I tried driving into her with my elbow, but there was no way to connect with enough force to do her any harm. I got one hand up, grabbing her by the hair, tucking forward abruptly so that her own weight carried her to the concrete with a soft grunt.

I caught a quick impression of weaponry, warned by a

whistling sound, but not soon enough to duck. I heard a sickening crack on impact. She'd come up with what looked like an ax handle, wielded with such force that I felt no pain at all at first. It was like that interval between lightning and thunder, and I wondered if there was some way to gauge the intensity of pain by how many seconds it took to register on the uncomprehending brain. The ax handle came whistling up at me again, and this time I got a hand up, protecting my face, taking the blow on my forearm. I didn't even associate the cracking sound with the pain that shuddered up my frame. My mouth came open, but no sound emerged. She drove down at me again, her eyes bright, her mouth pulled back in something that would pass for a smile among lunatics. I hunched, taking the blow on the shoulder this time. The pain was like heat licking up my side. My fingers closed around the handrail. I hung on to the stairs for dear life. A bright cloud was reducing my vision to a pinpoint, and I knew once the aperture closed I was dead. I sucked air in, shaking my head, noting with relief that the dark flooded back.

I pulled my right fist back. With a low cry, I pushed off, driving forward with everything I had. I connected, and the blow rang all the way back down my arm. I felt the pain arc from my battered knuckles to her face, and she made a low sound I liked. She staggered back and I launched myself at her, getting a headlock on her that closed her throat. I swung her sideways, keeping her off-balance, moving backward at the same time so she couldn't get her feet under her. She was being hanged by the force of her own weight. I braced myself then and concentrated on narrowing the V of my arm where her neck was caught. I heard a loud pop, and for a moment I thought I'd broken her neck. She sagged to the floor. I released my hold to keep from being pulled down on top of her. I looked down at her blankly and then looked up. Leonard was standing there with a .22 that was now aimed at me.

Marty was wheezing. "You shot me, you fool." Her voice was hoarse.

Leonard's gaze shifted to her with dumb amazement.

I stepped back. The slug had caught her in the side; not a

atal wound but one that had taught her a little respect. She was on her knees, clutching at herself. She hurt and she made little mews of outrage and pain.

I was winded, still heaving for air, but I felt the strange exhilaration of victory. I had almost killed her. I'd been seconds away from converting her live body to a quite corpselike state. Leonard couldn't shoot straight, so he'd felled her himself, thus spoiling the fun, but the battle had been mine. I wanted to laugh, until I caught the look on his face.

The craziness that had consumed me for the last few minutes drained away, and I realized my troubles were starting all over again. I was dead on my feet. Somehow, I'd taken a blow right across the mouth and I was tasting blood. I felt gingerly to see if a tooth was broken, but everything seemed to be intact. It was a dumb time to worry about the possibility of a cap, but that's what I did.

I was trying to pay attention, but it was very hard. I had this weird desire to grovel around on the floor with Marty, the two of us snuffling like wounded animals looking for a way to crawl off and hide. I would have to go after Leonard soon. Already too much time had passed, and I knew I was losing ground.

He was staring at me without expression. I didn't know how to read him anyway.

"Come on, Leonard. Let's pack it in."

He said nothing. I tried to keep my tone conversational, as if I spent part of every day talking guys out of shooting me dead.

"I'm tired and it's late. Let's go home. She needs help."

Wrong move. Marty seemed to rouse herself, focusing on him. She didn't represent any kind of threat at this point, but he was teetering on the brink, maybe testing, as I had, the odd new sensation that death-dealing brought.

"Shoot the bitch," she gasped at him. "Shoot!"

I used every last ounce of strength I had, pulling myself together. He fired at me as I moved forward, but by then I was carried along by my own momentum. I yelled, "*No!*" and kicked him in the kneecap so hard I heard it crack. He dropped, warbling with pain like some kind of weird songbird. The gun skittered off across the floor. I thought Marty would try for it, but she only stared, making no move at all as I bent to retrieve it. I released the cylinder and popped it out. There were four more live rounds in the chamber. I snapped it back and made sure the safety was off, turning so that I could keep them both in my line of fire. Leonard was sitting up now, rocking back and forth. He looked at me with momentary venom.

I extended the gun, aiming at his face. "I'll kill your ass if you move, Leonard. I've had a lot of practice of late and I'll drill you right between the eyes."

Marty started to cry. It was an odd sound, like an infant with colic. Leonard leaned over and put his arm around her protectively.

In that moment, I wished there was someone to comfort me. My left arm was hanging like a piece of wood with a loose connecting pin. I glanced down and saw blood spreading out across my sleeve from a rip the size of a pea. The sucker *shot* me, I thought with astonishment. I steadied the gun in my good hand and started yelling for help. It was May Snyder who finally heard me and called the cops.

Epilogue

ve been in the hospital now for two days with my left arm
a cast. There's an orthopedist coming in this afternoon to
sess the X rays and figure out what kind of rehabilitation
I need once I get out of here. I've talked to Julia Ochsner
phone and she's invited me to recuperate at her place down
Florida. She promises sunshine and rest, but I suspect she
es it as a chance to set me up as a fourth for bridge. My
al bill came to $1,987.35 but she says she won't pay me
til I arrive on her doorstep. You gotta watch out for little
d ladies—they're tough—which is more than I can say for
yself. I hurt just about every place there is. I look in the
irror and I see someone else's face: puffy mouth, bruised
eeks, the bridge of my nose looking flat. I'm feeling some
her kind of pain as well and I don't know quite what that's
ade of. I'm closing the file, but the story's not over yet. We'll
ve to wait and see what the courts do now, and I've learned
be cautious about that. In the meantime, I stare out the
indow at the palms and wonder how many times I'll dance
th death before the orchestra packs it in for the night.

—Respectfully submitted,

Kinsey Millhone

Sue Grafton
'A' is for Alibi £5.99
A Kinsey Millhone Mystery

'Aside from the hazards of my profession, my life has always been ordinary, uneventful and good. The day before yesterday I killed someone. The fact weighs heavily on my mind . . .'

He was a ruthless hot-shot, a lawyer, a cheating husband. A lot of people could have found a reason for killing Laurence Fife. In the end they settled for blaming his wife.

Now Nikki's out on parole and heading straight for the party who ended her marriage for good. Which is bad news for Kinsey Millhone – picking up the stone-cold trail of someone sharp enough to get away with murder once . . .

. . . and ready, willing and able to start all over again . . .

'E is for excellent. Ms Grafton' THE SUNDAY TIMES

'Smart, well paced and very funny' NEWSWEEK

'What Grandpa used to call a class act' STANLEY ELLIN

Sue Grafton
'C' is for Corpse £5.99

The medics could do something about the damage to Bobby Callahan's body but not for the broken bits of his brain.

Which is why he needs help from Kinsey Millhone. The car accident wasn't an accident. Somebody wants him dead and he can't remember who or why.

Three days later, whoever was trying to kill Bobby Callahan succeeded. Kinsey had been hired to stop a killing. The least she could do now for the kid was to find his killer . . .

'C is for classy, multiplex plotting, strong characterisation and a tough cookie heroine' TIME OUT

Sue Grafton
'D' is for Deadbeat £5.99

'Dawn was laid out on the eastern skyline like watercolours on a matt board: cobalt blue, violet and rose bleeding together in horizontal stripes . . .'

Kinsey thought the job was cut and dried . . . until the client's cheque bounced. Daggett was about as worthless as his cheque. An ex con, inveterate liar, chronic drunk . . . and deader than his credit rating.

Accidental death, according to the cops. But Kinsey finds a long line of could-be killers. A long-suffering wife and daughter; a lady who *thought* she was his wife (and had the bruises to prove it); out of pocket drug dealers; and the families of five victims of horror death crashes . . .

. . . a roll call of hatred that only Daggett's death could avenge . . .

'E is for excellent. Ms Grafton' THE SUNDAY TIMES

'Classy . . . D is for deft and diverting' THE GUARDIAN

'Kinsey Millhone has a lot more than the alphabet going for her' THE OBSERVER

Sue Grafton
'E' is for Evidence £5.99

'I could feel my face heat, the icy itch of fear beginning to assert itself. I said. "This isn't the report I saw . . ."'

It was a routine job – and it was Christmas. All things considered, a neutral verdict looked like a good bet.

But when a mystery well wisher weighs in with an unmarked bank deposit for $5,000, Kinsey Millhone's suspicions are finally aroused.

Too late to avoid the set up – and fighting for her life against the oldest trick in the book . . .

'A woman to identify with . . . a gripping read' PUNCH

'Kinsey Millhone is going to have herself a bright literary future' STANLEY ELLIN

Sue Grafton
'F' is for Fugitive £5.99

*'I slammed the phone down before the guy got out another word.
Sat straight up, heart thudding. Floral Beach. Already I was wishing
I'd never come . . .'*

It was an old man's dying wish. To clear his son's name and reunite
his family. But Bailey Fowler had been missing for 16 years and there
was more than one person in Floral Beach who didn't want him
found.

Until the cops turn him up – by accident. And suddenly murder is the
hottest game in town all over again. Kinsey Millhone was summoned
for the fairy tale ending . . .

And arrived at a tragedy – starring himself . . .

'A woman to identify with . . . a gripping read' PUNCH

'Quiveringly alive' THE DAILY TELEGRAPH

'Private Ey-ette Kinsey Millhone gets more interesting by the book'
THE TIMES

All Pan Books are available at your local bookshop or newsagent, or can be ordered direct from the publisher. Indicate the number of copies required and fill in the form below.

Send to: Macmillan General Books C.S.
Book Service By Post
PO Box 29, Douglas I-O-M
IM99 1BQ

or phone: 01624 675137, quoting title, author and credit card number.

or fax: 01624 670923, quoting title, author, and credit card number.

or Internet: http://www.bookpost.co.uk

Please enclose a remittance* to the value of the cover price plus 75 pence per book for post and packing. Overseas customers please allow £1.00 per copy for post and packing.

*Payment may be made in sterling by UK personal cheque, Eurocheque, postal order, sterling draft or international money order, made payable to Book Service By Post.

Alternatively by Access/Visa/MasterCard

Card No.

Expiry Date

Signature _____

Applicable only in the UK and BFPO addresses.

While every effort is made to keep prices low, it is sometimes necessary to increase prices at short notice. Pan Books reserve the right to show on covers and charge new retail prices which may differ from those advertised in the text or elsewhere.

NAME AND ADDRESS IN BLOCK CAPITAL LETTERS PLEASE

Name _____

Address _____

_____

_____

_____

8/95

Please allow 28 days for delivery.
Please tick box if you do not wish to receive any additional information. ☐